"If we a...
but we are n...
then where...

"I'll tell you where we are, we're in no-man's-land."

"No-man's-land," Flora repeated. "Our own private land."

"For the time being."

No-man's-land. A place where only one man existed, she thought. A man whose eyes glittered darkly down at her, mesmerizing beneath the thick curtain of his lashes. A man who, by his own admission, confided in no one, yet had confided in her. A dangerous man. A lonely man. A challenging man. And a very enticing one. "I think I like no-man's-land," Flora said.

"So do I," Geraint said softly, closing the space between them. He slid his arm around her waist. His fingers were delicate on her jaw, her cheek, making her catch her breath in anticipation, making her tremble, scattering her inhibitions to the four winds.

Her body was pliant, melding itself to his hardness as she reached up to put her arms around his neck. As his lips touched hers, her eyelids closed. His tongue ran along the soft skin on the inside of her lower lip, and she shivered at the shocking intimacy of it. It was like the first sip of a fine French cognac. Warmth flooded her.

* * *

Never Forget Me
Harlequin® Historical #1198—August 2014

MARGUERITE KAYE

—

Never Forget Me

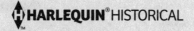

Recycling programs
for this product may
not exist in your area.

ISBN-13: 978-0-373-29798-6

NEVER FORGET ME

Printed in U.S.A.

Did you know some of these novels are also available as ebooks? Visit www.Harlequin.com.

Author Note

War, conflict and the impact it has not just on those who fought, but on those left behind, have been recurrent themes in my books. While the First World War has long been a subject which I found compelling, I've always shied away from it as the backdrop to romance. The sheer scale of the suffering, death and destruction seemed prohibitive, and the war itself is still very much present in the memories of the families of those who fought in it.

With the centenary of the start of the "war to end all wars" coming around though, I began to seriously rethink my stance. Between 1914 and 1918, the world, or at least the world of those countries involved in the conflict, really did change utterly, and it wasn't all negative. Out of such suffering, those who fought and those who lost loved ones were determined some good must come—not just the long-term peace that the League of Nations was established to protect, but "good" for the individual. And it did. Of course, there were other influences and dynamics of change that were in train before the war, but no one can deny (though no doubt someone will now!) that the war gave women's liberation a kick start, not only in enfranchising them, but in getting them out of the home and into the workplace, and in Britain making a start on sexual discrimination by allowing them into the legal profession and the higher echelons of the civil service. A maximum working day (and week) and a stronger trade union movement were just some of the measures that protected workers.

I could go on, but this isn't a history lesson. What I'm trying to say is, the idea of somehow showing the impact of these huge changes on my characters really appealed to me. But how to do this, and at the same time capture the essence of the war? I decided that rather than pick one key moment in the conflict, I would write three different stories set at the beginning, the middle and the end. Building on my experience from working on the Castonbury Park series, I'd have some continuity characters who would act as landmarks for the changes, and so I came up with the idea of having a house and a family central to all three stories, who would then represent the shift from the old world to the new.

All very well, but finding a way of setting not one but three romances against a backdrop of war without shying away from the reality was a tough one. What I hope runs through all the stories is the triumph of the human spirit, and the power of love.

My own spirit, I must admit, was at times crushed by this book. Thanks once again to my Facebook and Twitter friends for all their help and encouragement. You kept me going, and you fed me ideas—having letters form a key part of my second story is just one of them. Many thanks to Alice, who shared the amazing story of her grandfather's war and allowed me to borrow his surname for one of my heroes. And finally, a huge big thank-you to Linda F. at Harlequin Mills & Boon for taking a chance on this book, and as ever to my wonderful editor Flo, who hauled me out of the mire that my third story had become entangled in.

This has been by far the most challenging book I've written, but because of that it's also been the most rewarding. I truly hope you find it as rewarding to read.

A Kiss Goodbye

Chapter One

Argyll, Scotland—October 1914

Corporal Geraint Cassell, late of the Royal Welsh Fusiliers and currently seconded to the Army Service Corps, gazed out of the window as the staff car swept up the impressive driveway. There was something about the quality of light, the way it filtered through the battleship-grey clouds, casting a soft haze over everything, that made him think of home. The picturesque villages they had skirted on the journey north, though, looked nothing like the gritty Welsh mining village in which he had been raised, where the narrow houses huddled into the valley, their tiny windows looking blindly out onto the road, which rose steeply towards the pit head and the winding wheel that dominated the skyline. In contrast, the whitewashed Highland cottages seemed like something out of a child's fairy tale.

Private Jamieson pulled the car to a halt in front of Glen Massan House. Geraint surveyed the place with a jaundiced eye. It was more like a castle than a house. Built in the Scots' baronial style, he had gleaned from the requisition orders, it sat on a promontory with a commanding view over Loch Massan. A large tower five stories high with crenellated battlements bolstered one side of the grey granite building, while the main body of the house, with its steep-pitched roofs and its plethora of smaller, conical towers, seemed to have been added higgledy-piggledy. The result was strangely attractive. It was easy to imagine generations of Carmichael lairds striding out from that massive portico in their plaids, hounds yelping at their heels, to go off on a stag hunt or whatever it was that Scottish lairds did.

Generations of crofters and serfs had no doubt dutifully served their lord and master here, working the land for a pittance and shivering in their thatched cottages, Geraint reminded himself. Whatever this war brought, one thing was certain, it was the end of the line for people like Lord Carmichael and his privileged family.

The war would see the end of the line, too, with a bit of luck, for the 'Old Contemptibles' like Colonel Aitchison, whose ilk were bumbling about with General French over on the Western Front. Geraint belatedly turned and saluted as his so-called superior officer finally stumbled out of the staff car juggling gloves, hat and swagger stick. No doubt the Carmichaels of Glen Massan House would resent being evicted from their pretty Highland castle, but Geraint refused to feel sorry for them.

'I simply can't comprehend why the army wants our home. Why Glen Massan?'

The question was rhetorical, though Lady Elizabeth Carmichael had asked it repeatedly since the requisition order had arrived. Her daughter, Flora, looked up from the newspaper in which she had been reading the first encouraging reports of the battle being waged at Ypres. 'Perhaps it really will be over by Christmas,' she said, 'in which case, we will only have to decamp to the Lodge for a few months.'

'A few months! The place is tiny. There are only three bedrooms.'

'Then Robbie will have to bunk with Alex the next time he comes up from London,' Lord Carmichael said patiently.

'But that means you and I will have to share a bedroom.'

'We *are* married, Elizabeth, and there *is* a war on, in case either fact had escaped your attention. It is up to all of us to make sacrifices.'

Lady Carmichael took a sip of tea. 'Do you really think it will be over by Christmas as they say?' she asked her daughter.

Flora's opinion was so rarely consulted that for a moment she was quite taken aback. 'I don't know,' she answered simply. 'If the newspapers are to be believed...' She halted mid-sentence, because the growing casualty lists and the claims of imminent victory seemed to her at odds. The reports in the papers were unrelentingly cheerful, full of praise for the bravery of the men who went 'over the top'. At times, they made life in the trenches sound like some sort of Boy Scout camp. In the first weeks, Flora had been as enthusiastic as everyone else, but now that men from both sides were dying in unimaginable numbers, she was beginning to have the most unpatriotic doubts about the ability of those in charge to do their job.

Not that she would dream of saying so in front of her parents, who considered any talk of casualties defeatist. Leaning across the table to clasp her mother's hand, she smiled weakly. 'Perhaps it will be over soon. I sincerely hope so.'

'It is selfish of me, but you know how much your brother Alex wishes to join the older boys from his school who have already enlisted.'

'Alex is only seventeen,' the laird said pointedly. 'He is at no risk.'

But Robbie, Flora's other brother, who was twenty-five and currently running his wine-importing business from London, certainly was. The laird did not say so, but it was obvious to her that all three of them were thinking that Robbie's joining up was a distinct possibility. 'It's almost a full year before Alex is eligible to enlist,' Flora said, trying to sound more reassuring than she felt. 'If it's not over by Christmas then it certainly will be long before then.'

'I hear that our ghillie's son, Peter McNair, is talking of joining up,' Lady Carmichael said. 'Mrs Watson from the village shop told me that they are attempting to form one of those units Kitchener made such a fuss about.'

'A Pal's Battalion,' the laird said dismissively. 'Foolish name, foolish idea. This is a small community, we can ill afford to lose significant numbers of men.'

'I quite agree,' Lady Carmichael said. 'Our local young men would be better served tending to the fields. Not that I would dream of saying so outside these four walls,' she added hastily. 'We are at war after all. Though why that requires us to be cast out of house and home…'

'We shall know soon enough,' her husband retorted sharply. 'The army are due this morning.'

Lady Carmichael sighed. Weak autumn sunshine filtered through the voile curtains draped over the two long windows of the dining room, bathing her in its unforgiving light. Her mother's stern beauty had held up remarkably well, Flora thought. They were so unalike, mother and daughter, sharing little but the same grey-blue eye colour. She would have liked to possess some of her mother's curves, but she had inherited her father's physique, being tall and slim.

'Would you like me to deal with the army chaps?' she asked, thinking that at least she might spare both her parents and the unsuspecting officer in charge.

Lady Carmichael, however, looked horrified. 'Don't

be ridiculous. You cannot possibly take on such a task, it would be quite beyond you.'

'I am twenty-three years old, and since you trust me with little more than flower arranging, I don't see how you can have any idea what I am capable of.'

'Flora!'

Lady Carmichael looked scandalised by this unexpected riposte. Flora was rather surprised at herself, for though she often disagreed with her mother, she rarely allowed herself to say so. 'I beg your pardon,' she said, feeling not at all contrite, 'but I would very much like to feel useful, and I wished to spare you what can only be a painful process.'

'Flora is quite right,' the laird said, coming unexpectedly to her aid. 'It will be difficult for us to relinquish the house. Perhaps we should delegate the task to her after all.'

'Father, thank you.'

'Andrew! You cannot mean that. Why Flora is— She has no experience at all. And besides, think of the proprieties. All those rough young soldiers.'

'For goodness' sake, Elizabeth, those rough young soldiers are British Tommies, whom I'm sure will treat both the house and our daughter with respect. Whatever the army's intentions are for Glen Massan, it will require our home to be stripped of its contents. I am trying to spare you the trauma of witnessing that, and frankly I have little stomach for the sight, either.' Lord Carmichael patted his wife's hand. 'Best you concentrate your energies on making the Lodge comfortable for us, my dear. If Flora makes a hash of things, I can always step in.'

It was not quite the wholehearted endorsement she would have liked, but it was nevertheless more than she had hoped. What was more, loathe as she was to admit it, her father was entitled to his reservations. 'I shall do my best to ensure it doesn't come to that,' Flora said, pleased to hear that she sounded considerably more confident than she felt. It was wrong to think that any good could come from this horrible war, but it would be equally wrong for her not to seize the opportunity it provided to prove herself.

Outside, a horn honked, gravel scrunched and in the distance, a low rumble could be heard growing ever nearer. Flora ran to the window. 'Speak of the devil. It's an army staff car. A Crossley I think, Father. Alex would know.' She gazed out in amazement at the convoy of dusty vehicles following behind the gleaming motor car. 'Goodness, there are so many of them. Where will they sleep?'

'Certainly not in the house. At least—I suppose we could accommodate some of the officers,' Lady Carmichael said unconvincingly.

'My dear,' the laird said, 'this will be *their* house very soon. They will sleep where they choose. In the meantime, I expect they will put up tents.'

'On the lawn! In full sight! Andrew, you cannot…'

'Elizabeth, you must allow Flora to worry about the details.'

As truck after truck pulled to a stuttering halt and what seemed to Flora like a whole battalion of men began to descend, she struggled not to feel quite overwhelmed.

'It is like an invasion,' her mother said in horror, and Flora couldn't help but think that she was right.

The driver of the staff car pulled open a door and a polished, booted foot appeared. Flora straightened her back and took a deep breath. *These are our brave boys,* she reminded herself. 'I think we'd better go and see what we can do to assist them.'

Her father gripped her shoulder. 'Bravo,' he said softly. 'Get your mother to the Lodge first. Join me as soon as you can.'

Feeling anything but brave, Flora watched him leave before turning to her mother and pasting on a smile. 'Well, it looks as though the war has arrived in Glen Massan.'

Chapter Two

Geraint listened distractedly as Colonel Aitchison droned on, reading out the army regulations, statutes and by-laws governing the requisition of the house in the manner of a judge delivering a death sentence. Across from him, seated on an ornately scrolled and gilded sofa, Lord Carmichael held himself rigidly, his face expressionless, though judging from the way his fingers curled and uncurled compulsively, this was merely the aristocratic stiff upper lip on full display.

A tall, thin man with a helmet of red hair and a neatly trimmed beard, the laird looked more like an academic of some sort than the exploitative landowner he surely was. There was an aesthetic quality to that long, narrow face, intelligence in that wide brow and those piercing eyes. Very piercing, Geraint thought, catching the man's glance and finding himself being scrutinised with disconcerting thoroughness. He squared his shoulders and glared back, and was surprised when the laird gave him a wry smile in return.

As the colonel turned to the specifics of recompense, Geraint's attention wandered. The drawing room was huge, the cornicing of the high ceilings formed in a geometric pattern that looked vaguely Oriental. A bay window at the far end looked out onto the gardens at the rear of the house, and at the opposite end, a massive white marble fireplace was flanked by a pair of statues bearing gilded torches. Aphrodite? Artemis? Athena? Knowing that he had not the slightest chance of attending university, and having besides a natural antipathy towards anything that smacked of privilege, Geraint had been dismissive of the classical elements of his education. All Greek goddesses looked pretty much the same to him.

The door opened and a girl burst in, startling the colonel into temporary silence. Her bright head of auburn hair gave her away immediately as the laird's daughter. Geraint got to his feet several seconds before the portly colonel could manage to do the same. Not a girl, but a young woman in her early twenties. Tall and slim, clad in one of those white dresses that only the well-heeled could afford to wear, she had around her neck a strangely masculine little black silk cravat that served to emphasise her femininity.

'Colonel, may I introduce you to my daughter, Flora.'

She didn't walk across the room so much as float, though Geraint could see that her feet in their delicate little shoes were firmly planted on the antique rugs that covered the floor, and he saw also, because he took the trouble to look, that her ankles were as slim and elegant as the rest of her. Her hair, which she wore piled on top of her head, was a shade darker than her father's, the colour more lustrous. Beneath it, there was just a touch of haughtiness in her startling blue-grey eyes and humour, too, in that generous mouth. She was no Greek goddess, but she *was* lovely.

And she was looking enquiringly at him now. 'Corporal Cassell,' her father said by way of introduction.

'Corporal Cassell. How do you do?'

The hot dart of desire that made his belly clench took him entirely by surprise. Flora Carmichael, spoilt little rich girl, was most certainly not his type. She turned to him with one dark brow raised, holding out her genteel little hand. He caught a waft of her flowery scent and it was intoxicating. For a moment, for just a moment, he actually thought she felt the jolt of connection, too, as his fingers touched hers and her eyes widened a little. Then he remembered who he was and where he was. Women like Flora Carmichael did not look twice at men like him, and men like him did not fraternise with the enemy. He dropped her hand abruptly and sat back down, realising too late that he hadn't even returned her greeting and had thus most likely confirmed her assumption that he was a complete boor before he'd even opened his mouth.

Flora took her place by her father's side on the sofa, somewhat confused. Had she just been snubbed? Across the room, the rude corporal kept his eyes firmly on his commanding officer, allowing her to study him covertly. He looked to be about Robbie's age, perhaps two or three years older than herself, though it was difficult to tell, for there was a hard edge to him that her elder brother did not possess. Jet-black hair, cropped ruthlessly short. Was he, then, a recent recruit? Dark eyes rimmed with thick dark lashes were set under a high, intelligent brow. His face was all angles, softened only by the fullness of his lower lip. It was a memorable face and a handsome one, though not in the least gentle or kind.

His attention switched, and he caught her staring at him. She refused to avert her gaze, though she could feel the colour creeping up her neck. What had she done to earn such overt antagonism? He was positively bristling with it.

'Flora?'

She stared at her father blankly, her fingers straying to her cravat.

'The colonel has been explaining that Corporal Cassell will be in day-to-day charge of the requisition handover. Unfortunately the lieutenant assigned to the role is indisposed.'

'Naturally I will be keeping tabs on things,' the colonel said. 'I'm staying with an old colleague who lives just next door, a Colonel Patterson—do you know him, Lord Carmichael? We fought the Boers together, you know.' Colonel Aitchison paused, looking somewhat confused. 'What was I…'

'The guided tour. Sir,' the corporal prompted, none too subtly, 'to ascertain which rooms can be utilised for what.'

His voice was unexpected, his accent softly lilted. 'You are Welsh,' Flora exclaimed in some surprise.

'I am a soldier, Miss Carmichael.'

It was not just antagonism, he had obviously taken an instant dislike to her, which shouldn't matter one whit, and most certainly should not hurt her. Flora got to her feet, forcing the colonel and the rude corporal to stand. He was taller than she expected, more intimidating as he stood there in his pristine uniform, his feet in their gleaming boots planted slightly apart, as if he was on guard duty and would challenge her right to pass. In her own home!

'Let us proceed with the tour at once.' *Because the sooner this is over, the sooner I shall be rid of you,* she implied as she strode past him, her nose in the air, knowing that she must look perfectly ridiculous as well as appearing dreadfully rude. 'Good morning, Colonel.'

'My daughter is right,' she heard her father say, 'the sooner the better. If that is all for now, Colonel?'

'A few signatures, the rest can be ironed out later. As I said, I shan't be far away. Hoping to bag a few grouse while I'm here, actually. Maybe even a salmon. Patterson was telling me there is excellent fishing on his stretch of the river. In the old days…'

The meeting was clearly over. Flora fumbled with the latch.

'Allow me.'

Corporal Cassell reached around her, the sleeve of his jacket brushing her arm, ushering her through the open door. She was absurdly conscious of how slight she was compared to his broad physique. 'Thank you.'

'You're welcome.' She had expected him to return to the drawing room, but instead he followed her out to the Great Hall, wandering over to the stone fireplace and studying the display of claymores ranged in a wheel on the wall above it. 'Do you keep these in readiness to repel an invasion by the English?' he asked.

Flora rarely lost her temper, but she felt her hackles rise. This man was insufferable. 'It may have escaped your notice, but we are actually fighting on the same side in this particular war.'

'I doubt you and I will ever be on the same side, Miss Carmichael,' Corporal Cassell said, turning his attention to the array of muskets in a case by the window. 'You'd do well to make sure the colonel doesn't clap eyes on these, else he'll be requisitioning them.'

'They would be of little use, since they are over a hundred years old.'

'I'm willing to bet they're still a damn sight more effective than what they've been giving our boys to train with,' he exclaimed with surprising viciousness. 'Broom handles, pitchforks, guns minus bullets if they are very lucky,' he added, in answer to her enquiring look. 'This war has caught the army on the hop. If you could but see…' He stopped abruptly.

'If I could but see what, Corporal Cassell?'

He shrugged and turned away to look at a large flag displayed on the wall.

'The standard you are looking at was borne at Culloden,'

Flora said, addressing his back. 'Though some of the clan fought for Bonnie Prince Charlie, others were on the side of the crown.'

The corporal made no reply. Thoroughly riled, and determined to force him to acknowledge her presence, Flora went to stand beside him. 'Above the standard is our family crest, which is also carved over the front door. *Tout Jour Prest*. It means...'

'Always ready. You see, I am not wholly uneducated.'

'I did not think for a moment that you were. Why do you dislike me so much, Corporal?'

He twisted round suddenly, taking her off guard. 'I bear you no ill will personally, Miss Carmichael, but I do not approve of your type.'

'My type?' His eyes, she realised, were not black but a very dark chocolate-brown. Though he clearly intended to intimidate her, she found the way he looked at her challenging. It was deliberately provocative. 'And what, pray tell, do you mean by that?'

'All this.' He swept his arm wide. 'This little toy castle of yours. All these guns and shields and standards commemorating years of repression. A monument, Miss Carmichael, to the rich and privileged who expect others to do the filthy business of earning their living for them.'

'My father works extremely hard.'

'Collecting rents.'

'He does not— Good grief, are you some sort of communist?'

She could not help but be pleased at the surprise on his face. 'What on earth would you know about communism?' he demanded.

'You haven't answered my question.'

'I am a socialist and proud of it.'

'Like Mr Keir Hardie? He has made himself most unpopular by campaigning against the war. Are you also a pacifist?'

'A conchie? Hardly, given my uniform and my rank. What do you know of Keir Hardie? I wouldn't have thought someone like you would be interested in him.'

'Someone like me! A female, do you mean, or one of my class? Do you have any idea how patronising that sounds? Silly question, of course you do.'

'I did not intend to insult you.'

'Yes, you did, Corporal Cassell.' Flora glared at him. 'Please, feel free to continue with your barbs. Being a patriot, I am delighted to afford you the opportunity to practise something that gives you such obvious pleasure.'

To her astonishment, he burst out laughing. 'I will when I can think of one. I must say, you are not at all what I was expecting.'

His backhanded compliment should most decidedly not be making her feel quite so pleased. Quite the contrary, she should have taken extreme umbrage by now, and left him to his own devices. Instead Flora discovered that she was enjoying herself. Corporal Cassell was rude and he made the most extraordinarily sweeping assumptions, but he did not talk to her as if she was witless. 'I have never met a socialist before. Are they all as outspoken as you?'

'I don't know. I've never met a laird's daughter before. Are they all as feisty as you?'

'Oh, I should think so. Centuries of trampling over serfs and turning crofters out of their homes into the winter snows leave their mark, you know.'

He smiled wryly, acknowledging the hit. 'And then there is the red hair. Though it would be a crime to label it something so mundane as red.'

She knew she ought not to be standing here exchanging banter with him. She was also quite certain she should not be feeling this exhilarating sense of anticipation, as if she were getting ready to jump into the loch, knowing it would be shockingly cold but unbearably tempted by its deceptively blue embrace on a warm summer's day. 'What, then, would you call it?' Flora asked.

The corporal reached out to touch the lock that hung over her forehead, twining it around his finger. 'Autumn,' he said thoughtfully.

She caught her breath. 'That's not a colour.'

'It is now.'

The door to the drawing room opened, and he sprang away from her. 'Flora?' her father said.

'I was showing Corporal Cassell our collection of fire-arms.'

The laird drew her one of his inscrutable looks before turning back to the colonel. 'Good day to you. I will see you in a few days, but in the meantime you can reach me by telephone, and I'm sure my daughter will keep me fully briefed.'

With a gruff goodbye to the corporal, her father picked up his walking stick and headed for the front door where the deerhounds awaited him. He'd be off for a long tramp across the moors. Her father supported the war unequivocally and would like as not have enlisted himself if he'd been of age, but Glen Massan House was in his blood, and giving it up was no easy sacrifice to make.

A horrible premonition of the other, much more painful sacrifices her family might ultimately have to make made Flora feel quite sick, but she resolutely pushed the thought away. There was no point in imagining the worst when there was work to be done. Besides, neither of her brothers was currently in the firing line, for which she was guiltily grateful.

She turned her attention to the forecourt, where the corporal was in earnest conversation with his colonel. The engine of the staff car was already running. She could not hear what was being said, but she could tell the Welshman was not happy. Eventually, he stepped back and saluted. The car drove off in a flurry of gravel, and the corporal re-joined her.

'What do you intend to use our house for?' Flora asked.

'It's supposed to be hush-hush, though I can't imagine why. You're not a German spy by any chance, are you?' he asked sardonically. Pulling off his cap, he ran his fingers through his hair. 'It's been earmarked for special training. That's all I know, and even if I did know more I couldn't tell you. One thing I do know, though, we only have a few weeks to get the place ready before the first batch of Tommies arrive, so me and the lads are going to have to get our skates on.'

'Which means that I, too, will have to get my skates on. I would not wish to be responsible for delaying the British army,' Flora said, trying not to panic. Outside, the soldiers were playing an impromptu game of football on the croquet lawn. She prayed her mother had for once done as she was bid, and kept to the Lodge. 'How many of you are here as the—what is it, advance guard?'

'Just the one section, me and twelve men.'

'Goodness, when you arrived it seemed like hundreds.'

'It most likely will be soon, but for now it's just us. And the colonel, of course, whenever he deigns to join us.'

Flora eyed him sharply. 'You sound positively insubordinate, Corporal.'

'Do I?'

'The colonel strikes me as the kind of man who is rather more efficient in his absence than his presence,' she ventured.

'And you are qualified to make such a judgement, are you?'

'Oh, for goodness' sake, why must you be so abrasive?' Flora snapped. Though he raised his brows at her flare of temper, he made no attempt to apologise. She suspected he was the kind of man who made a point of not apologising for anything, if he could avoid it. 'Look, the truth is, I have no idea whatsoever what it is that you expect of me,' she said with a sigh. 'So if you can bring yourself to let me in on your plans, I would very much appreciate it.'

His expression softened into a hint of a smile, which did very strange things to Flora's insides. 'Since I've only just been dumped with— Since I've only just assumed responsibility, I don't actually have any plans. You're not the only one who is in uncharted territory.'

'Thank you. I know that shouldn't make me feel better, but it does.'

'As long as you don't go bleating to your daddy.'

'I am not a lamb, Corporal,' Flora snapped, 'and I am certainly not in the habit of telling tales.'

'I apologise, that was uncalled for.'

She glared at him. 'Yes, it was.'

Once again, he surprised her by laughing. 'You really are a feisty thing, aren't you, Miss Carmichael.'

And he really was rather sinfully attractive when he let down his guard. 'Call me Flora. We shall sink or swim together, then,' she said, holding out her hand.

He did not shake it, but instead clicked his heels together and bowed. 'If we are to swim together, then you must call me Geraint.'

He held her gaze as he turned her hand over and pressed a kiss to her palm, teasing her, daring her to react. His kiss made her pulse race. Seemingly as shocked as she, he dropped her hand as if he had been jolted by an electric current.

They stared at each other in silence. He was the first to look away. 'We should start by making the tour, and take things from there,' he said gruffly.

Had she imagined the spark between them, or was the

corporal intent on ignoring it? Flora was so confused that she was happy to go along with him. 'Yes,' she said, aware that she was nodding rather too frantically. 'That sounds like a plan.'

'In the meantime, my men will unload the trucks and set up temporary camp.'

'Oh, please, not on the lawn. My mother specifically asked…'

'What, is she worried that we'll dig latrines next to her rose beds?'

'Actually, manure is very good for roses.'

She caught his eye, forcing a smile from him that relieved the tension. 'Perhaps you could suggest somewhere more suitable, Miss Flora.'

'At the back near the kitchens might be best. The house will shelter the tents from the wind coming in off the loch, and they will be near a good water supply.'

'Practical thinking. I'm impressed.'

'Goodness, a compliment Corporal—Geraint.'

'A statement of fact.'

'Did I pronounce it correctly? Your name, I mean. Geraint.'

'Perfectly,' he said shortly.

Really, his mood swung like a pendulum. 'What have I said to offend you this time? I can almost see your hackles rising,' Flora said, exasperated.

'Nothing.'

She threw him a sceptical look.

'I don't think I've heard my Christian name spoken since I joined up, that's all,' he finally admitted. 'I'd almost forgotten how it sounded.'

She was instantly remorseful. 'But don't you get leave? I am sorry, I am afraid I know nothing of these things.'

Geraint shrugged. 'Why should you? No, we don't get

leave. Leastways, nothing long enough for me to go back to see my family.'

'Your family! So you're married,' Flora exclaimed, inexplicably appalled by this.

'Good God, no! I wasn't married when the balloon went up and I'd be a fool to get hitched while there's a war on. Even if there happened to be someone I wanted to marry, which there is not,' Geraint said. 'I meant my parents, my brother and sisters.'

'Yes, of course you did,' Flora said. 'I knew that.' Which she had, truly, for she also knew instinctively he was not the kind of man to flirt with another woman if he was married. Not that he had flirted with her. Had he? She sighed inwardly, wishing that she was not such an innocent. 'You must miss them,' she said, trying to pull her thoughts together. 'Your family, I mean.'

But Geraint merely shrugged, his face shuttered. 'We didn't see much of each other this last while, frankly,' he said, and when she would have questioned him further, turned his attention elsewhere. 'I must go and see to the men, else they will happily kick a ball about all day. I'll see you in a couple of hours.'

Which was definitely not something she should be looking forward to, Flora thought, watching him stride off purposefully.

The men were lined up on the driveway now. She could not hear what the corporal was saying to them. He seemed not to be the kind who barked orders, but rather spoke with a natural, quiet authority that made the troops pay attention. Once dismissed, they started to pull back the tarpaulins on the trucks, revealing iron bedsteads, tents, trestle tables and a host of other equipment including what looked horribly like field guns. Flora headed back to the Lodge. It had been an extremely eventful day already, and it was only lunchtime.

Chapter Three

Three days later, Geraint was in the morning room with Flora, where a phonograph sat incongruously on an antique marble-topped table. Like the rest of the house, the room was a mixture of styles, reflecting the changing tastes of the Carmichaels through the generations. Glen Massan House was too eclectic to be aesthetically pleasing. It was not a showpiece, but a home. Flora Carmichael's home. Which it was now his duty to pillage.

He must not allow himself to think about it in that manner. She and her ilk neither deserved nor required his sympathy, yet he found it increasingly difficult to think of Flora as belonging to any clique. She seemed slightly out of place, a misfit. A bit like himself, if truth be told. 'I can't quite work you out,' Geraint said, surrendering to the unusual desire to share his thoughts.

Flora looked up from her notebook, her smile quirky. 'I thought you had me neatly labelled from the minute we met.'

'That's what I mean. You should be empty-headed, or your head should be stuffed full of fripperies—dresses and dances and tennis parties. I'm not even an officer. You should be looking down that aristocratic little nose at the likes of me.'

'The likes of you?'

She eyed him deliberately up and down. If anyone else had appraised him so brazenly, it would have provoked a caustic riposte. Instead, Flora, with her sensuous mouth and her saucy look, made him want to kiss her.

'I am not in the habit of categorising people, as you are,' she said. 'In any event, I very much doubt there is anyone quite like you. Which is why, despite myself, I find your company stimulating.'

Stimulating! She certainly was. 'Then that makes two of us,' Geraint said, trying not to smile, 'though let me tell you, it is entirely against my principles.'

Flora gave a gurgle of laughter. 'You are the master of the backhanded compliment. I am sorry that you find you cannot dislike me when you have tried so hard to do so.'

'You sound as if you wish me to try harder,' he retorted.

'Perhaps I do. Your barbs, Corporal Cassell, have been a welcome distraction while we dismantle my home.'

Which was the nearest she had come to saying what she felt about the requisition. Her father wasn't the only one with a stiff upper lip. Guessing that sympathy would be most unwelcome, Geraint gave a mocking bow. 'I am delighted to have been of service.'

Flora's smile wobbled. 'It is silly of me, but I feel as if we are doing something very final. I doubt things will return to what they were, even when this war is over.'

'I sincerely hope they do not.'

She sighed. 'No, of course you don't, and you're probably right.'

The perfume she wore had a floral scent. Not cloyingly sweet, but something lighter, more delicate and springlike. 'I don't understand you,' Geraint said. 'You're not some empty-headed social butterfly. Don't you feel suffocated, stuck here in this draughty castle with nothing to do but— what, arrange flowers and sew samplers?'

'Do not forget my playing Lady Bountiful for the poor of the parish,' Flora snapped. 'Then there is the endless round of parties and dances, the occasional ceilidh in the village that I must grace with my presence. Added to that, there is tennis in the summer and...'

'It was not my intention to patronise you,' Geraint interrupted. 'You just baffle me.'

'So you said.'

Her eyes were over-bright. Annoyed, as much for having allowed himself to notice the soft swell of her bosom as she folded her hands defensively across her chest as for having been the cause of the action, Geraint spoke in a gentler tone. 'It just seems to me that you're wasting your life, shut away here. Aren't you bored? Why don't you leave?'

She stared at him blankly. 'I cannot just leave. Where would I go? What would I do?'

'I don't know,' he said impatiently. 'What do you want to do? You must have thought about it.'

'I have never had to,' Flora said, looking troubled, 'which is a shocking thing to admit, but the truth, for it is not as if I spend my days idly, is that there is always something to do here. I suppose it has always been assumed that I would marry well.'

'You mean replace your father's patronage with that of another wealthy man so that you can carry on arranging flowers ad nauseam.'

'That is a very cynical way of looking at matrimony,' Flora said coldly, 'and quite beside the point, since I have no intention of making such a match. The problem is, I am not actually qualified to do anything else. Thank you very much for bringing that fact to my attention, incidentally.'

'You are making a pretty good fist of managing this requisition, despite your claim that you had no idea how to tackle it,' Geraint pointed out.

'That is because I have had your expert lead to follow.'

He shook his head firmly. 'Do not underestimate yourself.'

'I doubt that is possible.'

'Flora, I meant it. You are bright, quick-witted, practical and articulate. You've a talent for organising, for creating order.'

'Do you really think so?' She spoke eagerly.

'I wouldn't have said it otherwise,' Geraint replied, touched by the vulnerability her question revealed. 'You should know me well enough by now to know I don't say anything I don't mean.'

'My parents are both fairly certain that I will make a hash of things.'

'Then you shall surprise them by proving them wrong.'

He was rewarded with a smile. 'Perhaps I shall surprise you, too, at the end of it,' she said. 'Despite the melancholy nature of our task, I have to admit that I am enjoying the challenge. Perhaps I should reconsider joining the VADs, like Sheila.'

'Sheila? You mean the maid? Blonde, pretty girl?'

'Do you think she's pretty?'

Geraint laughed. 'I think that's the first predictable thing you've ever said to me. Yes, she's very pretty and I'd have to be blind not to have noticed.'

'We went to school in the village together until I was removed to an academy for young ladies,' Flora said, making a face. 'Sheila is counting the days, waiting to be assigned to a hospital. I shall miss her terribly when she goes. I did consider volunteering, but my mother was appalled. She thinks it would be most improper work for me, and my father thinks that I would find it far too taxing, and the demoralising fact is that he is probably right.' She held up her hands for his inspection. 'Lily-white and quite unsullied by hard work, as I am sure you have noted.'

Which so exactly mirrored his own, original opinion of her that Geraint felt a stab of guilt. 'There are plenty of other things you could do, I'm sure,' he said gruffly.

'Would that I had your confidence in me. Which sounds really rather pathetic. You are right, I am stuck in a rut and have no purpose whatsoever in my life save to look decorative while waiting for a suitable husband to appear,' Flora replied brightly. 'Thank you, as I said earlier, for pointing that out, but if you don't mind, I have had quite enough picking over my empty life and my character flaws for one day.' She picked up her notebook and pencil. 'I think we should get back to work.'

Her smile was fixed, her cheeks flushed, though she countered his scrutiny with a determined tilt of her chin. Geraint was not fooled, but he was not such an idiot as to ignore the signs. *No trespassing.* He ought to be pleased with himself for making her face up to some unpalatable truths, but he wasn't. She had taken his criticisms on the chin, too. She would have been within her rights to tell him to mind his own business, which was what he would have said had the roles been reversed. Flora Carmichael might look as if a puff of wind would blow her away, but she had backbone. He had to admire her for that. In fact, the more he got to know her, the more he liked her....

The realisation set him quite off-kilter. Geraint got to his feet and made a point of consulting his wristwatch. A gift from his parents on his twenty-first birthday, it was a plain, functional timepiece, but it was one of his most precious possessions. 'You carry on without me. I need to check on the lads.'

The door closed behind him, but Flora remained where she was. Geraint did not, as Robbie would say, pull his punches. It was a dispiriting thought, but she suspected she had been merely marking time with her life without even realising it. Forcing herself to think about it now, the very idea of turning into her mother, which she would, if she continued to allow herself to drift with the tide, made her shudder. Her parents expected so little from her that it was ridiculously easy to please them. And it would, sadly, be ridiculously easy to disappoint them, were she to pursue some sort of independent course.

'Whatever that may be,' Flora muttered to herself. Pacing over to the window, she stared morosely out at the loch. The problem was that now Geraint had pointed it out, she could not deny the creeping dissatisfaction she had been feeling, and nor could she ignore it, though to do something about it would be to fly in the face of her parents' expectations. 'So I am damned if I do, and damned if I don't,' she said wryly. 'Which brings me no nearer at all to knowing what it is I am going to do.'

You are bright, quick-witted, practical and articulate, Geraint had said. None of those epithets had ever been applied to her before, yet Geraint never said what he didn't believe. He was blunt to a fault, but he also saw things in her that others did not, and expected much more of her than anyone else did, which both pleased and scared her a little. What if she failed?

Think positively, Flora castigated herself. She would not fail, because that would reflect badly on Geraint, and she wanted Geraint to succeed. Almost more than she wanted to succeed herself. Which was a novel, not to say startling, thought. 'Sink or swim,' Flora repeated, remembering the pact they had made.

An image of a naked Geraint swimming beside her in the loch, rivulets of water coursing down his muscled back and buttocks, sprang shockingly vivid into her mind's eye. 'Swim it shall most definitely be,' Flora muttered, pressing the backs of her hands against her flaming cheeks.

Chapter Four

A few days later, as October was coming to a close, Flora and Geraint were in the attics, a jumble of rooms at the top of a narrow staircase. Though the main part of the house had electricity, which ran from a generator, there was no light here, save for what crept in through the occasional dusty skylight and what was given off by the two oil lamps they had brought with them. It had been Flora's idea, since the outhouses and the old stables were already full to overflowing with displaced furnishings, to put the smaller and more valuable artefacts here, but she was beginning to wonder if it had been a mistake. 'I hadn't realised there was so much up here already,' she said, looking around her in dismay.

Geraint was standing just inside the doorway, clutching the low frame, staring past her into the cramped room, his eyes unfocused. 'Geraint? Are you feeling unwell? You look quite pale.'

Flora set her lamp carefully down and put the back of her hand on his brow. It was clammy with sweat. 'It's nothing,' he said brusquely, before pushing her hand away and ducking his head to enter the attic. 'I see what you mean. I've never seen such a collection of junk.'

His voice sounded brittle to her, but his colour had returned. If he was feeling ill, he did not care to admit to it.

Flora edged her way into the confined space, which was strewn with bric-a-brac. Old trunks, dusty boxes, broken furniture and huge empty picture frames comprised the majority of it, but there were also moth-eaten rugs, several stacks of account books, and an assortment of stuffed animals in various states of decline. 'I doubt I'd recognise that thing if it were alive,' she said, pointing to a decrepit mound that looked like a large shoe with fangs. 'What on earth is it?'

Geraint picked it up gingerly. 'It appears to be a baby crocodile or alligator. Did one of your ancestors have a penchant for taxidermy?'

'I have absolutely no idea. Why do you ask?'

'I'm just worried we might stumble across a stuffed laird or two.'

Flora burst into laughter. Geraint, now seemingly quite restored, was smiling at her in a way that made her heart beat erratically. It was an intimate smile, a complicit smile, and at the same time a very sensual smile. His eyes looked more black than brown in the dim light and there was a warmth in them that triggered a corresponding heat in her blood. Tearing her mind back to the job in hand, she looked around despairingly. 'I shall have to clear some space, though how I am to decide what can be jettisoned…' She took the crocodile from Geraint and eyed it distastefully. 'You can go for a start, my lad.'

'And what about this?'

She whirled around to find him draped in an ancient sheepskin cloak, clutching a dagger. The leather was worn, the fleece was moulting in places, the blade of the dirk was rusted through, and yet he managed to look both fierce and proud, not just a warrior, but a warrior king.

'What do you think, wench?' he growled.

She thought, rather fancifully, that she could understand why a woman would let herself be carried off by such a man to be—well, who knows what? 'You look very—convincing.' There was a smear of dust across his cheek. His hair was dishevelled. The cloak emphasised the breadth of his shoulders and his chest, just as the army puttees so tightly bound around his legs showed off the muscles of his calves. 'They'd have worn that thing over a plaid originally,' Flora said.

'Shall I take off my tunic for the sake of authenticity?'

They both knew he meant it for a joke, but as she looked at him, the smile died on his face. She touched the fleece, which was hemmed with a complicated design of coloured wools. Her hand brushed against the rough khaki serge of his tunic. She snatched it away. 'It must be like wearing a hair shirt,' she mumbled.

His eyes were dark, dangerous. She stood rooted to the spot, unaccountably certain that he was going to kiss her. Then he took a deliberate step back and discarded the cloak. 'No worse than a plaid would be, I imagine,' he said.

Did she imagine it, that almost kiss? She did not think so, but she had so little experience, she could not be sure. She had wanted him to kiss her. Had been wanting him to kiss her since that first day when he had pressed his lips to her palm. Had it been her own latent desire that had made her mistake his intentions? Slanting a glance at him, she received an inscrutable look.

'Is this the only attic?' Geraint enquired.

'No, though it is the biggest,' she replied, which caused him to flinch slightly, before he turned away quickly and picked up the oil lamp. 'Let's take a look, then.'

They began to work their way through the rooms, deciding what could be moved, what could be thrown out and which items Flora would have to consult with her father about. Two hours later, they had completed about half of the task, and Geraint stopped to push open a skylight, taking greedy breaths of fresh, cold air. Alone in this cramped space, he'd undoubtedly have parted company with his breakfast, but Flora's presence was proving a welcome, and surprisingly effective distraction.

Leaving the skylight slightly ajar, he sat down on an old steamer trunk. 'Do your family never throw anything away? There's enough stuff up here to furnish the entire valley back home.'

Flora perched beside him on a moth-eaten stool. 'You know all about my family, down to the intimate details of how we live, yet I know nothing of yours. You mentioned sisters and brothers, I think.'

'Three sisters between myself and my brother, Bryn, who's the baby of the family. Bethan and Angharad are in service, Cerys is training to be a nurse.'

'And your parents, what do they think of you joining up?'

Geraint shrugged. 'What every parent thinks, I suppose. My father will be proud I'm doing my bit for my country, though he'd prefer I did it down the mine.'

'So your father is a miner?'

'He is, as I was until a few years ago. As Bryn will be in a year, unless I have a say in it.' Geraint frowned. 'Bryn is such a bright lad. He could do so much better for himself. He's at the grammar school on a bursary, just like I was, but he has no ambition to stay on as I did until I was eighteen. Worships my dad, does our Bryn—he wants nothing more than to follow in his footsteps down the mine. All the more so, since I've so signally failed to keep up the tradition.'

'But surely, with a grammar-school education, you had no reason to work in the mine at all.'

Geraint laughed bitterly. 'I had every reason. I am my father's son. It's what the men in my family do. *Not* becoming a miner would have been viewed as the ultimate act of disloyalty, because any other white-collar job I could have got above ground would have entailed working with *them*. The bosses, the owners.'

'Surely you exaggerate.'

'That is how it would have been seen by my family, our neighbours. A betrayal.'

'And yet you gave it up all the same,' Flora said, looking puzzled. 'Why?'

It was an innocent enough question and a perfectly natural one, but it made Geraint realise how personal a turn the conversation had taken. He never talked about his family, had a policy, forged of bitter experience, of not explaining himself. 'I had my reasons. So I left.'

I left. Such a simple phrase to describe one of the most difficult decisions of his life. So many nights spent lying wide awake in bed. The long days when he was due on late shift, walking in the nearby hills, trying to talk himself into staying on for just another year, month, week. Geraint leaned back against the attic wall, turning his face up to the skylight, to the wide, grey-blue sky above, which was the colour of Flora's eyes. 'I left,' he repeated sadly. '*To find something better*, is the reason I gave my dad, and he took offence, thinking I was demeaning his life's work'

'There is nothing wrong with trying to better yourself,' Flora said indignantly.

'Tell that to the toffs at the grammar school.'

The words did not come over as light-heartedly as he'd intended. Flora had her arms clasped around her knees. His own legs were sprawled in front of him, so that they were almost touching hers. 'It must have been very difficult for you there,' she said. Her hand touched his knee tentatively.

'I coped. I fought my corner. Literally. It was a long time ago. I really don't know why I'm telling you all this.'

'I am glad that you have.' Flora twisted the little pearl ring she wore on her pinkie finger round and round. It was a habit she had, he'd noticed, when she was struggling to voice her thoughts. 'We have more in common than you might think. You've made me face the fact that I don't want what my parents have planned for me, either. I was— I suppose I was simply avoiding facing the issue before. Now you've forced me to look, I can't pretend I haven't seen. I have no choice but to hurt them.'

She was saying that she understood, and Geraint could tell she did. He covered her hand with his. 'My dad thought I was ashamed of him, of our family, our village,' he admitted painfully. 'I had no choice but to leave, when my presence there was a daily reminder of my betrayal.'

Flora reached up, touched his cheek fleetingly, but to his relief she sensed that her pity would not be welcome. 'So you joined the army,' she said. 'I confess, I've wondered why a man so radical as you, who has such contempt for hierarchy and tradition, would enlist in an institution that sets such store by it.'

'I didn't, not straight away. I went to London and found a job in the office of a factory that manufactured automobiles. A job with prospects,' Geraint said mockingly, remembering the interview. 'Maybe it would have been, if I'd stuck it out. I have a head for figures, and a talent for organising, just like you, but I also have a nose for injustice, thanks to my dad. Those poor lads on the factory floor worked bloody hard—beg pardon—for a pittance in conditions almost as dangerous as those down the pit. I was working for the Labour Party in my spare time. Eventually my employers found out, and that put paid to my prospects. By then it was obvious war was going to be declared, so I enlisted.'

'I still don't understand why,' Flora said.

'I joined the Royal Welsh Fusiliers,' Geraint replied.

'To fight alongside your own people, was that it?'

'It was. Brothers in arms and all that. But the moment

they got wind of my accounting experience, they transferred me to the Army Service Corps and I washed up here, destined once again to play the pantomime villain by desecrating Glen Massan House,' Geraint said with a twisted smile.

Flora frowned. 'Do you really believe *we* are on opposing sides?'

'I'd hardly be confiding in you if I did.'

'So we are fighting on the same side?'

'I wouldn't go that far, Miss Daughter-of-the-Laird-Carmichael,' Geraint said, grinning and getting to his feet. He held his hand out to help her up. Her fingers were slender, perfectly manicured, her palm smooth against his rough calloused hand.

'If we are not enemies but we are not on the same side, then where on earth are we?'

'I'll tell you where we are, we're in no man's land.'

'No man's land,' Flora repeated. 'Our own private land.'

'For the time being.'

No man's land. A place where only one man existed, Flora thought. A man whose eyes glittered darkly down at her, mesmerising beneath the thick curtain of his lashes. A man who, by his own admission, confided in no one, yet had confided in her. A dangerous man. A lonely man. A challenging man. And a very enticing one. 'I think I like no man's land,' she said.

'So do I,' Geraint said softly, closing the space between them. He slid his arm around her waist. His fingers were delicate on her jaw, her cheek, making her catch her breath in anticipation, making her tremble, scattering her inhibitions to the four winds.

Her body was pliant, melding itself to his hardness as she reached up to put her arms around his neck. As his lips touched hers, her eyelids closed. His tongue ran along the soft skin on the inside of her lower lip, and she shivered at the shocking intimacy of it. It was like the first sip of a fine French cognac. Warmth flooded her.

Her heart pounded. His kiss deepened, his tongue tangling with hers, sending sizzles of heat coursing through her veins. His hand cupped her breast. They staggered back, stumbling over the steamer chest, until her back was pressed against the attic wall, directly under the skylight. He slid his hands down, cupping her bottom, lifting her. The rough stone grated on her back as she arched against him, encountering the hard length of his erection through his uniform. He moaned, a low growl that made her spine tingle. And then he dragged his mouth from hers.

For a long moment they stared at each other, eyes glazed with desire, breathing shallow and fast. Then slowly, reluctantly, he released her. As her feet touched the dusty wooden boards of the attic, Flora caught at his sleeve to steady herself. 'I think the air in no man's land has rather gone to my head,' she said.

Geraint laughed softly. 'I could tell you what it's done to me, but I suspect you already know.' His smile faded as his eyes met hers. 'I didn't mean to get so carried away.'

'I ought not to have let you,' Flora said, realising this very belatedly. Which made her realise that the thought had not occurred to her, any more than it had occurred to her to be embarrassed. On the contrary, what she felt was a kind of elation. This strange, interesting, dangerous man wanted her, and she wanted him. 'No man's land,' she said softly, looking at him with a deliberately teasing smile, 'is a dangerous but exciting place to be.'

Chapter Five

'You actually kissed him! Oh, my, who would have thought it?'

Sheila and Flora were in what Lady Carmichael termed the garden room, which was in reality an old scullery at the back of the house used mainly for flower arranging. At this time of year it lay empty and quite unoccupied. Outside, a neat row of army tents had been erected amongst which soldiers bustled around, some in full uniform, some minus jackets, in singlets and braces. Unfamiliar accents echoed over the once-peaceful loch. Sporadic bursts of raucous laughter punctuated the Highland air. 'I don't know why you look so astonished,' Flora said. 'I've been kissed before.'

'Not like that, I'll bet,' Sheila replied, grinning. 'Your Welsh firebrand looks like a man who would know how to kiss. I would kiss him myself if he gave me the chance, but he's not shown the least bit of interest. To be honest, I find him a bit intimidating. Not exactly stand-offish, but a bit of a loner. I suppose I'm—well, just a wee bit envious.'

'Are you shocked?'

'Your ma would be. *The man is not even an officer,*' Sheila said in an excellent imitation of her employer.

'I'm not my mother,' Flora said.

Sheila raised her brow. 'Do I hear the sound of a worm turning?'

Outside, one of the soldiers, sitting on a box cleaning his boots, was singing, 'Daisy, Daisy, give me your answer true.' Flora turned away from the window. 'I kissed him because I wanted to. I've been wanting to from almost the first moment I set eyes on him,' she admitted sheepishly. 'But you're right, it's not just that. He's made me realise that I've taken too much for granted.'

'You just make sure that Corporal Cassell doesn't take too much for granted,' Sheila said. 'You're from different sides of the fence, you and the corporal. Kiss him, why not, there's no harm in it, but what I'm trying to say is, be careful, Flora.'

'You're making too much of one kiss.'

'Good. And good for you!' Sheila rubbed her eyes. 'I was up till all hours last night sewing my new uniform. I heard in the village that Mrs Oliphant got a telegram yesterday. Her Ronnie is missing.'

'Oh, no! Oh, the poor woman.'

'I really hope I'll get my posting to one of the hospitals soon. News like that, it makes you want to be doing something.'

'I've been thinking again about volunteering myself.'

She expected to receive an approving smile, but Sheila frowned. 'I'm not so sure. It's very physical work, Flora, and you've no experience.'

'Nor likely to get any if no one will let me try.'

'I'm just pointing out the truth. There's no need to take the huff.'

'Actually, there is every reason,' Flora exclaimed. 'It's bad enough to know that my parents think I'm useless, but you are supposed to be my friend. Just because I've never lit a fire or mopped a floor or ironed a shirt doesn't mean I can't learn. You have never washed a wound or applied a splint or given an injection of morphine, but you are pretty certain that you'll be able to. You haven't ever seen anything worse than a nosebleed, yet you have every confidence you won't faint at the sight of blood, and just as much confidence that I will.'

'Flora! What on earth is the matter with you?'

'I don't need to be pampered and cossetted. I'm not a lap dog.'

'Right now, you're more like an angry terrier.'

She was forced to laugh. 'I'm not angry, I'm just disappointed. I thought you would be on my side. I need to be doing something.'

'You're managing the requisition.'

'That will be complete in few weeks.'

'And then your corporal will probably be sent off to the front, I suppose.'

'He's in the service corps.'

'For now. Didn't you just tell me that he signed up with the Welsh Fusiliers?'

'I hadn't thought of that.' Flora shuddered. 'I'm terrified that Alex will lie about his age to enlist. His letters from school are full of talk about the boys from the year above him who have joined up already. And Robbie—it's probably only a matter of time before he leaves his job and joins up. I don't want to think of Geraint on the front line, even if it is what he wants.'

'No point in worrying about it until it happens.' Sheila smoothed down her apron. 'I must get on, I've a hundred things to do. Look, forget what I said. If you think you're capable of volunteering, then you volunteer. Better to try and fail than not to try at all, as my mum would say.'

Which was hardly likely to fill her with confidence, Flora thought as the door closed behind her friend. Examining her hands, their white, unblemished state the mark, her mother was forever telling her, of a lady, she felt quite dejected. Perhaps Sheila was right.

Or perhaps not. What was it Geraint had said? *You've a talent for organising, a talent for creating order.* Picking up her notebook, Flora looked at the neat list of tasks, the ticks that were steadily accumulating, and felt a glow of satisfaction. She was making a good job of this. There must be some way of applying her newfound skills elsewhere.

Her eye fell on the last task. *Sign off paperwork and complete handover.* If they kept to the tight schedule Geraint had set up, that would be in just a few weeks time. Glen Massan House would be a fully operational military training school, and their time in no man's land would come to an end. *'Carpe diem,'* Flora muttered to herself. 'Seize the day. That's what we'll all have to do while this dreadful war rages on. And I intend to do just that.'

The list of tasks was nearing completion by the middle of November, the requisition proceeding exactly to schedule. 'There, now, what did I tell you, is this not the most spectacular view?' Flora pointed down at Glen Massan House, several hundred feet below.

They were at the peak of Ben Massan, a short but steep climb. Her eyes were sparkling, her cheeks flushed, her hair blowing in wild, fiery tendrils around her face. She wore an old mackintosh coat that was far too large for her, the sleeves turned up to form a cuff, the hem flapping around her ankles. On her feet were sturdy brown brogues, much worn and eminently practical.

'Spectacular, but not as pretty as you,' Geraint said, pulling her into his arms and kissing her hard.

Laughing, she put her arms around his neck and pulled him closer. Her lips were cold, but her tongue was warm. She kissed him back as fiercely as he kissed her. He felt the familiar rush of blood to his groin and reluctantly let her go.

'Why do you do that?' Flora was staring up at him, her expression hurt. 'Stop kissing me, I mean. Don't you like kissing me?'

It hadn't occurred to him that she wouldn't understand. 'Don't look at me like that,' Geraint said, putting his arm around her, pulling her onto the soft, peaty ground in the lea of the cairn that marked the summit. 'It's because I like it too much.' He cupped her face, smoothing her hair away from her cheeks. 'Flora, it's all very well to joke about being in no man's land, to talk about seizing the day, but we have to be careful. We have to see this for what it is, a bit of fun.'

'Fun.' She said it as if she were turning the word over, inspecting it from every angle. 'What you really mean is that there's no future in it. I already know that, Geraint. There is no need to warn me off.'

But there seemed to be a need to remind himself of that salient fact. 'When the war is over, I intend to go into politics,' he said. 'Things need to change for the better for ordinary working people.'

She smiled wryly. 'You mean we shall end up on opposite sides again.'

'Something like that.'

'And because of that you don't want to take advantage of the situation,' she said with a crooked smile. 'I know,' she said, putting her fingers over his mouth to prevent him replying, 'that the idea of being called a gentleman appals you, but nevertheless, your sense of honour would put a lot of so-called gentlemen to shame. And I suppose I should be embarrassed now, for I have admitted to a very unlady-like wish that you would not behave so very honourably.'

'Which I am delighted to hear,' Geraint said with a gruff laugh, 'because behaving honourably is just about killing me.' He pulled her to him, running his thumb over the soft, sensual skin of her lower lip. 'The things I imagine us doing together would make you blush to the roots of your hair.'

She caught his hand, closing her mouth around his thumb, pulling it into the moist heat of her mouth before releasing him. 'Tell me,' she said.

He shook his head. 'Certainly not. *That* would be most ungentlemanly.'

'I already told you that I feel most unladylike. Please tell me, Geraint. I know we cannot, but I would like to know what it would be like if we could.'

She was smiling, one of those smiles that did strange things to his guts, and he thought he had never found any woman more irresistible. In the throes of passion, he had been able to ask—Do you like this? Do you want this? Harder? Slower? Faster?—but he had never before articulated his own desires. *I want to know what it would be like if we could.* He pulled Flora closer to him out of the wind, resting his chin on the silky mass of her hair. 'The reality could never match my imaginings,' he said, willing himself to believe it.

'I would still like to know.'

She had slipped her arms under his greatcoat, wrapping them around his waist. Geraint closed his eyes, drinking in the scent of her perfume, her soap, the fresh Highland air and the intangible something else that made the heady mixture uniquely Flora. 'When we kiss,' he whispered, 'I feel like I am diving into a deep, dark pool. And the more we kiss the deeper I want to dive.' His fingers found the warm, delicate skin at the nape of her neck. 'I want to touch you. All of you. I want to taste you, every part of you.'

Flora shuddered. He pulled her closer so that she lay half over him, her leg between his. 'I want to kiss your mouth,' he said, unable to stop himself doing just that. 'I want to kiss your breasts.' He undid her coat, cupping her through the soft wool of her dress. She rolled onto her back. He covered her with his body. 'I want to kiss your breasts until you can't take any more,' he said, his voice ragged, his thumbs stroking her nipples.

Flora arched under him, her eyes glazing over. 'What else, Geraint? What else would you do?'

He was already hard. 'I would kiss your belly.' He flattened his palm, sliding it over her. 'I would kiss the inside of your thighs. Soft, your skin would be. So soft and so warm. When I kiss you there, I can feel you want me, feel it here,' he said, pressing down on the taut muscles of her stomach, then farther down. 'I want you every bit as much, but I don't want it to be over too soon, so I touch you. Here.' Flat palm gliding over her sex. Flora's hands on him, clutching at his tunic. Her eyes wide, dark, her cheeks bright with colour. Her breath shallow, fast. 'I have never wanted anyone as I want you,' he whispered.

'Never. Not ever,' she answered.

'I want to taste you. Here. This. I want to taste all of you.' The words, shocking, stark, raw with need, formed without thinking. He touched her, just covered her, through her dress, and felt her arch up under him just as he had dreamed. 'I taste you,' Geraint said, his eyes fixed on hers, stroking now, just stroking, 'and I kiss you. Here. Like this.'

Her mouth under his. Her lips soft, velvet, clinging. Tongues tangling. His erection throbbed. She bucked under him, moaning softly as he kissed her, as he touched her until she shuddered. She was going to come. He saw it in the faraway look, felt it in the way her body reacted. And if he did not stop…

He rolled abruptly away, closing his eyes tight, thinking of cold snow, of army drill, and when that did not work, of the cramped recesses of the mine workings. Sweat of a different sort broke out on his brow, and the danger passed.

Flora sat up, pulling her coat around her, feeling as if she had been caught, yanked back at the last moment from falling. No, it was more like a dream where she fell and fell, and woke up just before she hit the ground. Beside her, Geraint had his eyes screwed shut. She stared down into the glen at her home. Her former home.

Geraint got to his feet, holding his hand out to help her up. 'Well, I think that rather proved the point,' he said shakily.

'That reality is no match for your imaginings?' she asked, still keeping her eyes on the view.

'I think we had better stop this before we get in too deep.'

She turned to face him. His mouth was set, resolute. *Before we get in too deep.* It would pain him to know it was already too late. It would be painful for her, much more painful, if she let herself fall any deeper. 'You're right,' she said, summoning a bright smile and rummaging in her capacious coat pocket for her notebook. 'We should concentrate on what we came up here for before the light fades. Tell me, then, which parts of the grounds do you think best suited for target practice.'

'So, given the two new sections that have arrived, and with the main body of men due on the seventh of December, which is next week, we felt it prudent to establish a regular patrol in the village.'

Flora glanced up from her notes at her parents, who were seated opposite her at the dining table in the Lodge. She would have held the meeting in the parlour over tea. She would not have called it a meeting, but a chat. It was Geraint who insisted she formalise matters. 'Else they will not take you seriously,' he had told her. 'You need to stamp your authority on this, make them realise that the decisions are already made, and not up for discussion.'

'Wouldn't it be better if you did it?' she'd asked him, but he shook his head.

'I'm not the one with something to prove.'

And he had been quite right, on all fronts. 'I see no need to patrol the village,' her father said. 'Simply keep it out of bounds to the men, and there ends the problem.'

He spoke in his don't-be-a-silly-girl voice. Flora counted to three and made sure to reply in her well-rehearsed voice of reason. 'First, making the village out of bounds will only encourage the men to want to go there. It is human nature to wish to do what one is told one cannot.' A lesson she had been learning on a daily basis, these past couple of weeks, since agreeing her pact with Geraint on top of Ben Massan. 'Second, drawing demarcation lines between the village and the House will create unnecessary tension. We are all in this together, Father. Third, it is inevitable that without some sort of patrol as a safeguard, there will be trouble between the village lads and the Tommies. And that leads me to my next point. The Christmas concert and children's party. We feel this will provide an ideal opportunity for the men to help maintain good relations with the village, so Corporal Cassell and I have decided…'

'You and Corporal Cassell seem to have decided a great deal,' Lady Carmichael interrupted. 'I thought Colonel Aitchison was in charge.'

'The colonel has naturally approved the details of the plan,' Flora said, which was essentially true. The colonel having been given a brief summary by Geraint and listened to Flora's assurances that the laird was in full agreement, had nodded, signed the latest batch of requisition orders and returned to his fishing.

'You seem to have spent an inordinate amount of time with this corporal,' Lady Carmichael said pointedly.

'It has been necessary in order to carry out my duties.' Which was true.

'Duties you have discharged very thoroughly,' the laird said. 'I must say, Flora, you have surprised me.'

She had surprised herself, but she remembered just in time to suppress her gratified smile as her father got to his feet. Flora cleared her throat. 'I am not quite finished yet, if you don't mind.' The laird sighed, but sat back down again. 'The main convoy arrives next week, as I've said,' Flora continued. 'There will be a company of over two hundred men complete with a major, four lieutenants and a number of ancillary staff including officer trainers, cooks, medics and drivers.' She paused, reminding herself not to sound apologetic. 'The kitchen garden will form a shooting range. The high walls make it an ideal location. Artillery practice will be carried out on the grouse moor. And the croquet lawn—the croquet lawn will form the main area for parking and storage of large equipment.'

'The croquet lawn?' Lady Carmichael said icily.

Beneath the table, Flora clasped her hands together tightly. Despite not being the least bit interested in croquet herself, and the fact that the hoops had long been removed for the winter, Flora had been anguished, too, when Geraint raised the issue. Losing the beautifully manicured lawn set aside for the genteel pursuit seemed almost an act of vandalism. 'Since the forecourt will be used for drilling the troops, this is the most convenient area.'

It was a full thirty seconds, which felt like thirty minutes, before her father broke the silence. 'What about the cellars? All that valuable wine your brother Robbie has stored there?'

'Corporal Cassell was equally concerned, so he had all the wine moved to the cellars here at the Lodge. There was just about enough space.'

Flora frowned, remembering how Geraint had been

that day. The cellars at Glen Massan House were deep, a warren of narrow passageways from which various rooms led. 'Like going down the mine,' she had joked at the time, standing over the hatch, watching Geraint slowly descend alone, for she had no intention of encountering the rats she was certain lived down there. He had emerged no more than fifteen minutes later, sweating profusely, his pallor ghostlike. She thought he was going to faint, though he brushed her offer of water away, just as he also brushed away her concern. 'Were there rats down there?' she'd asked fearfully, foolishly staring at the wooden staircase as if they might have followed Geraint up. 'I'll get Hopkins to deal with this,' he'd finally said, ignoring her question, pushing past her hurriedly and out of the basement.

There must have been rats after all, she had decided. And he simply didn't want to admit his dislike of them. Although you'd think he'd be accustomed to rats, working down a mine. Presuming mines had rats.

'Are we quite finished?' the laird said, looking pointedly at his watch.

Flora dragged her mind away from Geraint and hastily consulted her list. 'Unless you can think of anything we have omitted?'

He shook his head. 'You have been most thorough. Forgive me, but I must— I need some air.' The laird patted his wife's shoulder as he got to his feet. 'Flora has only done what was required of her. What is required of us is to accept these very painful decisions with good grace. Excuse me.'

The door closed behind him. 'This *bloody* war,' Lady Carmichael exclaimed. 'I think the world going to hell in a handcart.'

Flora dropped her pencil, staring open-mouthed at her mother, who never swore.

'I do not, as you know, have any time for those women

who claim we females should be enfranchised,' Lady Carmichael continued, 'but I'm beginning to wonder, if we did have the vote, whether we'd have avoided this dreadful situation in the first place. I had a letter from your brother Alex this morning. He wants to leave school at the end of this term. Your father had a separate communication from him, asking permission to enlist.'

'Oh, no!'

'He will refuse, of course, but—I can't bury my head in the sand for much longer. It is inevitable that my sons will join this war, and I do not want...' Lady Carmichael dabbed frantically at her eyes.

Flora got up and knelt at her mother's chair. 'There's nothing to apologise for—what you're feeling is perfectly natural. We can be as patriotic as the next woman and still wish that our loved ones did not have to do what other people's loved ones are doing.'

Her ladyship sniffed. 'I am sure there is something quite flawed with the grammar of that sentence, but I must endorse the sentiment. Now the handover of Glen Massan House is nearing completion, I can admit that I have never been entirely comfortable with you having to be so much in the company of that corporal. A most intimidating young man, and insolent with it. It's not so much in his words, but he has a way of looking at one. You will be able to spend more time with me again. I thought we could take a trip to Edinburgh next week, to do some Christmas shopping.'

Flora sighed. 'Mother, you know that I am considering joining the VADs.'

'You cannot, Flora. I need you here.'

'Nonsense. These past few weeks while I have been working with Geraint, you have managed perfectly well without me.'

'Geraint? You mean Corporal Cassell, I take it? You do

realise, Flora, that he is not our sort. I sincerely hope that you have not allowed the man to take liberties.'

'Geraint is not the sort of man to take unwelcome liberties,' Flora said, which was true. Another thing Geraint had taught her—always tell the truth when confronted, even if you tailor it to suit your needs. And in fact, since that kiss on the top of Ben Massan they had both been at pains—extreme pains—to avoid anything but the most casual of contact.

'Well, I am pleased to hear it,' Lady Carmichael said. 'I expect he will be posted somewhere else soon, in any event, since his task is nearly complete.'

'I suppose so,' Flora replied. She did not want to think about that. 'Mother, what I'm trying to tell you is that I shall be looking for something else to do.'

'Such as what, precisely? And please, Flora, do not persist with this notion that you can become a volunteer nurse. You are quite simply not cut out for it.'

'I can learn. I do have some skills. I am an excellent organiser, and I am a good negotiator, too. It was I who agreed the terms of the regular local deliveries, and many of those coming from Glasgow. I did those on the telephone.'

'Well! So it has come to that, my daughter discussing terms with tradesmen.'

Flora burst out laughing. 'For heaven's sake, Mother...'

'It is not funny.' Lady Carmichael pushed her chair back violently. 'It is very far from funny. This war will not go on forever, Flora Carmichael. When it ends, if you are not careful, you will discover that you have become quite unsuited for real life. Think about that before you ruin your hands with carbolic soap and ruin your chances of making any sort of match by compromising your reputation nursing common soldiers.'

'So much for my determination to have the last word,'

Flora said as the door swung shut behind her mother. Picking up her notebook and pencil, she got to her feet, staring out of the window at the darkening sky, all her pleasure in having completed her meeting exactly to plan quite spoiled by her mother's reaction.

But beneath her mother's bluster there was genuine concern. Leaving home, flying in the face of her parents' wishes, would change things irrevocably between them. What was more, if the war continued as it seemed inevitable it would, into 1915 or even 1916, there was a good chance they would lose all of their children to it, one way or another.

Chapter Six

Several days later, in the drawing room, Flora's shoes echoed on the bare boards. It looked enormous without its furnishings, the last of which had been shrouded in old sheets and in placed in the stables. Dust motes danced in the air as a faint streak of winter sun penetrated the gloom. 'Is it selfish of me,' Flora asked Geraint, 'to want to leave here just when my parents may need me the most?'

'What about your needs?'

'I need to leave,' she replied without hesitation, 'though it makes me feel horribly guilty just saying it.'

'I know how that feels.'

'Of course you do.' She touched his arm sympathetically. 'Do you regret it, Geraint?'

His hand covered hers briefly before he snatched it away. 'It's tough, walking away from the life you know, the people you love. I—I miss them.'

'I find it appalling that you have not had sufficient leave to go to Wales since joining the army.'

Geraint flushed. 'I haven't been home in three years.'

'Three years! But I thought— You said— I assumed...'

'It's not that we're estranged. I write every week.'

Geraint was staring down at his boots, the toes of which were polished to a mirror-like smoothness, which, he had told her, severely compromised their waterproofing. 'But you have not seen them since you enlisted,' Flora said.

'I told you, when I left the pit, they thought I was being disloyal.'

'Don't you think that perhaps the problem lies more with you, and not them? Geraint, they will surely be more hurt by your staying away than the fact that you left in the first place.'

When he finally looked up, his eyes were bleak. 'You don't understand,' he said.

I don't want to discuss it, his tone made very clear. *Make me understand, explain it to me,* Flora wanted to say, but the pain in his eyes stopped her. 'The news from the front is as gloomy as the weather,' she said instead. 'The Battle of Ypres continues on into its fourth week, although the press claim that we have repulsed the last German attack.'

'I saw the latest figures. Fifty thousand British casualties so far and the French have lost over eighty. Small consolation that Jerry has lost the same amount combined.'

'And every one of them someone's husband or brother or son,' Flora said sadly. 'In the village, the talk is all of the boys who enlisted alongside Ghillie McNair's son, Peter. Ten of them in total, and no doubt hundreds more from the rest of the county, all now training with the Argyll and Southern Highlanders.' She smiled weakly. 'One piece of good news, if you can call it that. Mrs Oliphant's son has rather miraculously turned up alive at a hospital in France, though he has lost a leg and the sight in one eye.'

Geraint grimaced. 'It could have been much worse.'

'My mother said that it would have been better if Ronnie had remained missing.' Flora flushed with embarrassment at the memory. 'She said that now he will forever be a burden to his family.'

'Maybe she's right, for once,' Geraint said roughly.

'You don't mean that.'

'I do, Flora, I mean it sincerely. Maybe not if it was just a leg, or just one eye, but if it was worse—and there's an awful lot worse, from what I've heard—if it was me, I wouldn't want to be packed off home to be looked after like a baby for the rest of my life. And if you're honest, really honest, if it was your son or your husband, you wouldn't want it, either.'

'Don't say that. Don't talk like that.'

She covered her ears, knowing it was a childish gesture but unable to stop herself. Geraint pulled her hands down. 'Imagine what it really means, to devote your entire life to a man who can't lift his own fork, or who can't eat anything but soup because he's lost most of his face,' he said brutally. 'Think about how it would be, tied to a man who might not ever be a man in any real sense ever again.'

She shook herself free angrily. 'Stop it! Why are you saying these things to me? Do you really think so little of me, that I would actually prefer one of my brothers to die?'

'I wasn't talking about your brothers. I meant me. *I* could not stand it. *I* would rather die.'

The blood drained from her face. 'Have you had orders to go to the front? Geraint, please, is this your way of telling me that you are going to France?'

'No.' He swore, catching her as she swayed, holding her tight against his chest. 'Flora, I'm not going anywhere just yet. They want me to stay on until this place is established. I'll be around at least until the new year. Flora, do you hear me?'

'I'm fine.' She was shaking, but she pushed herself free and went to stand at the window. Across the loch, the clouds were gathering, turning the water on the far shore iron-grey in stark contrast to the deep blue, white-crested waves lapping the shore nearest to the house. It was one of the things she loved about Glen Massan, the sheer drama of the constantly changing weather, but as the sun disappeared behind the scudding, rain-sodden clouds and the drawing room darkened, she could not help but think it was an ill omen. Winter was approaching here in the Highlands, and it would descend, too, on the trenches of the Western Front. It signalled the end of the campaign season, which meant months waiting for the conflict to resume in the spring, though it also meant that the men at the front would be relatively safe in the interim. Cold, but safe. The war would not be over by Christmas. Even the most jingoistic of supporters acknowledged that much.

'I don't think you're selfish.' Geraint stood at her shoulder. 'To want to leave here, I mean. I think your parents are the selfish ones, wanting to keep you here.'

She turned around to face him. 'You don't think I'm being disloyal?'

'No. And before you say it, I know that's contradictory of me.'

'Can't you find a way to make your peace with your parents?'

Geraint shook his head sadly. 'It's complicated.' He looked at his wristwatch. 'They'll be setting up this room this afternoon. The last one. Why don't we get out of here, get some of your fresh Highland air?'

'Won't they need you here?'

'I've put one of the new lance corporals in temporary charge. When the company arrive tomorrow, we move into full service mode. It might be our last chance to get out together for a while, though it looks as if it's about to pour.'

Flora smiled, looking out of the window where the rain clouds were already passing overhead. 'Four seasons in one day, that's what we get here. I think we've missed the worst of it. Let's take our chances.'

* * *

They left by the front door, but instead of taking the path down to the loch with which Geraint was familiar, Flora led the way through a gap in the huge rhododendron bushes that grew on one side of the driveway, and onto a narrow track. She had pulled on her old mackintosh coat, which sat incongruously over her emerald-green dress. As usual, she seemed to glide rather than walk, which had the odd effect of making it look as if the coat itself was floating along the narrow, rutted path as he walked behind her.

Geraint had tried very hard since that day on Ben Massan not to give in to the temptation of kissing her again. For long periods of time, when they were involved in the detail of packing up the house and writing out the various lists and inventories, he'd succeeded, after a fashion. Then Flora would laugh at something he said, or stop in the middle of wrapping some object to tell him its history or, more often, some story associated with her own childhood. She would go misty-eyed on those occasions, and her smile would soften, especially when she spoke of her brothers, both of whom she adored unreservedly and in equal measure, just as he loved his own siblings. Listening to her speak of their games of make-believe, their childish squabbles, the endless aligning and re-aligning of loyalty that went on as they grew up, made him think of his own childhood. It disturbed him, this affinity, more even than the depth of his desire for her. He had warned her they must not get in too deep. He would do well to heed his own warning.

Flora stumbled on a tree root and righted herself, looking over her shoulder at him, her face flushed with the fresh air and the cold. 'You haven't asked where I'm taking you.'

Because he didn't much care, so long as he was with

her. Geraint quickly cornered this thought and bundled it away. 'Go on, then,' he said. 'Where are we going?'

'It's a surprise.'

He laughed. 'Then I won't ask.'

She stopped and turned towards him. The wind had whipped her hair, loosening long tendrils from the confines of her elaborate bun to cluster around her face. She seemed, now they were away from the house, to have cast off her oppression. 'Don't you want to guess?'

'I prefer to be surprised. You smell of flowers.' He hadn't meant to say it, but for once spoke without thinking. 'Flora,' he said. 'You were well named.'

'Geraint was a knight at King Arthur's court. I wish you had a white charger to carry me away from here, just for a while.'

He brushed her hair from her face. 'I'd do it gladly, if I could.'

She caught his hand and to his surprise pressed a kiss on his scarred knuckles. 'Does it all feel unreal to you? I read the reports in the papers of the fighting, and I think, this can't be happening. It is almost Christmas. Alex will be home then, but our soldiers will not. Christmas in the trenches. I cannot imagine…'

'Then don't.'

'But I have to, I have to try to make it real. You were right to try to open my eyes about the—the horror of it. I'm frightened about the future.'

He caught her to him, wrapping his arms tightly around her, resting his chin on the damp silkiness of her hair. 'You're right to be,' he said, wishing he could say otherwise but knowing her well enough to understand that her need for reassurance was second to her need for the truth. Her hands rested on his chest, caught in the warmth of their bodies pressed together. 'Let's not talk about it,' he said. 'Just for this afternoon, let's pretend it's not there. That there's only us.'

'A brief return to no man's land,' Flora said.

'If you like, yes.'

When his lips touched hers, it was all she wanted. Pressing herself against him, opening her mouth to his, she wrapped her arms around his waist and kissed him back fervently. He pulled her with him under the shelter of a tree. Raindrops fell from the bare branches onto her hair, her face, stinging cold on her skin, mingling with the heat of his kiss.

It was not like before. There was an urgency in both of them, in the way their lips clung, their tongues touched, their hands clutched and stroked, hindered by the damp, by the layers of their clothes. Heat and desire flooded her, making her reckless, beyond thought. An urgent need possessed her to prove that she was alive, that he was alive, that here was something that had nothing to do with war and destruction and the real world. Something ephemeral yet utterly earthy. The primal urge to connect, unite, join with another.

His hands were inside her mackintosh, sliding up her back, cupping her bottom, stroking her sides, her waist. Her breasts were pressed against his tunic. She stroked his cheeks, ran her fingers through his hair, flattened her palms on his chest. His kisses deepened. She slid her hands down to rest on his flanks and he moaned, pulling her closer. He was hard. It excited her, knowing that she was doing this to him, that this man, so different from any other she had known, so determinedly difficult, at times so deliberately obtuse, the fascinating, intriguing, lethally attractive, determinedly solitary, dangerous Geraint Cassell desired her. Wanted her. Knowing all this made her want him even more. She had never wanted any man like this.

Never, in such a basic, uncomplicated way, wanted to use her body to show what she felt.

When he tore his mouth away from her, she had to bite back a moan of protest. 'I'm not going to apologise this time,' he said. His hands were still on her waist. His cheeks were flushed, his eyes dark and heavy lidded. 'I've not been able to stop thinking about it since the last time I kissed you. It is a very bad idea. You know it and I know it, but right now, I don't give a damn.' He looked up at the sky, now guilelessly blue. 'Come on, you'd better show me this surprise of yours while the rain holds off.'

They walked to the end of the woods, emerging suddenly at the edge of the loch where the path skirted round the rocky shore to a small inlet. The ruined church stood on a raised promontory surrounded by a low perimeter wall. 'It dates from the fourteenth century,' Flora said, 'though there was a monastery here from about the sixth. They say the Vikings razed that.'

They entered the burial grounds through a creaking gate. The gravestones, some flat, some lurching at haphazard angles into the soil, were ancient. Wandering slowly around, they read what they could of the faded stones until they came to the wrought iron enclosure set apart from the rest that contained the Carmichael family graves. The crypt faced out over the loch.

Geraint gazed out at the choppy waters, which turned from blue to iron-grey to blue again as the clouds scudded over the sun. 'It's a beautiful spot,' he said. 'There's something about it. Peaceful. Calming'

Flora squeezed his hand. 'Enduring. This place has survived so much. It gives me hope. Don't laugh at me.'

'I'm not.'

They walked back up the hill towards the ruined church. There was shelter from the wind here, and a wider panorama that swept out over the loch to the mountains beyond. Aside from the distant bleating of a sheep, there was not a sound. Geraint drew her down to perch beside him on one of the inner walls, putting his arm around her and hugging her close into the shelter of his body.

'I know we agreed not to talk about it today, but I hate to think of you being ordered to the front,' Flora said, after a short silence.

Geraint's expression tightened. 'I joined up to fight with my countrymen. The men I enlisted with are at the front. It's where I should be.'

'I know it's wrong of me to say it, but I don't want you to go to war and I don't want Alex to sign up or Robbie, either.'

Suddenly it was all just too much. She had not allowed herself to cry, not once since the army had arrived. There were others enduring so much more than her, she had not felt as if she had the right to cry, but now the tears came, hot and acrid and unstoppable. She tried desperately to brush them away with her hands, rubbing her eyes furiously. 'I'm sorry. It's unpatriotic of me.'

Geraint laughed. Not a humorous laugh, but a bitter one. 'Unpatriotic but healthy. I sometimes wish I could cry.'

This unexpected admission brought her tears to an abrupt end. 'I cannot imagine such a thing.'

He flushed. 'Because tears are for women?'

'No. No, I did not mean that at all. Are you afraid, Geraint?'

'A coward, you mean?'

'I meant nothing of the sort! I cannot believe there is a man in uniform who has not been afraid at some point. I merely meant…'

'Forget it.' Geraint pulled out a handkerchief from one of the capacious pockets of his tunic.

His expression was closed, unreadable. 'I didn't mean to offend you, or to imply…'

'I said forget it.' He closed his eyes, took several deep breaths before opening them again. 'Let's not talk about the war, Flora,' he said in a gentler voice. 'Let's pretend it's not happening, for just one day.'

Hurt. He was hurt, and he was hiding something. What had he said earlier? *It's complicated.* Flora longed to ask him what, exactly, was so complicated, but he was so very determined that she should not know, and she could not bear the thought of him walking away from her. Not today. She shivered. 'It's getting cold, but I know a place nearby, a shepherds' bothy, which has a fire.'

Chapter Seven

The bothy was a rough hut used by local shepherds to shelter from the weather. Pulling a box of lucifers from her coat pocket, Flora set light to the kindling, which was always left for the next occupant.

'What a surprising wee lassie you are,' Geraint said in a fair attempt at a Scots accent.

Relieved that his mood had lightened, Flora laughed. 'I'm five foot eight. Not so wee, thank you very much, though beside you I feel like a skelf.'

'You've lost me now.'

'A skelf is a Scots word for splinter.'

'Given that a splinter is something that gets under your skin, you might have a point, Miss Carmichael.'

'I doubt I'd get under anyone's skin in this old thing,' she said, holding out her mackintosh and making a twirl, as if she was wearing a ball gown.

His smile was completely unguarded, a rare thing for Geraint. He pulled her to him, his arm circling her waist, and spun her around again in the tiny stone hut, making her giddy. Her laughter faded when he looked down at her, his eyes dark with the passion she had witnessed earlier.

'You have certainly managed to get under mine,' he

said, pulling her backwards into his embrace and kissing her.

This time he did not stop. He kissed her, and she kissed him, and it was as if they had not left off kissing in the woods at all. They sank to the hard earth floor in front of the spluttering fire, still kissing. He kissed her eyelids, her cheeks, her throat. Her mackintosh fell onto the ground as he nuzzled the hollow at the base of her neck.

Lips. Tongue. His. Hers. She could not tell, and did not care. Who would have thought kisses could make you feel like this, melting and on fire at the same time? Who would have thought that so quickly, kisses would not nearly be enough?

She struggled with the brass buttons on his tunic. Geraint swore and unfastened first his belt and then the buttons, still kissing her. He shrugged out of the jacket. His singlet was pristine white, stretched taut over his chest. His arms were muscled, just as she had imagined them, smooth skin, knotted underneath, like whipcord. The hardness of his body made her shiver, made the tension twist low inside her. She smoothed her palm over his chest, feeling the heat of his skin through the cotton, feeling his heartbeat, slow and certain, enjoying the sharp intake of his breath as she touched him.

He pulled her to him, wrapping his arms tight around her so that she was pressed against his chest, and she felt the heat of her passion rise another notch. The dry wood on the fire sparked and crackled as Geraint slid his hands over the soft woollen sleeves of her dress, flattening his palms on her breasts in an echo of her own action, making her shudder. Her nipples hardened. He stroked them through the layers of her garments, so delicately it was almost painful. She moaned his name, shocked by the strength of her response, even more shocked by how much more she wanted.

He managed the hooks and buttons of her gown far too deftly to have been anything but familiar with such impediments. She wouldn't think about that. The emerald-green woollen dress was worn under a tunic patterned in the new jersey fabric, but Geraint managed to pull both from her shoulders at the same time, sliding them down her arms, leaving her in her camisole. She had always thought it would be embarrassing, to have a man look at her in her underwear. Geraint's breathing quickened, his eyes darkened as he looked at her, leaving her in no doubt about what he thought. She felt powerful, liberated.

He laid her down with the mackintosh to protect her, sliding her gown out from under her before stretching out at her side, his legs tangling with hers, half-covering her with his body. He kissed her more languorously this time, deliberately slowing her, when she would have touched him, gently putting her hands aside. 'Wait. Let me,' he said. His touch was like the whispered breath of a warm breeze on her skin, fingers and lips. Her arms, his mouth warm on the sensitive skin inside her elbow. Her chest, the valley between her breasts, stroking and licking his way along the lacy frill of her camisole. He cupped her breasts and circled her nipples with his thumb, then he kissed them, his mouth warm, dampening the rayon, making it cling.

He undid the ribbons of her camisole and pulled it open. His hand on her skin, so much more. How could there be so much more? His mouth enveloping her nipple, sucking, licking, making her shiver, making the knot inside her tighten.

She could feel the hardness of his erection pressing into her thigh. His kisses became more heated. He slid his hand down, under the waistband of her knickers. She tugged his singlet free of his trousers to run her hands up the knotted length of his spine, revelling in the way his muscles flexed beneath her trembling touch.

His hand cupped the heat between her legs. 'More,' she gasped, not meaning to say the word aloud, even though she was thinking it. He slid his finger inside her so easily. Deeper. Then he touched her, a sliding, stroking touch that made her lose all sense of everything except what he was making her feel. His mouth on hers. Her hands on his skin, clinging, digging into him, and his fingers sliding, stroking, until she could bear no more, and it was as if she was tearing apart. Her climax ripped through her. When she finally opened her eyes, it was as if she was another, quite different Flora.

He was gazing at her, dark eyes, flushed cheeks, unreadable expression. 'Geraint?'

He rolled away from her and got hurriedly to his feet. Dazed in the aftermath of her climax, she stared at him as he tucked his singlet hurriedly back into his trousers, picking up her gown, holding it out for her to step into. 'It's gone too far, Flora. Much too far.'

His voice sounded curt. As he turned her around to fasten her dress, she flinched. *Fool. What a bloody stupid fool he was.* 'I'm sorry.'

'Don't say that.' She turned on him, her face stricken. 'Don't apologise. It makes it worse.'

She was searching for her shoes under her mackintosh. It had grown dark outside, though it couldn't be much after four. He stooped to help her. 'Here.'

She snatched the shoes from his hands and tried to put them on, hopping on one foot, and when he tried to help her, she pushed him away. 'Leave me alone.' She dropped onto the wooden bench, staring dejectedly into space.

He took her shoes and knelt before her to put them on before sitting down beside her on the bench. 'Flora, it's not that I don't want you, you must not think that. I have never, ever wanted anyone as much as I want you, but it would be wrong. You know that. We both do.'

She refused to meet his eyes. 'Flora, it's because I care for you that I stopped.'

Finally, she looked at him. 'Do you?'

'More than I realised. More than is right.'

'Right? *Please* don't tell me that it's because of who I am, Geraint. Please don't tell me that it's because we are from—what did Sheila call it?—different sides of the fence.'

'Is that what Sheila said? She's right, but it's not that. Not just that.' Geraint got to his feet and picked up his tunic. Sitting next to Flora was distracting. His body still yearned for satisfaction. The more clothes, and distance, he could put between them the better. 'You're still a virgin, Flora,' he said bluntly. 'I won't take that from you when there can be no future for us. That honour will go to your husband, the lucky man. And don't tell me that it doesn't matter, because I know damn well it will. I won't compromise you.'

'You make me sound like some sort of Victorian heiress, for goodness' sake. We are in the twentieth century, not the nineteenth.'

'But some things still matter, and that's one of them. Another thing that matters is this damned war. I'll be going to the front sooner or later, and the chances are, if I come back at all, I'll not be the man I am now. Even if things were different, even if we did want the same things from life…'

'I have no idea what I want.'

'But you're finding out.'

'Thanks to you.'

He shook his head. 'You're doing it all yourself. You can do so much more than you think, Flora. This war could be the making of you, if you wanted it to be.'

'But you will not allow it to be the making of us?'

He had not allowed himself to consider it until now, any more than he had allowed himself to consider her feelings might run every bit as deep as his. One step, and he could take her in his arms. Just one step. The temptation was shockingly, terrifyingly, strong. Dear God, but he really was in over his head.

Appalled, Geraint picked up his belt and tightened it viciously. 'No, I won't,' he said brusquely. 'It would be the most selfish thing I could do. It would never work.'

'Why must you always harp on about the differences in our station?' She jumped to her feet and began to shake out her mackintosh furiously. 'I am sick to death of our friendship being a source of shame to you!'

He could never tell her that his shame had nothing at all to do with class. His horrible, loathsome, cowardly little secret accounted for that. He took her mackintosh from her and helped her into it. 'As it is, it will be hard enough for both of us when I leave here,' he said, pulling her back against him, wrapping his arms around her. The unmistakable scent of female arousal overlaid her usual perfume, made his blood thicken. He let her go reluctantly. 'Think how much harder it would be if we allowed ourselves to care more deeply, Flora. Think how much more difficult it would be to get through every day, living in fear of what will happen. I might be killed. If I don't die, it's possible I'll be maimed. I won't be a burden. I wouldn't do that to you. I can't.'

'Do I have no say in the matter?'

He shook his head.

'Why not?' she asked.

He couldn't tell her. Not the definitive reason. He simply could not. 'You just don't,' Geraint said. 'Trust me, it's for the best.'

Flora fastened up her coat, tucking her hair into the

collar. 'I love you, you know. I didn't know it until today, but I do.' She dashed a hand across her eyes, digging her knuckles into them painfully.

He had not thought he could feel worse. For the tiniest moment, Geraint felt the most utter elation, which made the guilt-fuelled plummet back down to earth an agony. She loved him. She could not, *must* not love him. 'Flora…'

She shrugged herself free when he caught her to him. 'Please don't tell me again how impossible it is. You've made yourself very clear. I know it makes no difference. I told you—I told you because it seemed wrong not to. I am sorry, I should not have said anything.'

She waited, looking at him expectantly, her blue-grey eyes glittering with unshed tears, but he could think of nothing to say. She loved him. Those most perfect of words and most dreadful. They tore him in two. As she turned away from him, out of the bothy and into the dusk, Geraint forced himself to hold his ground, not to go after her. He had done more than enough damage already. No more.

It started to rain as Flora made her way back to the Lodge, not inconsequential drizzle, but thick, no-nonsense drops that were wetter than should be possible. Clutching her mackintosh around her, she stumbled along the well-known path, too numb to cry.

Geraint had said nothing because there was nothing more to say. Her declaration had been the final nail in the coffin, as far as he was concerned. At least she had not embarrassed herself by begging. He wanted her, she had no doubt about that, despite her relative lack of experience, but he did not want her love.

'And I do love him,' she whispered, coming to a halt at the place where they had kissed earlier. 'I love him so much.'

It had crept up on her so stealthily she had hardly been

aware of it. She had been so caught up in the wholly new experience of falling from attraction to desire to love that she had not realised she'd fallen until it was too late, and she had not been able to admit it to herself until it was too late, either. Too late to retreat. Too late for it to make any difference. He did not love her. He *would* not love her. And perhaps he had a point.

These past few weeks, she had changed so much, but was she really different inside? Would she cope with a husband who required a nurse rather than a wife? A man who thought his injuries made him no longer a man. Would she fail him? Would she resent him? Right now, she could not imagine doing anything but loving him, but she was so horribly aware that she remained untested. Should anything happen to one of her brothers, she was pretty certain her mother would crumble. Was she really so sure that she herself was any different?

And even if he did survive unharmed, there was Geraint's political ambition. A laird's daughter would be no asset to a working-class hero. He was probably just letting her down gently.

Miserably, Flora plodded on along the forest path, which was fast churning into mud underfoot. It didn't matter, because Geraint was determined she would never be tested. Not by him. She loved him, but he did not want her. It kept coming back to that. That, and the niggling suspicion that he was keeping something from her. But whatever it was, it didn't matter, either. He wanted her to leave him free to get on with his life. Or death. She shuddered. The only way she could prove her love was to do as he bid her. And the only way she could do that was to leave Glen Massan as soon as possible.

No point in weeping and wailing; there was already too much of that in a world at war. 'I will find something useful to do,' Flora muttered as she emerged from the path into the grounds of the House. 'I will find something that challenges me, something that everyone else will think I can't possibly do. And I will prove them wrong. All of them. It doesn't matter that Geraint will probably never know.'

The skies had once again cleared, and the moon was rising over the loch by the time Geraint arrived back at Glen Massan House. Once in the Great Hall he hesitated. The drawing room, which would serve as the officers' mess, was unoccupied, but a burst of laughter came from the dining room, the designated mess for the men. The gramophone was playing 'Keep the Home Fires Burning'. It was the kind of sickly-sweet sentimental song designed to make mothers cry. The men sang it when they were maudlin. It made Geraint cringe.

'Till the boys come ho-ome.' The song finished and he opened the door, quickly calling out to the men to be at ease, before helping himself to a glass of beer from the barrel that stood in the far corner.

'All right, Corp, what've you been up to?'

'Walking out with that Miss Flora again, sir?'

'One up for the enlisted men, eh, sir? She's got good taste, she has.'

'Here's mud in your eye, Corp.'

'I Wonder Who's Kissing Her Now' started up on the gramophone, causing a fresh burst of laughter.

'Put a sock in it, you lot.' Geraint took a long, refreshing swallow of beer and sat down on the window seat, one of the few fixtures that remained. From here he could survey the room without seeming to, and at the same time, he was sufficiently detached not to put a damper on his men's enjoyment.

He had no cause to feel guilty, but it was there all the same, gnawing at him. Guilt at having failed to tell her the whole truth when she had stripped herself bare for him, literally and metaphorically. In his world, admitting to a weakness meant admitting to being less than a man. But Flora's honesty put him to shame.

The clock on the wall above the mantel showed past midnight. It was a functional piece, army issue, but Geraint checked it against his own watch all the same, before calling time on the remaining stragglers. After a few token protests, the room cleared quickly. The clatter of boots on the bare boards of the staircase was succeeded by silence as the men made their way up the second flight of stairs to the newly created dormitories on the third floor.

He stood at the window gazing out at the moon suspended high above the loch. He should not have allowed her to fall in love with him. He should not have allowed himself to get so close. He had no right to that soaring, exhilarating joy when he thought of her loving him. He didn't deserve her love. Not someone as damaged as him, who would let her down, shame her. He would speak to the colonel tomorrow and claim a severe bout of patriotic guilt. With the new company arriving, he would be easy to replace. At the front, he would confront his fears and overcome them. Or not.

He cursed under his breath, a Welsh oath that his grandfather had used, whose meaning he had never known. He liked the way it sounded. Wearily, Geraint switched out the electric light and locked the door of the mess.

Chapter Eight

The first heavy snow of winter was falling steadily as Flora sat in the parlour of the Lodge. The cold mid-December weather seemed to have no effect on the army's routine. The now-familiar sound of men drilling on the driveway, the crunch of boots interspersed with the staccato barks of the sergeant major formed a permanent backdrop to all conversation.

She had barely seen Geraint since the afternoon in the bothy. Most of the tasks they would have undertaken together, he had delegated. 'I need to concentrate on the training side of things,' he had told her. She watched him obsessively from a distance whenever she could, but studiously avoided being alone with him lest she embarrass them both by throwing herself at him and begging him to love her, please love her.

Instead she concentrated on making her own plans. After many painful hours of contemplation, writing out lists of her meagre skills, perusing every detail of the war effort in the press, interrogating anyone and everyone with power or influence, she had concluded that she would be best suited in some sort of organising role. She had proved that she could negotiate, order, cater. The hotchpotch of hospitals, which stretched out along the Western Front and was staffed by volunteers from as far afield as America, required specialist medical help. But for the men in transit from the front or waiting to go, convalescing, taking their leave, in dire need of food and beer and cigarettes, for those she could help organise comfort. In France, she would see the effects of war first-hand. In France, she would at least be in the same country as Geraint, though he would never know it. In France, she thought with some trepidation, she would either crumble or thrive.

Across from her, Lady Carmichael was laboriously knitting socks for the war effort. 'You seem to have a great deal of correspondence of late,' she said. 'Who are all these letters from?'

'This one is from Sheila.' Flora unfolded the closely written sheets from the envelope. 'She is being kept very busy. The hospital she has been assigned to takes those surgical cases who are well enough to be transferred from France.'

'I visited Mrs Oliphant today. As you know, Ronald is home. The woman is so determinedly optimistic, one has not the heart to try to make her face reality.' Lady Carmichael laid down her knitting and rubbed her brow. 'To be honest, Flora, I can't help but wonder if I'd be the same myself if it were—if it were— If I were ever to be so unfortunate as to be in her shoes.'

'Neither Robbie nor Alex have enlisted yet,' Flora said.

'You've heard Alex arguing with your father since he came home from school. I suspect he will wear him down eventually. And as to Robbie…' Flora's mother sighed and picked up her knitting. 'It won't be long. I know my sons.'

Flora folded Sheila's letter and placed it on top of the cream, embossed envelope addressed to her in an elegant script. She had already sent her reply accepting the post. If things went to plan, she would be on her way to France at the end of January, but she could not bring herself to tell her parents just yet. There was someone else she needed to share her news with first. Someone else she would be forced to say goodbye to. And despite the fact that she told herself over and over that it was for the best, she knew it would be the most difficult thing she had ever had to do.

A week before Christmas, the audience in the packed village hall was on their feet clapping and cheering. On the stage, the soldiers from the Glen Massan camp concert party took another curtain call. Seated in the front row beside her father, mother and brother Alex, Flora dabbed frantically at her handkerchief.

'Splendid my dear. Just what was needed to raise everyone's spirits at this difficult time.' The laird leaned across his wife and smiled at his daughter as the makeshift orchestra sounded the opening chords of 'Silent Night' and audience and cast began to sing along.

The carol sent everyone home in a subdued mood, their thoughts occupied by the men and boys of the village who were absent. Ghillie McNair had received a letter from his son Peter the day before, informing him that he had been awarded best marksman in the whole of the division in which he was training. 'Chip off the old block,' the father said proudly to anyone who would listen. 'All that grouse shooting paying off. He'll give Jerry what for.'

Flora's brother Alex's unremitting demands to be permitted to enlist made her want to scream at him about the futility of it all. There were times when she believed she could easily side with the pacifists. Only knowing that it would also mean taking sides against those she loved most prevented her.

When the glossy black car pulled up in front of the Lodge the next day, she was alone in the house. Expecting one of the officers with a message for her father, she had to clutch at the door handle as she watched Geraint ease his long legs out of the driver's seat.

'I need to talk to you.' He had on a greatcoat over his uniform and wore a pair of thick leather driving gloves. He looked tired. There were shadows under his dark eyes. 'Come for a spin with me.'

'That's a staff car,' Flora said stupidly.

'Lent to me by one of the Red Tabs who owes me a favour. Will you come? Please, Flora, it's important.'

She nodded, afraid to speak lest she burst into tears. Pulling on her coat and gloves, wrapping a plaid shawl around her head, she managed to regain control over herself, but the shock of seeing him, the rush of affection that enveloped her, was quickly replaced by a sense of foreboding. He had been so very careful to avoid being alone with her, only something momentous could have changed his mind. Love? But Geraint didn't look like a man about to speak of love. He looked like a man about to…

'You've received your orders,' Flora said flatly as she took her seat in the front of the car.

Geraint, concentrating on manoeuvring the car through the narrow gate posts and onto the public road, nodded curtly.

'When do you leave?'

'Off to a training camp tomorrow, then France in a few weeks.'

'So this is goodbye.' Flora closed her eyes, leaning back against the soft leather of the car seat, willing the tears not to fall. She would not have him pity her, she would not make him feel guilty, she would not have his last memory of her as weak and snivelling.

He reached over to touch her hand briefly. 'I know it might have been better if I had simply left…'

'No!' Flora sat up, her eyes wide with horror. 'Don't say that.'

He winced. 'I simply wanted to spare us both something that cannot be anything but painful, but I can't because I can't go without telling you the truth. You've been so completely honest with me, I owe you that.'

'What truth?' The ominous feeling flooded back.

'Wait. Let me find somewhere we can stop and talk properly.'

They were speeding along the main road west. Geraint glanced across at Flora, who was huddled deep down in the plush leather seat, her shawl pulled tightly around her shoulders. Her face was set and pale as she stared blankly ahead. He'd found it painful, these past few weeks, to shun her company, but that was nothing compared to the pain he felt, knowing that he was about to change her opinion of him irrevocably. It had to be done. He could not allow her to live a lie. Between them, if only ever between them, there would be honesty. That would be his consolation.

Though he had put the canvas roof up, the wind whistled through the space between it and the doors. The road was a narrow strip hewn into the hillside. Waterfalls gushed at sporadic intervals from the rock face on one side. On the other, far below, a ribbon of a stream meandered along the valley floor. At the top, the summit known locally as the Rest and be Thankful, he pulled into a clearing and cut the engine.

Flora shifted sideways to face him. His resolution wavered as he gazed at her. Her love was the most precious thing anyone had ever given him. He did not doubt her ability to cope without him, but he wished fervently that he did not have to make her do so. He had to make her see that what he was actually giving her was her freedom. Knowing that would be enough. It would have to be enough. Geraint clenched his gloved hands around the polished steering wheel. 'The truth is,' he said determinedly, 'I'm not the man you think you love. I can't leave you with false illusions about me, Flora, it wouldn't be fair.'

'Do you mean you've lied to me?'

He shook his head. 'No, but I haven't been entirely honest, either.'

'You're married, is that it?'

'No! I swear to you Flora there is only…' *Only you.* He stopped himself just in time. 'I'm not married. It's not that.'

'Then what?' She furrowed her brow. 'Something to do with your family? Is that the reason you have not been home for so long, despite the fact that you obviously miss them. It's complicated. I remember that's what you said.'

The wind had died down. Outside, a golden eagle soared high above them then plunged suddenly out of view. Geraint unfurled his fingers from the steering wheel. 'They think I left because I thought I was too good for the mines. They don't know it's because—because I couldn't cope.' He gritted his teeth. 'It's not the dark, as such,' he said. 'It's knowing that you can't get out. The first time I went down in the cage, I was sick. I got the shakes just standing at the pit head. The mineshaft was the worst, but it's not the only place. Any small room, any tight space…'

'Like the attics at Glen Massan?' Flora asked gently.

'Was it that obvious?'

'At the time I put it down to strain. Overwork.'

'Overwrought, maybe, blubbing like a girl,' Geraint said grimly. 'That's what they used to say, those toffee-nosed bullies at the grammar school.'

'What did they do to you?'

'They called it the coffin. It was a cellar, really. The older boys used to lock the younger ones in it, as a punishment for breaking their pathetic so-called rules. Needless to say, once they saw my reaction, I was targeted mercilessly.'

Flora stared at him in horror. 'Of course, that day in

the wine cellar at Glen Massan—that's why you looked so dreadful, it must have been a horribly painful reminder. My God, Geraint, they locked you up, knowing that you were afraid of such places, knowing what it would do to you. That is monstrous. Surely your father—when you told him…'

'Tell him what, exactly, that I'm a nancy boy afraid of the dark?'

'So you did nothing?'

'I became a better fighter.' He couldn't bear the pity on her face, and gazed directly ahead at the windscreen. 'I didn't tell you this to win your sympathy. I need you to understand. I left the mine because it got to the point where I couldn't sleep, worrying about whether or not I'd be able to force myself to get in the cage, whether I'd get through the day without throwing my guts up or giving in to the need to get out, up, away. I was good at covering for myself, but there were times…' He stopped, shuddering, remembering the close calls. 'There's a sort of code among miners. It's a bit like the army. You can't let on that you're afraid. You daren't admit to weakness—it's shameful and it's there to be exploited. My father wouldn't have been able to hold his head up if anyone found out how I felt, and he is a very proud man, Flora.'

'So you suffered—my goodness, how you must have suffered. And then you lied to protect him. Even though he's your father, and he might have understood?'

'He wouldn't have.' Geraint ran his fingers through his hair. He'd had it cut, more hacked than cut, by an army barber. 'Even if he did, he'd blame himself for expecting me to go down there in the first place, or for not spotting that I was struggling. I wouldn't want that.' He covered his wristwatch, twisting the strap around and around.

'You love him very much,' Flora said.

'Quietly like,' Geraint replied, his accent deliberately

broad. 'It wouldn't do to say it, mind.' His faint smile faded. 'I signed up partly because I wanted to make him proud of me. Because I wanted to prove that I wasn't a coward. I signed up before we had any idea what this war would become, and what it's become is a— It's my worst nightmare, Flora.'

Her hand went to her throat. 'The trenches.'

Geraint clenched his fists, forcing himself to finish what he had started. 'I panic. It's not just the nausea and the sweats, I panic. I want to run. I can't explain, but it's almost impossible to stop myself. And sometimes I freeze. Can you imagine how that will look?' He closed his eyes, partly to avoid seeing the realisation dawn on her face, partly to remind himself of the harsh reality of his condition. 'What if I can't even get into the trenches in the first place, never mind live there for weeks at a time, like a rat in a sewer? What if I run? They shoot you for cowardice, you know. They court martial you, and they tie you to a post in front of a firing squad.' He dropped his head into his hands. 'Imagine what that would do to my parents, having their son shot as a coward. Imagine what it would do to you, Flora, learning that the man you love is a traitor to his country.'

He forced himself to look at her. 'I'm not afraid of fighting, I've done enough of that in my time, but I'm afraid I won't get the chance to fight. I'm afraid that my weakness will be the cause of other men's pain and suffering and death. My comrades. My countrymen. The men I enlisted to fight beside, to prove myself to. I'm afraid I won't be able to hide it, that they'll see my fear. There will be no glory for me in this war, Flora, you have to understand that. The best I can hope for is to be killed in action, but the most likely thing is that I'll die a coward. You can't love a man like me. I won't let you. You deserve better.'

* * *

Flora stared at him, unable to make sense of what he was saying. 'You think you're a coward?' she finally managed, bewildered by this more than anything. 'You think this fear that you have no control over makes you weak?'

'If I was stronger, I'd be able to overcome it.'

'How long did you work in the mine?'

'Two years.'

'Two years! For two years, you went down into that pit, knowing what it would do to you, struggling to keep it under control, and you think you are weak!'

'Flora, you saw what I was like in your father's wine cellar. I virtually passed out. I didn't tell you this to have you try to make me feel better about myself.'

Her head felt as if it might explode. 'Then why did you tell me?'

'Because I need someone to know the truth, and because I need you to see how pointless it is, wasting your love on someone like me.'

She thought she might be sick, then a wave of fury swept over her. 'You told me this…this terrible, awful thing about yourself to stop me loving you!' She stared at him in utter disbelief. 'Do you really think I am so shallow! And so weak!'

'Flora!'

She shrank from him. 'You are the one who has been telling me all along that I am stronger than I thought I was. It was you who encouraged me to look beyond Glen Massan. It's your voice I could hear when I wrote all those letters applying for various posts.'

'What posts?'

'I'm leaving for France. Next month, in January sometime, to help establish field canteens behind the lines.' Determinedly, she bit her lip and met his gaze full on. 'I thought you would approve, since I cannot have you…'

He caught her hand, gripping it painfully tight between his own. 'It's impossible. Have you not been listening to me?'

'You mean it. I don't doubt your sincerity, Geraint, and I am touched beyond words that you have confided in me today, but you are utterly wrong.' Her voice sounded so cold, but it was the only way she could keep control over herself. Later, she would be devastated, but for now, she was angry, not with Geraint but with what had shaped him.

'You said that you wanted honesty between us. Very well, then, here is my version of it, though it will pain you. I love you. I think you are the bravest man I have ever met, and I think you are possibly the most stubbornly pig-headed, too. I don't know how you will cope in the trenches, but I do know that you will always put others first. No, don't interrupt, just listen. Your compassion is what drives you. You have gone to extreme lengths to protect your family from the knowledge of your condition, to save them embarrassment, hurt, guilt. Something so deep-rooted will not fail you if you go to war.'

'You don't understand.'

'I do. I know you. I love you. If something happens—if you die—I will feel as if part of me has died, too, but I will carry on, because I know it is what you would want. I will know, no matter the circumstances, that you have died a brave man, Geraint. And if you were wounded, I know I would cope then, too. I don't know how, or how well, but I would cope because you would still be you, the man I love, and I would rather have that than nothing.'

'Flora…'

She shook her head, pulling her hand free. 'I know you don't feel the same way. I've thought about it and thought about it, and it's the only explanation, because if you loved me, you'd want to take a chance on us having some sort of future, no matter how brief. But you don't.'

'I want you to be free of me.'

The lump in her throat made it impossible to reply to this. Flora nodded, biting hard on the inside of her cheek. 'I know,' she whispered.

His eyes were dark, his expression unbearably sad. 'You'll survive. I need you to survive.'

Without him, he meant. 'I'll do my best.'

'I know you will, and your best is infinitely better than you ever imagined it could be.'

Putting on his cap, Geraint got out of the car and turned the starting handle. The powerful engine roared to life.

Chapter Nine

He had lied to Flora. Twice. The travel warrant dated today, not tomorrow—his white lie—had been folded inside his top tunic pocket when he drove her back to the Lodge from the Rest and be Thankful. He had turned straight around and onto the main road after he left her, parking the staff car at the tiny local train station where it would be picked up by a returning officer later that day. It was not for fear that Flora would try to change his mind that he had lied, but fear that he would allow her to.

The ill-fitting windows in third class blew a permanent draught through the carriage. The slatted wooden seats were uncomfortable. The train trundled slowly through the isolated stations, making countless unscheduled and seemingly pointless stops at lonely farmhouses and road junctions. Geraint sat deep in thought, oblivious of both the train's discomfort and snail-like progress. His second lie lay black on his conscience. Flora thought he did not love her.

He loved her, all right. He loved her so much that every second, every passing mile that took him away from her felt like a stab to his already bruised heart. And she loved him. Flora's words rang in his ears, circled his head, gnawed at his resolve. She loved him, despite his secret shame. She believed in him. She wanted him, no matter how maimed. She loved him. She loved him. She loved him. The words merged themselves into the rhythm of the metal wheels on the track.

And he loved her. Painfully. Deeply. Utterly. Brave Flora, who was willing to test herself to the limits, knowing that she might fail. Flora, who had not pleaded or attempted blackmail or even wept. Flora, who had loved him enough to let him go, though she believed he was wrong. *Was he?*

He was afraid of being a coward, yet here he was, running away from the most astounding, wonderful, perfect thing that had ever happened to him, and telling himself that he was being brave and noble for doing it. Looking down at the stripes on his arm, it occurred to him that he had never, not once, allowed himself to believe he would survive the war. Yes, he had talked of his political ambitions, but they had faded the moment the reality of life in the trenches became clear. He assumed he would die because he thought he did not deserve to live. He had acted as judge and jury on his own conduct before he'd even had a chance to prove himself, just as he'd judged Flora and her family before he'd ever met them. And he'd been wrong on that one.

Flora was not afraid of failing. He had failed her, was failing her, with every mile of railway track that stretched between him and the woman he loved. The woman he was wilfully surrendering for no other reason than that he was afraid! What was he more afraid of, his claustrophobia or losing her?

As the train clanked into another tiny station, Geraint grabbed his kit back and cap. *Carpe diem*, Flora was forever saying. 'Bloody right, I'll seize it,' he told the bewildered guard as he jumped onto the platform.

The next morning, Flora sat at the dining room table in the lodge staring down at her notebook. She was attempting to prepare a list of tasks she must complete before she left for France, but the page remained stubbornly blank as her mind drifted back once more to those last moments with Geraint. He had made no attempt to kiss her goodbye. She was relieved, in a way, though it was one more piece of evidence that he didn't love her. She had decided it would be too painful to seek him out again. Just as well, as she had learned this morning from one of the other men, ribbing her about needing a new boyfriend, that he had left yesterday. As she had lain in her bed last night, imagining all sorts of impossible scenarios in which they met in the bothy to make love for the last time, he was already on the train heading south.

She was picking up her pencil for the umpteenth time when the doorbell rang, swiftly followed by a rapid, insistent thumping on the door itself. Her mother was in the village folding yet more bandages. Her father was also out. Sighing heavily, Flora got up and pulled open the front door.

Geraint was haggard, unshaven and wild-eyed. 'What on earth are you doing here?'

'I need to talk to you. Urgently.'

'But—you left.'

'That's what I need to talk to you about. Flora, for pity's sake, I've hardly any time. Please.'

She stood aside to let him past, ushering him into the dining room. 'Is something wrong? You look dreadful.'

'I've been trying to get back here since yesterday evening. Missed the last train. Had to spend the night in the station.'

'You're shaking. Sit down. Can I get you some food? Something hot to drink?'

'No!' Geraint threw his cap down on the table and ran his fingers through his hair. 'Sorry, but there's no time. If I'm not at the station in Arrochar in two hours to pick up the train south, I'll be officially absent without leave by the time I get to my barracks.'

'If it's because you didn't say goodbye, I understand…'

'No, you don't. I don't want to say goodbye, not ever. That's the whole point. I thought…' He smiled weakly. 'I love you,' he said baldly. 'I let you think I didn't love you because I thought it would be kinder, but it was wrong and I was a complete idiot and you were right and—and I love you.'

Flora's legs almost gave way beneath her. She dropped extremely ungracefully into a chair. 'You love me.'

'I do. And as long as you love me, that's all that matters. You were right. We can cope with anything, if we have each other.'

Geraint loved her. She couldn't believe it. She couldn't let herself believe it, not just yet. 'But yesterday you said…'

'Some things haven't changed.' He looked down at her earnestly. 'I am still terrified that I won't be able to cope in the trenches, but I know that I'll try my hardest, and I know that if I fail you'll still love me. I've realised that the only way I can let you down is by walking away from you, by being too afraid to give what we have a chance.'

'And if you are hurt, Geraint? If you are wounded, scarred, worse? Will you come home to me?'

'I promise.'

'And afterwards, after the war, what then? What about your political ambitions? I'm not exactly a poster girl for the socialist movement.'

Geraint grinned. 'Oh, but all that's going to change. No more us and them. We'll work together, you and I, to change the world. Or at least, to change that part of it. With you by my side, I'm know we'll succeed.'

He dropped to his knees before her, taking her hands in his. 'Knowing you love me will give me something more precious than anything to fight for. If you'll take me, if you can forgive me for being so blind, if you still want me, I can think of nothing I want more, and no bigger honour than to have you as my wife. Will you marry me?'

She had held herself in, kept her emotions strapped so tightly down for weeks now that it was almost impossible to let herself go. But Geraint was looking at her, his face stripped bare for her to read, and his train left in less than two hours, and she loved him and he loved her and that really was all that mattered.

'Yes,' Flora said in a tight little voice that did not sound a bit like her own. Happiness, like a sudden burst of summer sunshine, caught her unawares. She threw her arms around his neck. 'Yes, yes, yes. Oh, dear heavens, yes.'

Laughing, kissing, crying, she clung to him. 'I love you,' he said over and over as he returned her kisses. 'Are you certain?' he asked her as she kissed him back.

'Absolutely. Completely. Utterly.'

'Then tell me what we need to do.'

'Do?'

'Banns. Paperwork.'

'You mean you want me to marry you now? But we are both leaving for France.'

'All the more reason, but if you'd rather wait I would understand.'

'No. No, I don't want to wait a second longer than we have to. I'll postpone my departure. I'll make a list,' Flora said, laughing. 'It's one of the many things I've discovered I'm rather good at.'

Six weeks later

'Did I tell you that you look quite radiant, Mrs Cassell?'
'Several times. Did I tell you that I love you, Mr Cassell?'

'No matter how many times you do, it will never be often enough.'

They were in Flora's bedroom, having appropriated the Lodge for their wedding night. Alex had returned to school most reluctantly. Flora's parents were spending the night as guests of Colonel Patterson. Her mother was very far from reconciled to the marriage, but the laird had proved a surprisingly fervent supporter.

The two sets of parents had been rather awkward with each other, but to Flora's relief her brother Robbie had dashingly stepped into the breach. Charming, and as ever the life and soul of the party, Robbie had abandoned his elegant girlfriend, Annabel, to dance several reels with Mrs Cassell before persuading Geraint's father to down a few wee drams of the laird's oldest and finest malt.

'What on earth did you two find so fascinating to talk about? You were chatting away for hours,' Flora asked him at the end of the evening, but Robbie merely grinned.

'Wouldn't you like to know,' he said, enveloping her in a bear hug. 'I've never seen you look so happy, sis. Don't worry about the new in-laws, I'll take good care of them.'

True to his word, Robbie and Annabel remained with Geraint's parents until they left to spend the night at the drover's inn in the village, having politely but firmly refused the laird's offer to join him and his wife at Colonel Patterson's stately pile. 'We'll be more comfortable in the pub,' the senior Mr Cassell had said.

'Not too comfortable, mind,' his wife had retorted. 'We've a long journey back to Wales in the morning.'

In the morning, Robbie and Annabel would return to London. In the morning, Geraint would be going back to camp. In the morning, Flora herself would be packing to go to France. In the morning, she would be alone. A bride of less than a day. She didn't want to think about the morning.

The lamp cast long shadows on the faded wallpaper.

She was nervous as she removed her cape and gloves. One night was all they had together. Geraint had been unable to persuade his CO to grant him more. They both knew it was because he had orders to mobilise, though neither of them had alluded to it.

'We'll manage, my darling, because we have to,' Geraint said, as if he had read her mind, which she supposed was not so very difficult.

'When I am in France, perhaps it might be possible for us to see each other.'

'Perhaps, but let's not talk of France or the war just now,' Geraint said. 'I love you.'

'I know.'

'Yes, but you don't know how much.' He smiled at her, a wicked smile she had not seen before. 'Come here, Mrs Cassell. Let me show you.'

He kissed her slowly, as if they had all the time in the world. He kissed her brow and her cheeks and her neck as he pulled the pins from her hair. Then he kissed her mouth, lingeringly, lovingly. He kissed her throat and her shoulders as he undid the fastenings of the Poiret evening gown she had gone to such lengths to acquire. The soft folds of the gauzy overdress were fashioned in the Roman style, worn over a heavy lace underdress that made the most of her tall, slim frame. The gown fell to the floor and pooled at her feet. Geraint led her to the bed and removed her silk slippers. He kissed the soft skin at the top of her stockings, the back of her knee, her calf, the fluttering pulse at her ankle.

She watched, her pulse racing, as he hastily removed his own clothes, casting them carelessly onto the floor beside her own discarded gown. Broad shoulders tapering to a narrow waist. Long, lean legs. Her breathing quickened. She had never seen a naked man before. She could not tear her eyes from the sleek arc of his erection.

He pulled her from the bed and kissed her again. He was hard, hot against her belly. He undid the ribbons that held her camisole in place and kissed the valley between her breasts. She wriggled free of her silk knickers, the last scrap of her clothing. He was breathing heavily. He bent his head to take one of her nipples in her mouth. Low inside her, the thrumming started. He took her hand and curled it around him, showing her how to stroke him, and slid his fingers inside her, stroking, slowly, to the same rhythm. She began to quiver with the pulsing inside her. He laid her on the bed, parted her legs and put his mouth on the throbbing core of her. She came quickly, crying out, bucking under him. He held her, kissed her, then he entered her, thrusting gently in on the ebbing waves of her climax until she enveloped him and the ebbing changed direction.

His skin was damp with the effort it was costing him to hold back. She didn't want him to hold back, and wrapped her legs around him, pulling him towards her to kiss him greedily. He groaned and thrust. She thought she might die from the sheer bliss of it, until he thrust again, and it intensified. Thrusting, harder now, deeper, she heard wild cries that might have been her own as she came again, as his own climax took him, and he spilled himself inside her, clinging to her, rocking her with him, murmuring her name.

It was true what they said, she thought, drifting, floating. It was true, it was a union. They really were one.

'Are you tired?' she whispered to her husband some very little while later.

'Not in the least.'

'Good,' Flora said, running her hands suggestively over the taut muscles of his buttocks, 'because we've got all night, my darling, and I am anxious that we make the most of it.'

She felt rather than heard the low growl of his laughter. 'Then why don't you make a list of what you want us to do,' Geraint said, and kissed her.

Dearest Sylvie

Chapter One

Paris—28th October 1916

The nightclub was packed with revellers. The air was stale, a cocktail of cigarette smoke, alcohol and sweat combined with the faint but distinctive smell of the trenches, which clung to the uniforms of the soldiers huddled round the tiny tables. Hostesses, like exotic birds in their revealing evening gowns and garish make-up, laughed coquettishly and smiled ceaselessly as they worked the room. Glasses were emptied and refilled at an alarming rate as everyone sought that ultimate of prizes, oblivion. The atmosphere was one of frenetic gaiety laced with desperation. A stranger entering would be forgiven for thinking that this was a party to celebrate the end of the world.

On a tiny podium, an exotic dancer clad only in a jewelled headdress and a transparent tunic was doing her dubious best to impersonate the infamous Mata Hari. Ribald cheers and catcalls accompanied her every gyration. Seated alone at the back of the room, Captain Robbie Carmichael of the Argyllshire Battalion, Argyll and Southern Highlanders, squinted down at the letter in his hand.

My Dear Alex,

My wound has finally healed and I go back on active duty in two days. In your last missive, you begged me to use whatever influence I have to effect your transfer from Egypt to join me in the trenches of the Western Front. I cannot, WILL NOT, do as you ask.

You are my only brother, Squirt. Our parents have only two sons. With the odds stacked against me, you must see that it is your duty not to come here to die but to stay where you are and to fight to survive.

You have to stop thinking of me as a hero, Alex. I'M NOT!!! Being wounded in the line of fire isn't honourable or brave, and it's certainly not glorious. Getting hit means one is careless or unlucky.

Despite what we officers write in those hateful letters to the families of our men, death is rarely either quick or painless and it is NEVER heroic. This war must be won, and it will be, but the cost is an obscene waste of life—there's hardly a lad left from Glen Massan in my company who hasn't been killed or wounded.

Alex, forget what they told you in that school of ours. War doesn't bring out the best in men but the worst. We are not noble brothers in arms but savages who will do anything to survive.

Please, I beg of you, forget this business of a transfer and concentrate on staying safe.

Your brother,

Robbie

Robbie tore the letter into tiny pieces and stuffed them into his tunic pocket. Alex was just nineteen, and despite having seen very limited action in Gallipoli, his letters showed him to be still the naively patriotic boy not long out of school. Robbie himself had no illusions left about mankind. He could not bear to destroy his brother's. The war would do that soon enough.

Picking up the bottle of red wine, he emptied the last of it into his glass. He hadn't ever intended to send the letter, had written is as a form of catharsis. Stupid idea! All it had done was reinforce the reality of what he would have to face again in two days. It was late, he was exhausted, but he was not nearly drunk enough to go back to his digs, not nearly drunk enough to sleep. The nagging headache that had been his constant companion since waking up in the field hospital several weeks before was concentrated behind his eyes tonight. The scar throbbed. A thin angry red line beneath his newly grown hair, it ran from his temple to the base of his skull, a memento of the shrapnel that had almost killed him and the reason for his sojourn in the French capital. Convalescence. As if any of them would ever truly recover from this conflict.

Robbie stretched out his long legs and drained his glass in a single gulp, at the same time raising his hand to summon the waiter. *'La même chose,'* he said, and once more declined the man's offer to send the next bottle over with *une petite copine.* In the time he had taken to drink the first bottle, several of the club's so-called *jolies filles* had offered to sit with him, despite the fact that he'd ostentatiously placed his hat on the only other seat. Like almost everyone in Paris, the nightclub hostesses were on the make, vultures who fed off the war, leaching on the fervour of soldiers who hadn't seen anything remotely *jolie* for months. Though he would concede that they provided a much-needed service, it was not one he wished to make use of. The old, carefree Robbie had enjoyed sex and female company enormously. The Robbie that the war had created shunned it as he shunned almost every other human contact that was not strictly necessary.

The dancer had finished her performance and was now

drinking champagne and laughing wildly with a group
of admirers. Robbie leaned back in his seat, surveying
the room with a jaundiced eye. The pain stabbed behind
his eyes, as if someone were turning a white-hot skewer
around and around in his brain. Another glass of wine,
even another bottle, would make no difference. He would
not sleep, and the headache would only get worse. He was
trying to summon up the energy to cancel his order when
he saw her.

She was standing at the end of the polished zinc bar.
Tall, for a woman, her face unmistakably French in some
indefinable way, it was the blankness of her expression as
she stared sightlessly across the room that caught his attention. She was beautiful. Glossy black hair cut fashionably
short, tucked back behind her ears to show a classic profile. High, wide cheekbones, a very Gallic nose. Her brows
were dark, finely arched above deep-set eyes that looked
like two black pools in the shadowy light of the club. Pale
skin that drew his attention to her mouth. Full, sensuous
and pink, it was a mouth made for laughter, though she
looked as if she did as much of that as he did. A mouth
also made for kissing. Robbie smiled bitterly. Working
here, as she undoubtedly did, he bet she did a great deal
of that. For the right price.

Her gown was dark blue, draped softly over her breasts
in the style of a Roman tunic, revealing just enough of her
throat to make a man want to see more. Robbie was surprised to discover that there were some parts of him not
quite so moribund as he had imagined. Beneath the gown
he imagined her lush body, soft, creamy flesh to sink into,
to envelop his own battle-hardened and scarred shell. She
would smell of summer, of flowers, of that delightful sweet
spiciness that was so peculiarly female. She would not
smell of mud or despair.

He groaned. To the dull ache in his head was now added

the throb in his groin. Across the room, the woman was staring at him, her mind dragged back from whatever dark place she had been inhabiting, alerted no doubt by the intensity of his gaze. He willed himself to look away, but he could not, though he regretted it immediately when he saw her take the tray from his waiter containing the fresh bottle, threading her way through the crowds towards him.

'Your wine, *Monsieur Capitaine*.'

She spoke in English. He replied in French. 'I already told the waiter I'm not interested in company.'

'You flatter yourself, *monsieur*, I am not offering that kind of company. I think you have drunk too much, perhaps.'

'Correction. I've not drunk nearly enough.'

'I suspect there will never be enough for someone like you.'

Which chimed so accurately with what he'd been thinking himself that Robbie couldn't help but stare. Close up, her skin had a surprising freshness. The paleness he had taken for powder was natural. The pink of her lips seemed natural, too. 'I'm sure there are plenty of other men here who will be more than happy to pay for your services,' he said.

'You are mistaken, *Monsieur Capitaine*. I do not provide the kind of services the other girls offer. I work here, yes, but as a waitress only. *Monsieur le Patron* is from my home town and I needed the job. He's short-staffed as most of the waiters have gone off to fight. What are you doing here?'

'Getting drunk. Or I would be, if you would give me that bottle. Why didn't you let the other waiter bring it over?'

She shrugged. 'I don't know. Why were you staring at me?'

'I don't know.' He glared at her, not because he wanted

her to leave, but because now that she was here, he desperately wanted her to stay. 'For heaven's sake, since you are here, please sit down,' he said, snatching his cap from the chair.

She hesitated. 'I am sorry, I should not have— I can't think why I— I should go.'

Robbie cast a look over at the *patron*. 'Will you get into trouble?'

'I've finished my shift.' She put the tray down on the table and took the seat he had pushed towards her. 'My time is my own.'

'Then use it to save me from myself by sharing this bottle, *mademoiselle*,' Robbie said, pouring the wine. 'If you are in no rush to go home?'

She shook her head, offering him a small smile. 'It has been a long night, I confess I would very much like a glass of wine, and I am in no hurry.'

Robbie eyed the club's animated *patrons* sardonically. 'Then you're the only person in this city who is not.' He lifted his glass. '*Santé, mademoiselle.*'

'*Santé.*' Sylvie Renaud took a small sip of the cheap, rough wine and studied the man seated opposite her. Dark auburn hair with a natural wave fell over his brow, shaved almost to the bone on one side of his head. A head wound, she surmised, and no doubt the reason for his being here in Paris. Dark shadows told the same story of exhaustion she saw on every soldier's face who visited the club. His eyes, the grey-blue of the sea in winter, had the blank look of a man who had seen too much. She was accustomed to the sadness and desperation that clung to the men returning from the front, but this man seemed empty, a husk of a man wearing his aristocratic good looks like a borrowed suit of clothes. It was that singular trait that had caught her attention from across the room, though why it had led her to act so uncharacteristically, she had no idea. She closed her eyes and took another sip of wine.

His hand covered hers and her eyes flew open. 'Stop thinking,' he said. 'You stared at me, I stared at you. It doesn't matter why. So let us both stop thinking, and tell me your name.'

His hand was cool on top of hers. His fingers were long, elegant, extremely clean. 'You are right,' she said with some relief, because she really didn't want to persuade herself to leave him just yet. 'I am Sylvie. Sylvie Renaud.'

'Robbie Carmichael. *Enchanté.*' His mouth curled into what he obviously hoped was a smile. He looked as if he had to concentrate to make it happen.

'Robbie. That is a difficult name for me to pronounce.'

'It's Scottish.'

Which explained his accent, so much softer than the clipped tones of the English officers when they spoke French. 'But you are not wearing a skirt,' Sylvie said, trying one of her own practised smiles.

'Too cold this time of year.' His smile stretched a little farther this time. 'It's called a kilt.'

'Kilt.' He had a beautiful mouth. His legs were long, the calves beneath the ridiculous tightly bound gaiters all the British wore, were nicely shaped. Though his face was gaunt, his tunic loose fitting, his body, she suspected, was rather more solid-packed muscle and brawn than starved. He would have been the sort of man women swooned over before the war. 'You speak very good French,' she said. A trite remark, even if it was true, but she wanted to encourage him to talk, because then he would forget to drink.

He shrugged. 'I import wine, so I spent a lot of time here in France. Before.'

'Before,' Sylvie repeated. 'They all have a before, every soldier in this room.'

'And only a lucky few will have an after.' Robbie

Carmichael picked up the bottle and made to top up her glass, even though she had barely touched it. 'I won't be one of them.'

'Don't talk like that.'

She caught his wrist before he could drain his glass, causing him to slop wine onto the table, but he yanked himself free and took a large gulp. 'A well-kept secret, Sylvie, but the life expectancy of an officer in our wonderful British army is six weeks these days. I've seen action at Ypres, Festubert, Givenchy and the Somme. The odds are stacked against me. It is merely a question of time.'

He spoke not bitterly, not angrily, not even sadly. It was the very lack of emotion in his voice, the matter-of-factness, that got to her, wrenching unwanted feeling from her, that familiar terrible mixture of fear and deep-rooted sorrow that left her bereft. She had forgotten how that felt. More accurately, she had not allowed herself to remember. Blanking it from her mind had been the only way she could survive.

'You really are trying to save me from myself.'

She didn't understand what he meant until he nodded at her empty glass. She didn't even remember drinking it.

'What were you thinking about?'

His eyes were too focused on her. He saw too much. She pushed back her chair. 'I was thinking that I was right when I said there would never be enough wine. For either of us.' She held out her hand. 'Let's dance, Capitaine Robbie.'

If he'd thought about it he would have refused, but she gave him no option, tugging him up from his chair and weaving a path through the crowd to the tiny dance floor, forcing him to follow in her wake. The last time he had danced, it had been with Annabel, at the ceilidh following Flora's wedding. Annabel was also the last woman he'd made love to. Annabel, who had written to him for a few months following his departure to the front line before giving up for lack of a response. She was married to Duncan now, who was involved in something hush-hush at the Home Office, according to Robbie's mother, who took it upon herself to keep him up to date with such things. Though why he was thinking about that now, he had no idea. Thinking about his life before the war was like watching a moving picture starring a man who did a lot of laughing and smiling and had no idea that soon there would be nothing, nothing at all in the world, ever to laugh or smile about again.

'Robbie? We are here to dance, *non*?'

Sylvie's voice dragged him back to the present. Her scent, just as he'd imagined, was delicately floral. Her hair was thick, with a natural wave. The kind of hair that would be windblown on a bright, breezy summer's day. Her fingers were long, tapered, elegant. The music was slow. There was barely enough space to move, let alone dance.

He didn't want to dance, but he wanted nothing more than to be held. Just to be held. Just for a moment. It was to that he surrendered, the basic human desire for contact he had avoided for so long. He pulled her close, his arm on the curve of her spine, on the smooth, feminine silk of her gown, feeling the heat of her body beneath. Curves. He'd known there would be curves. And soft flesh, the antithesis of his own in every way. He closed his eyes and lost himself in the music and the moment.

It had been a mistake, asking him to dance. It made it impossible for her to ignore the fact that she was attracted to him. She liked the soft burr of his accent, which made her think of misty Scottish glens and rugged Highland scenery. She liked the combination of auburn hair and

grey-blue eyes and the latent strength she could feel in that
lean, hard body. She liked the hint of sensuality in his un-
smiling mouth. For once, she saw not the soldier but the
man. A vulnerable man who gazed out at the world from
behind his attractive carapace like a hermit crab living in
an abandoned shell.

And she so desperately wanted to be held. Not to think.
Just to be held. Sylvie relaxed a little, allowing him to draw
her closer. He smelled of expensive soap, unlike most of
the soldiers, and also a little of that dank, muddy smell that
clung to all of them. But mostly he smelled intoxicatingly
male. His body was hard, muscled, solid. The arm that
slid down her back to rest on the curve of her bottom was
warm. She could feel his breath on her cheek, the brush
of his thighs against hers. Her body tingled in response.
She slid her arm under his tunic, flattening her palm on
his back over the soft cotton of his singlet.

She closed her eyes. She forgot she was in the club. She
forgot the guilt at being alive that dogged her every waking moment, and she forgot to worry about whether she'd
be able to pay the rent if she continued to refuse the tips
the other girls earned so easily because there was a war
on and the world was utterly changed. She forgot everything save for the delightful heat in her blood caused by
this man's arms around her, this man's body sheltering her,
waking the desire that had long lain dormant, making her
want to lose herself in passion.

The music stopped. They stood still, two figures frozen
in time. And then the music started again and they moved
in rhythm, unspeaking, eyes closed, not dancing but holding, touching. His fingers played on her spine. Hers slid
down to cup the taut slope of his buttocks beneath his
tunic. His lips fluttered over her temple. She put her mouth
to the rough skin of his throat. He was aroused. She could
sense the thick shaft of his erection as they moved, though

he made no attempt to press against her. It had been so long since she had experienced the delicious frisson of such intimacy. So very, very long since she had even thought about it. It had been easy to repel the advances she inevitably attracted every night in this place. Yet now, when this man had made it clear he would make no such advances, it was all she could think about.

He was thinking about it, too. He could have stopped dancing at the last song, at the one before, or the one before that, but each time the music started up again he pulled her closer. Then the music stopped for the last time, and they were left alone on the dance floor.

'I don't want to let you go,' Robbie said. 'Not just yet.'

'Then walk me back to my apartment,' Sylvie said, without even considering the dangers of being alone with this stranger, a stranger who had been trained to kill without compunction. A man who represented all she hated and all that had damaged her life irrevocably. A soldier. A warmonger. But tonight, she found that she didn't want to be alone, either.

Chapter Two

Sylvie fetched her coat, ignoring the raised brows of the *patron* as he locked the nightclub door behind them. The night air was cold, the city streets eerily silent as Paris shut down for the night. All along the Boulevard de Clichy, the clubs were closing up, the last few customers reeling out into the dark. Two *poilus* in the distinctive pale blue greatcoats of the French army, propping each other up like bookends, sang a surprisingly melodic version of 'La Madelon'.

They walked along Clichy, not entwined but close enough to touch, Robbie Carmichael's shoulder brushing hers, looking straight ahead without talking. Awareness kept them leashed together, creating a tension that heightened with every step. On the corner of steeply rising Rue des Martyrs, Sylvie stopped. 'This is where I live.'

'So this is goodbye, then,' he said.

She thought he looked disappointed, but she could not be sure. She did not want to say goodbye, of that she was sure. 'It does not have to be,' Sylvie said, speaking before she could think, 'if that is not what you want?'

He laughed mirthlessly at that. 'I'd have thought that what I want was perfectly obvious when we were dancing.' He tangled his fingers in her hair, where the chic Parisian stylist had cropped it at her nape. Even after more than a year, Sylvie missed the weight of her tresses, could not get used to having her neck so exposed. 'You are very beautiful.'

His voice was low. His breath smelled of wine, but he did not look or sound in the least bit drunk. Desire warred with caution, but she was so tired of being careful, and it was so long since she had felt anything but numbness. 'I want you to know, I am not in the habit of doing this sort of thing,' she said urgently, because it was important he understood, even if she would never see him again.

'You told me, *ma belle*, and I believed you. I am not in the habit, either. At least not since— But I do want *you*. I want you very, very much.'

His words should have shocked, but she found them exhilarating. Her heart was beating erratically as they hurried along the Rue des Martyrs to the doorway next to the *pharmacie*. Up one steep flight of stairs and then another, where her fingers trembled as she unlocked the door to her apartment. Plenty of time to regret her impulsive decision, to call herself a fool for bringing a stranger here to her sanctuary. Not one of those thoughts crossed her mind.

The room was cold, the fire long since gone out. That was why she was shaking; it was the cold. She switched on the electric lamp, which as usual flickered alarmingly before casting an uncertain glow. She caught her breath in the dim light as he threw off his greatcoat and came towards her. Then his lips touched hers, and heat, neither warm nor gentle but raw and painful, seared them as they kissed.

All the pent-up passion from the dance floor, from the walk home, from the past two years since war had destroyed the life she knew, enveloped her, consumed her, turned her into a wild selfish creature whose only thought was release. His kisses were desperate, urgent, his tongue warring with hers. It was not a battle, Sylvie realised, but a race.

Her coat joined his on the floor. His hands were in her hair, on the bare skin at the nape of her neck, sliding down her spine to cup her bottom, pulling her tight against him, so tight that her feet left the ground and he staggered back against the wall. His passion was every bit as all enveloping as hers. The slash of colour across his pale cheeks, the harsh rise and fall of his rapid breathing, would have betrayed him even without the solid length of his shaft pressed between her thighs. His eyes clashed with hers, the pupils dilated. 'Too fast,' he muttered, almost to himself. 'Too fast,' he repeated, releasing his hold on her so that her feet slid back onto solid ground.

He was frowning down at her as if she were a book he had to study. He was a man women would swoon over, in another life. That was what she'd thought when she first saw him. A man who would put a woman's pleasure first. Who would not rush. She set about undoing the buttons of his tunic. 'Not fast enough,' she said, tugging it open, and flattening her palm over the broad expanse of chest covered only by his undershirt, over the dip of his rib cage, the tautness of his belly. It rippled under her touch. Down, to the rigid length of him tight against the wool of his trousers. 'Not nearly fast enough.'

Robbie bit back a moan as the blood rushed to his groin. He didn't think he'd ever been this hard. He didn't think he'd ever felt this overpowering, overwhelming rush to be there, inside her, as quickly as possible. Not like this. It shouldn't be like this. Before—but he would not think of before. Or after. Or anything except her hands on him, her mouth on him.

He shrugged out of his tunic and let it fall beside their coats. He kissed her, reeling at the way her mouth responded to his with equal fervour. She tasted exactly as he'd known she would taste: sweet, sinful, luscious. He cupped her breast with one hand, her bottom with the other. Such curves. Such beautiful female flesh, and such desire, as furiously ravenous as his own.

She was panting, her eyes wide, her cheeks flushed. Her nipples were hard beneath the filmy layers of her clothing. He bent his head to take one in his mouth, making her shudder.

She tugged at his undershirt. He pulled it over his head, then fumbled with the fastenings of her gown. Before, he had always made a performance of removing his lover's clothing. This was nothing like before. He tugged and yanked and she wriggled and pulled, and her gown fell away, and she stood before him in her shoes and stockings, in her garters and knickers and camisole looking so much more beautiful than he could ever have imagined.

The camisole was white, trimmed with satin ribbon, buttoned down the front. Her stockings were silk. He burrowed his face in the soft mounds of her breasts above her underwear, running his hands down her spine, over the curves of her buttocks, then round, to cup the curves of her breasts. She shivered. He undid the buttons, shaking now, taking a dark pink hard nipple into his mouth and sucking greedily, drawing a harsh moan from her that sounded like an echo of his own.

Her hands fumbled with the fastenings of his trousers as he sucked again, circling the other nipple with his thumb. He cursed inwardly, remembering the complexities of his army dress, and let her go, cursing aloud as he struggled with trousers and puttees and boots, finally kicking off his own underwear, conscious of her watching him all the time, blatantly studying his body, feeling a triumphant, ridiculous, wholly male pride as her eyes widened when he finally stood before her, hard and more than ready.

He should find the bedroom. The bed. His last coherent thought before she touched him, wrapping her hand around him and kissing him hard. 'Now,' she said.

It was an order, and Robbie had been trained to never disobey orders. Pulling her onto the floor, out of sight of the uncurtained windows, he rolled her onto her back, tugged her knickers down and thrust his fingers inside her.

Sylvie arched with pleasure. His mouth covered hers, and she kissed him, thrusting her tongue deep inside, her hands reaching for the satiny thickness of his manhood. She stroked him as he stroked her, sliding in and out and over the slick, throbbing heat between her legs. She thrust herself up shamelessly against his hand. 'More,' she gasped, 'please, more,' and heard him laugh, a guttural, innately male sound that sent shivers of pleasure up her spine. He tore his mouth away from hers to lick her nipples, first one then the other, still stroking. She tensed, then unable to control it any longer, her climax shook her, threw her, rocked her, making her cry out in wild abandon.

And it still wasn't enough. She pulled at him, tugged his shoulders, moaning his name, moaning, 'Now, now, now.' He rolled away from her, fumbling in his uniform, quickly pulling on a *préservatif*. Instead of pushing her onto her back, he pulled her on top of him.

The slide, the slow, delicious slide of his thickness into her, sent frissons of delight through her body. He was staring up at her, eyes wide but unseeing, his face rigid, biting his lip, struggling for control. She liked that. Sylvie tightened around him, and his moan drew a shudder from her. She lifted herself, then slid back down, drawing him in farther. She held him tight inside her and he tilted up under her. She lifted herself again to slide back down, and he thrust at the same time, making her gasp, and then it took over, the urge to climb again, the compulsion to reach that place, that peak, there. She arched her back, shuddering with delight at the way the movement slid him deeper inside her, and then he pulled her towards him and lifted her, and they found a new rhythm. Fast and hard. Until the swell of him threw her over the edge where her falling made him cry out, too, as he pulsed inside her, and she collapsed onto his chest and he held her there with arms as tight as steel bands, and they lay slick with sweat, breathing. Just breathing.

Robbie opened his eyes extremely reluctantly, dragging himself back from the velvet dark place that cocooned his sated body and kept his weary mind blank. He felt heavy, weighted down, yet curiously light-headed. He had never in his life experienced sex like that. He felt as if he had been wrung out, emptied and cast on the shore by a tempest. Carnal, it had been, and completely without finesse. He barely recognised himself. He ought to be ashamed. Except the woman lying over him, the lush, warm, beautiful woman lying over him, had been every bit as carnal, her desires every bit as raw and primal as his own.

He was not ashamed, but he was embarrassed. And confused. What on earth had come over him? Not once since he had found himself at the front had he desired this. Not ever, in his whole life, had he been so completely carried away. He felt as if he'd been swept along in a rip tide. And now that it was over he was afraid, because to his chagrin he found himself wanting her again. His hands rested on the curve of her spine. Her breasts were flattened against his chest. Her face was burrowed into his shoulder. The scent of their coupling mingled with her perfume. He was still inside her, spent, though not wholly spent, it seemed. What kind of an animal had he become?

Robbie began to ease himself up, lifting her away from him at the same time. She blinked, opened her eyes and stared at him as if he were a stranger, something of his own shock reflected in her face. 'It's very late. I should go,' he said, the first thing that came into his head. 'I've had my fun' was how it sounded. Sylvie flushed. He opened his mouth to retract, to explain, then closed it again, because even if he could have, there was no point.

'Very late. You're right.' She jumped to her feet. He had a brief moment to admire her curves, a brief moment when his traitorous body clamoured for her again, and then she grabbed her coat and pulled it on, and he covered himself, mortified, with his own coat that she threw at him, obviously wanting him gone. Which was exactly what he wanted, so he had no right at all to feel rejected.

'There is a bathroom through there,' she said, pointing to a door in the far side of the room. 'You can…'

He nodded, grabbing his clothes, fighting the urge to pull her back into his arms, which was patently the last thing she wanted. The bathroom was a small, meanly partitioned room lit by a naked bulb. It was spartan and freezing, but pristine. He washed and dressed hurriedly, fighting the sadness that was enveloping him. She had not used him, certainly no more than he had used her. It was not her he wanted again, but that feeling, far too short-lived, the velvet dark cloak of oblivion. No doubt that was what she, too, had sought. He had given her what she wanted, just as she had given him what *he* wanted. Only she had had enough and he had not. He tightened his puttees viciously and stamped his feet into his boots. It would have been wiser not to give in to temptation. Much wiser.

Checking his face in the mirror, surprised as ever to see the reflection of a gaunt, hardened soldier staring back at him, Robbie grimaced. He couldn't regret something that amazing. Smoothing his raggedly cut hair back from his brow, his hand went automatically to his scar, and he noticed that for the first time he could remember it was not throbbing. His headache was all but gone. When he got back to his hotel, he might even sleep. Maybe.

Closing the bathroom door behind him he found Sylvie gazing out of the window, still dressed only in her coat. She had removed her stockings. Her bare ankles and feet looked both vulnerable and erotic. Then she turned to face him and he recognised her smile as one of his own, fixed, rigid, forced. She blushed, tightening the belt of her coat around her waist. '*Pardon*, I feel a little embarrassed by my behaviour just now.'

Robbie crossed the room to join her at the window. 'It is I who should apologise. I did not— I am not usually so...' He paused, for lack of an appropriate word to describe his behaviour, and grimaced. 'Honestly, this isn't like me. I suppose—I suppose it's just been such a long time.'

She said nothing. He wanted her all over again, only this time he wanted to take his time, and that was what scared him more than anything else about tonight. 'I should go,' Robbie said roughly, wanting her to contradict him, and yet annoyed that he wanted her to do just that.

Outside, the night was fading into the dawn. Across the street, the shutters on the *boulangerie* were noisily raised. He waited for her to ask him to stay, wanting her to and desperately not wanting her to. She stared up at him for a long moment, then turned away to gaze out of the window again. '*Bonne nuit,*' she said.

He had never been dismissed before. Lovemaking had always been a play in three acts, beginning with a flirtatious prelude, ending with post-coital languor, sleep or a repeat performance. But this had not been lovemaking, it had been sex. Base instinct, a coupling with no other purpose than relief. Robbie's mood turned from grey to black as he kissed the cheek she offered instead of her lips, picked up his cap, turned to go, then changed his mind, because he would not let this cold, businesslike goodbye be his lasting memory of her. He caught her roughly to him and kissed her softly, drinking in her sweetness, capturing it to remember her by, before letting her go. *'Au revoir,'* he said, and left quickly without looking back.

Chapter Three

The road ahead was rutted, muddy and swarming with refugees. She recognised many of them. The school at which Papa was headmaster was the sole one in the town. She herself had taught many of the younger children who were clinging to their parents, balancing on the wheelbarrows and carts laden with whatever scant possessions they had been able to rescue. Little enough, since the bigger carts and all the horses had been requisitioned by the military. Sylvie's suitcase held her clothes and some treasured books. On her back, knotted in a sheet, was Maman's silver tea set, the family photograph album and the only practical items, the coffee grinder and the copper coffee pot. The spout was digging into her shoulder. Her mother's bundle contained the matching stoneware cups, along with who knew what from her store cupboard. On the cart that Papa and her brother, Henri, were pushing was piled an assortment of clothes and whatever else they'd been able to throw onto it in the four hours since they had been given notice to quit the town.

Dogs scampered backwards and forwards along the ragged line of people. Hens, cats, birds, a pet rabbit were carried in cages. By the time they reached the bend in the road that offered the last view of the town, the French army were approaching in the opposite direction. 'Don't look back,' Papa cautioned them. 'Don't look back.'

One of the cart wheels was coming loose. She could hear the irregular *thump, thump, thump* of it as it turned on the road. And then another thumping noise, though it was more like a crack, which made the earth rise up in a huge cloud. She thought at first the wheel had come off. Then she thought she must be the wheel because she was spinning, rolling along on the road. She felt something wet and sticky on her face. And then…

Sylvie jerked awake, heart thudding, skin clammy with sweat. She could still hear the crump of the artillery shell assaulting her ears. Dazed, shaking, her fingers clutched tight around the sheet, she realised the noise was someone knocking loudly on the door of her apartment. Surely it was too early? She glanced at the clock on her bedside table. Eleven. Late morning! At least it was Sunday, and she did not have to work. As she pushed back the tangled sheets and quilt, her unread book fell to the floor. The lamp was still on. She switched it off, clutching her head, which was also thumping.

'Attendez. Je viens,' she said, wincing at the sound of her own voice, staggering to the door simply to quiet the noise.

He was freshly shaven, though he looked as if he had slept even less than she. In the daylight the traces of his youthful good looks were much more evident. He could not have been more than twenty-seven or eight. Last night she'd thought him a few years over thirty. 'Robbie?'

'I woke you up, sorry.'

Sylvie looked down at her flannel nightgown that had once been red and had faded to pale pink. It had once been long, too, but she had been fifteen when Maman had made it for her, more than ten years ago. She had not been able to fasten the buttons properly for years, but she could not bring herself to stop wearing it. Blushing, she clutched at the neckline. It didn't matter that he had seen everything underneath. That had been last night. In the dark. 'What do you want?' she asked, much more brusquely than she intended.

She realised that he'd been trying to smile when it faded. 'I've obviously come at a bad time,' he said, backing away from the door.

'No.' She tried a smile of her own and held the door open. 'It is just—I was sleeping. It's Sunday. I was not expecting— *Entrez.*'

'Sorry to disturb you,' Robbie said again, standing awkwardly just inside the door.

'I am glad you did,' Sylvie said, shivering, thinking that at least he'd spared her the next part of her dream. The part with the blood and the screaming. 'I could do with some coffee, but as you can see, I've not lit the fire yet. Not that I'm actually permitted to brew coffee because it is not technically a kitchen, but still, what the landlord does not know, you know?'

She turned around from gazing helplessly at the empty hearth to find him studying her. She remembered thinking last night that he saw too much, and she'd been right. 'Bad dreams?' Robbie asked.

Sylvie shrugged. 'Nothing coffee won't cure.'

He did not press her, for which she was grateful, until she realised the reason why. 'You, too?' she said, touching her fingers lightly to the dark shadows under his eyes.

'Coffee sounds good,' Robbie replied, making it clear he wanted to talk about it as little as she. He took off his cap and pressed his fingertips against the shorn side of his head, tracing the long red welt that was just visible on his scalp.

Despite the chill in the unheated room, there was a fine sheen of sweat at his temples. Sylvie caught his hand in hers, forcing him to stop worrying at his scar. 'You will make it worse.'

'It's actually much better. I go back tonight.'

Her stomach plummeted. 'Back?' she asked stupidly.

'To the front line,' he confirmed. 'That's why I came. I needed to explain. About last night.'

'Can you explain it?' Sylvie wrapped her arms around herself. '*En vrai*, I don't think I can. I barely recognised myself, I was so—so out of control.'

'That's exactly how I feel. To be honest, I came here not knowing what I was going to say. I just knew that I had to, since I won't get another chance.'

Because he was going back to the front. Because he would never see her again. Because the chances were he would be killed. 'We need coffee,' Sylvie said firmly. 'Sit. I will light the fire.'

She did so quickly, leaving the wood to catch and fetching an ancient woollen jacket that was warm and all enveloping. No one could possibly find her alluring in this attire. She set a pot of water to boil over the flame, conscious the whole time of Robbie sitting, silently watching her. He was going tonight. To the front. She would never see him again because...

Don't think about that. The water boiled. She made the coffee in Maman's copper pot, the spout crooked from where she had landed heavily on her back after the explosion.

Don't think about that. 'I don't have any milk,' she said, handing Robbie a cup. Not the brown earthenware ones. They had been smashed into tiny pieces. He was going back to the front where he might also be...

Don't think about that. She pulled one of the hard, rickety seats from the table and sat down, taking a sip of coffee, then another. 'Better,' she said determinedly.

Robbie looked down at his own cup, seemingly surprised by its presence, and took one small sip before placing it on the floor by his feet. 'I needed you to know,' he said, 'last night. I don't— I have never— Not like that.'

Sylvie set her cup back carefully back in its saucer. 'You came back here to tell me you regret it.'

'No, I don't regret it. I should. I behaved like an animal, but I don't regret it.'

'I behaved like a harlot, but I don't regret it, either.'

'Don't say that.' Robbie jumped to his feet, narrowly missing his coffee cup. 'If anyone acted badly, it was me. Since coming here to France, not once in eighteen months have I behaved like that nor had any desire to. And yet afterwards I wanted more, even while I was still— I wanted you again. I tell you, I've never felt like that in my life.'

She should not feel relief at this declaration, but that was exactly what she did feel. 'Perhaps it was precisely because it had been so long,' Sylvie said, one of the many reasons she'd come up with herself to explain her wild abandon.

'Perhaps.' Robbie picked up his coffee cup and put it down on the hearth. 'But more likely because I've had everything civilised torn out of me.'

The naked suffering in his face took her aback. 'No, Robbie.' Sylvie got quickly to her feet, catching his hands between hers. 'You are not an animal. Or if you are, then I am just the same. Last night, I have never been so—so uninhibited,' she said, forgetting her embarrassment in the urge to assuage his guilt. And her own, perhaps. 'You were just a man a long way from home, looking to forget, find some comfort. It was the same for me.'

'Was it?'

He looked at her searchingly. The shadows made hollows under his eyes. She didn't think she had ever seen anyone look so utterly weary. He ran his fingers through her tangled hair. 'I thought that side of me was dead, until last night,' he said.

His touch made her shiver with awareness. 'I thought I would never— Not ever again,' Sylvie said, mesmerised by the blue-grey of his eyes, by the scent of him, by the breadth of him, which made her forget, as she had last night, that he was a soldier, made her think only that he was a man, a very attractive, extremely desirable man. 'I thought it would be enough. Perhaps it was too much,' she said.

'Not enough,' he repeated, his fingers feathering over the exposed nape of her neck. 'It could never be too much.'

He kissed her. It was the same as last night, though the edge of desperation was even sharper. She clung to him, forgetting everything save for the rampant need that bound them together, kissing him just as hungrily back. They stumbled towards the bedroom, discarding clothing. His tunic. Her woollen jacket. His boots and puttees. Kisses, punctuated by incoherent words, accompanied them as they shed clothes and staggered into the room.

But when he laid her naked on the bed, he slowed, tracing the lines of her body with his hands, then his mouth, tasting her, murmuring her name, and the knife-like need in her melted into a desire that caused her breath to catch in her throat. He kissed her breasts and her belly, the crook of her arm and the curve of her waist. She was liquid with longing as he kissed her knees, her ankles and then her thighs.

He licked into the crease at the top of her legs, and she moaned. Then he pushed her legs apart, kneeling between them, and slid his fingers inside her, and the melting need twisted into tension once more. Sylvie cried out as her climax took her, sudden and unstoppable, writhing under him, begging incoherently for more, panting wildly as he kissed his way back up her body to reclaim her mouth, as he slid inside her with one slow thrust.

She wrapped her ankles around him, digging her heels

into the tense muscles of his buttocks. He thrust into her, slowly and rhythmically, riding the waves of her climax to push deeper, tension and passion etched on his face until he could hold on no longer and cried out, a guttural sound wrenched from deep inside, clutching her to him as if she might save him from some fatal fall.

Robbie rolled onto his side, thanking whatever instinct it was that had reminded him at the last minute to use protection. His body was damp with sweat. This time there could be no blaming the night or the wine or the longing not to be alone among the teeming throngs of Paris. What on earth had he been thinking?

Not thinking. Again! Cursing under his breath, he got out of bed and made for the bathroom, grabbing his underwear and trousers. Unable to face the contraption that supplied hot water, he used cold, hoping that it would shock him into sanity. Emerging a few moments later, clean but none the wiser, he found Sylvie sitting up in bed clutching the sheet around her like a suit of armour. Her eyes were dark brown in the daylight, almost the same colour as coffee, her lashes as black as her hair. Were it not for the fact that she was looking at him with something akin to horror, he would have been very tempted to join her again.

'I didn't come here this morning expecting this to happen,' he said.

His words sounded a great deal more defensive than he had meant them to. Sylvie pulled the sheet higher. 'I hope you do not mean that I—that it was my fault.'

'Of course I don't.' Robbie's hand went automatically to his scar. It was throbbing. Seeing her pointedly watching his hand, he let it fall. 'It wasn't your fault, it wasn't mine. Or it was both of us. I don't have a clue what it was. I don't understand it.'

'You said that earlier.'

'And I think we've just proved me correct.' He felt his temper begin to rise, not in anger but frustration. The clock on her bedside table informed him it was two o'clock in the afternoon. How the hell had that happened? 'Look, I'm sorry.'

Her eyes flashed. 'I knew it!'

'I didn't mean that.'

'Then just what do you mean?' Sylvie jumped out of bed, grabbing her nightgown and the strangely shaped woollen thing, scrambling into both. 'I wish you had not come back.'

'You don't mean that.'

She glared at him, her breasts heaving. 'Why did you?'

'I told you, I wanted to explain, because I won't see you again.'

'Then why does it matter? Since you are so determined that you will die,' she said in response to his blank look, 'why does it matter that you explain—even if you could?'

A bloody good question. 'I don't know, I just know it does.' Robbie picked up his tunic and yanked it on. 'Look, maybe it was all a mistake. Maybe we shouldn't have—not last night, not today. I was perfectly fine until you came along, and now I don't know if I'm on my head or my heels. I haven't ever wanted anyone so much as you, and I don't want to, do you understand? I don't want to! I don't want to feel. I don't want to want. Not you. Not anything.'

'That at least is one thing we can agree on,' Sylvie said shakily. She picked up his boots and threw them at him. Her face was pale, the bright slashes of temper on her cheeks a stark contrast. 'You think it's easy for me, wanting you, when you stand for everything I loathe.'

He had been so caught up in his own turmoil, he had not quite realised how upset she was. 'You're shaking.'

She shook herself free. 'Don't touch me.'

She dug the heels of her hands into her eyes, gulping in

deep breaths of air. 'I hate this and all that it represents,' she hissed, pointing at his uniform. 'Not just yours—the French, the Germans, the British, all of them. None of them care about anything but their own squabbles, and if you are unlucky enough to get in the way—well, what does it matter in the grand scheme of things, as long as victory is won.'

'What do you mean?'

'What do you care?'

'You're from the north, aren't you?' Robbie said, though saying the words made him feel ominously sick.

'Picardy.'

Picardy, which had been rent in two and decimated by both sides in a gruesome game of tug of war from almost the first day of the onset. God knew which of the many villages and towns she'd been forced to leave, and by which army. 'I'm sorry,' Robbie said hopelessly.

'Please don't be! You don't want to feel anything, remember? Well, nor do I.'

She was crying now, though she didn't seem to notice. It was not so much the tone of her voice but the way she looked at him, as if he was the enemy, that made Robbie sick to his stomach. He was not angry with her but at them. The faceless hierarchy who had duped him, and thousands like him, into believing when he signed up that he was doing the honourable thing for king and country.

'These,' Robbie said, holding out his sleeve with its two captain's bands, 'simply mean I'm more likely to get killed than someone without them. Look, I don't know what happened to you, but believe me, I am sorry you've had to suffer. I'm sorry that anyone has to suffer, and that sometimes I am responsible for that suffering. That's just the way it is now, and I can't let myself think about that too much because if I do then I—I won't be able to function.'

Sylvie stared at him silently for a long moment, then she drew a deep, gulping breath and scrubbed frantically at her face with the end of her jacket. 'That, I do understand. I'm sorry.'

'You lost someone?'

She nodded, fighting the lump that rose in her throat. 'More than one. This war, what it does to everyone, I abhor it.'

He put his arms around her. 'It won't always be like this.'

'You don't believe that any more than I do,' she said sadly, tracing the contour of his scar. 'Things have changed forever.'

Robbie glanced at his wristwatch and winced. 'One thing hasn't changed. I have to go.'

Her fingers tightened around his arms. She bit back the protest, knowing that it was pointless, determined that the last thing he remembered of her would not be that. *The last thing*. Was this really the end? 'I can't believe it was only last night that we met.'

'I don't regret it, Sylvie. I have no idea what really happened between us, but I can't regret it, unless you do?'

'Blame the war,' she said, with a failed attempt at lightness. 'That's everyone else's excuse.'

'What happened between us wasn't like everyone else,' Robbie said fiercely.

'I know.' She wrapped her arms tightly around him, pressing her head against his chest. 'I know, but it is better if we pretend that it is.'

His arms held her just as tightly. 'I won't say goodbye.'

'No.'

'Don't see me out.'

'No,' she said again, trembling with the effort to control herself.

He kissed her forehead. *'Belle Sylvie,'* he said.

'Robbie?' She caught his arm as he turned away. 'Don't look back,' she said. Her father's words, and the words that had kept her safe. 'Don't look back.'

Chapter Four

7th November 1916

Dear Sylvie,

Ignore this if you see fit—I would not blame you—but
I simply had to write to you. I find I need there to be
honesty between us. It matters more and more with
every passing day since the earth-shattering night we
met. That's what it felt like—for me, anyway—like
an earthquake. You may laugh—how I would *love* to
see you laugh, by the way, truly laugh—but you made
me want things that I cannot have, feel things I am
afraid to feel, think things I can't bear to think about.
I thought I didn't want that. Since I came back here
to this hellhole, I have discovered that I do.

I can't say where I am, but it is an area familiar to
you—not that you'd recognise it now. In Paris, the
world still possesses some colour. Here, it is leached
out of everything, a landscape of greys and muddy
browns. The table in my dugout shudders every time
a shell falls. It's no secret that we're about to make
one last push to break through the German lines
before winter sets in. We go up the line tomorrow.
Over the shelling, I can hear some of my men

singing. It'll be their last rum rations for a while. Some of them will be writing letters home. Some of them will be praying. None of them want to go over the top. Sometimes I have to resort to threatening them with my revolver. My own men, Sylvie! I've never had to fire, thank goodness. Is it better to hope that I could, or that I could not?

I don't believe they are cowards, those who funk it, though the army does. I'm an officer— my duty is to the army, but more and more, I find myself questioning orders. Stupid ones, like foot inspection—who wants to take their boots and socks off in all this squelching mud!!!—and others, too, that I can't tell you because what I'm writing to you is treasonous enough. It's strange, I don't even know you, yet I feel I know you better than— I don't know, stupid thing to say.

If I read this over I know I won't send it, so I'll send it as it is. What I wanted to tell you was that you've woken me from my torpor and I'm—*grateful* is such a tepid little word. When I left you that day, I felt as if you had turned me inside out. Or I'd turned myself inside out. Whatever, you get the picture! I wish we were not at war, but I'm beginning to see in the midst of all this suffering and mud it is not all savagery, and it's not, as I was beginning to think, every man for himself. There is kindness here and nobility, too.

Sylvie, I am so very glad that our paths crossed. Thank you, and take care.
Robbie

10th November 1916

Dearest Brother,
I wrote you another, very different sort of letter, a

few weeks ago, but I tore it up. Listen, squirt, you must abandon this noble idea you have of joining me here, I beg of you. If one of us has to make the ultimate sacrifice, then let it be me. You know you've always been the apple of Mater's eye, and frankly, I know that Glen Massan has always meant a deal more to you than me. Let's face it, any Scotsman who prefers a good Bordeaux, as I do, to a fine malt doesn't deserve to be laird!!!

So as your elder and better, I'm ordering you to stay put and keep your head down, for my sake, as well as the P's.

Robbie

14th November 1916

Dear Robbie,

Your letter aroused so many emotions in me, I don't know where to start. Relief first, because though I did not want to admit it, I did not want to contemplate never hearing from you ever again. And then fear that even now makes my pen shake. *Are you safe?* The appalling thing is, unless you reply I will never know.

Your letter also made me feel ashamed, because you were brave enough to say the things you felt and I—I was trying very hard to pretend I did not feel *anything*. It has become a habit. Like you, I felt turned inside out—I felt as if everything had been bottled up in me and you somehow triggered its release—goodness, how utterly *dreadful* that sounds, but you know what I mean!

Since that night, like you, I have started to see things differently. I don't want to go back to *before*.

Funny, but now that word has two very different meanings. Before the war. And before Robbie.

You say you don't know me, and I hope that means you would like to, so let me tell you a little about myself.

As I told you, I am from Picardy, from a little town near Amiens. At the outbreak of the war, when it was captured by the Germans, we found ourselves behind enemy lines. Then, in September of 1914, long before you arrived in France, the French army liberated us, but we were not permitted to stay, because we were in the line of the fighting. While we were being evacuated, our convoy was shelled. My father, who was the head teacher in the local school, had gone back with my mother to help a neighbour. They were both killed. My only brother, Henri, survived but enlisted at the next town.

Henri was a man of the church, a man of God, and now he is a soldier. I saw him briefly at the start of this year. I am appalled to tell you that he had trophies from dead Germans. I barely recognised him. Revenge for the slaughter of our parents, he called it, though the truth is, we cannot even be sure it was German shells that killed them. Why is it that war kills so many who do not choose to fight?

I used to be a teacher, just like Papa. Now I work as a waitress in a nightclub full of men who think nothing of taking a life. Do you think it's wrong, Robbie, this licensed killing? Is it different for women, for those of us who have not experienced war first-hand? We are all casualties of war, I think—you, me and Henri. Is there a right and wrong anymore?

I find I have not the heart to teach now—there seems such little hope for the future. We are alike,

my brother and I, in that we have both lost our faith—
his in God, mine in human nature. Henri is fighting
at Verdun, I think. They say in the papers that it goes
well for the French—you notice I do not say 'us'—
but as usual the casualty lists tell a different tale,
and so, too, do the shortages that are starting to bite
here in Paris. No butter, no oil. Still plenty of wine,
though. I can see you smile—or pretend to smile—
at that. I wish I could see you smile, Robbie, as you
used to. Before. I think you once smiled a lot.

I was angry with you, that last day. I didn't want
to have to worry about someone else. I think I said
that. I don't remember all I said. I'm not angry now. I
have been thinking about my parents and my old life
a lot since you left. It hurts, but it means I'm alive.
There are so many refugees here, so much worse
off than me. In the nightclub, the atmosphere has
changed. There is an air of desperation now. A fear
that we might lose. We. You see, I told you I didn't
care, British, German or French, it was all the same
to me. That was a lie.

I have said too much. I will not ask you to take
care of yourself. I will not tell you that I miss you,
because how can I miss a man that I have known for
less than a day?

I will not beg you to reply, nor will I think about
how I'll feel if you do not.
Sylvie

20th November 1916

Dear Robbie,
I know it is too soon to expect a reply, but writing
to you seems to have opened the floodgates. I have
been besieged with memories of home. Shall I share

them with you? You said your world was leached of colour. Would it help if I painted some in?

You told me you imported wine, before the war. In Picardy, the wine is not so good, but the cider is excellent. We drink it from little cups, like small coffee bowls. It is not sweet, more like apple champagne. If you are not careful, it can go to your head just like champagne, too. It is especially good with oysters. We always had those on Christmas Eve.

There will be no oysters in Paris this Christmas, though it is the height of the season. I suppose nothing can get through. No butter, did I tell you that? In Picardy, we cook everything with butter. I am a good cook. Maman taught me well, though it is from Papa that I get my love of books.

I am wittering on, and all I really want to tell you is that I am missing you and praying for you. I tell myself that if I keep writing, then you will still be there to read my letters. That's what I tell myself. So I will keep writing.
Sylvie

21st November 1916

My dear son,
We received your telegram this morning telling us that you are safe as the hostilities go into abeyance for the winter. I must confess, my heart almost failed me when I saw the messenger at the Lodge door. To be completely honest, my heart sinks every time the doorbell rings, for fear it may be a telegram containing bad news. Your father can no longer bear to be in the room when I open them. But this time it was such wonderful news.

I know it is wrong of me, but I pray for an early and

long winter to delay any further fighting. I would pray for an early victory, but that is too much to hope for after all this time. You see how dreadfully unpatriotic I have become. Even my impudent Welsh son-in-law would be impressed by the extent of my sedition!

You write so rarely, and when you do you say nothing of how you really are. I promised myself I would not chastise you, and I do not mean to. I know that I have never been the most demonstrative of parents. I was brought up to believe it was not the done thing to show one's feelings. These days, I am awash with so many conflicting emotions that I am even upon occasion tempted to weep when I visit the latest of our people in the village to receive one of *those* telegrams, or when I see one of those brave boys limping past on one leg, or worse. I do not, of course, shed tears in public; one must, after all, maintain some standards when so many are slipping—for it seems to me that people are rather too eager to take advantage of the war by behaving most laxly.

Your father sends his regards. I fear this war has rather knocked the stuffing out of him. He has taken to spending even more time wandering the moors or locked in his study. I fear he misses all three of you dreadfully, though he would never say it.

There, enough of this. Flora, your frighteningly impressive sister, sends me letters full of fundraising suggestions she expects me to put into action. We have had blanket drives for the refugees, innumerable cake and jam sales in the village hall, and next month we will be holding our biggest event yet, over in the grounds of Colonel Patterson's estate. A Christmas Fayre of the most old-fashioned type. We hope to raise enough to send at least one ambulance to France. I have purloined a case of your best vintage for the tombola, I do hope you approve. Frightening to admit it, but I am quite enjoying all this organising. Perhaps it is from me that Flora inherited that particular talent. Who would have thought it?

I find the newspapers too depressing to read these days. There seems to be a growing voice in London dissenting against this dreadful conflict and I am becoming sympathetic to that point of view, though you must know that in no way reflects on the great sacrifices my children are making. I am very, very proud of all of you.

Speaking of which, your father had a letter from Alex just this morning, telling him he had asked you to intervene on his behalf with a transfer. I beg you, Robbie, to do all you can to persuade Alex to remain where he is. As a mother, I can be forgiven for taking a little comfort in knowing my youngest is in a place where the fighting is less fierce.

One of the officers from the house has just arrived, and I must go to see what he wants since the laird is out. He is a rather shabby boy with the most dreadfully common accent. I cannot imagine that he would have been deemed officer material in peacetime—heaven knows what school he attended!

I am sending my best love. I torture myself that I said it so little to your dear face, my darling. Looking back on how we were before the war, I want to laugh at some of the things that seemed so important. Please keep safe.

Your mother

23rd November 1916

My dear Sylvie,
I am safe, and overwhelmed to receive so many let-

ters from you. Thank you. I would have sent you a
telegram if I'd known you were so worried, though
perhaps it would not have been such a good idea
to have it arrive out of the blue. I know from my
mother what emotions the sight of those things can
do these days.

Before—before the war, long before Sylvie, you
see, I think there are two befores now, as you do—a
telegram usually signalled good news. *I'm arriving
on this train. I will meet you at this time.* Even
something as simple as *Happy Birthday.* Looking
back on it now, that life seemed to consist of a string
of parties and dances and picnics. Not true, of course,
lest you think I was a complete dilettante, because I
did work for my living. Not that I had to. As you've
probably guessed, I come from a relatively privileged
family, but I wanted to.

I've lost the thread of what I wanted to say. I miss
you, Sylvie. Is that permitted? Too late, I've said it.
I think about you all the time—no, that's not true,
and I've resolved to tell you as near to the truth as
I can. Only you. I think about you all the time that
I'm me, just me—in the moments that I'm Robbie
and not Captain Carmichael, and believe me, they've
been few and far between this last fortnight.

Do you want to know how it's been? I never tell
anyone. Usually, all I want to do is forget. I'm back
behind the lines, another trench, another little dugout
cut into the earth that I share with another captain—or
I will do, when they replace the one we lost. There's a
brazier fashioned from a large metal drum, and coals
to burn. There's a lamp, and two bunks with straw
mattresses. My man brings me hot water. I have no
idea where he gets it from. Of course, there are rats,
too, and the smell—no, no need to describe the smell.

It's eerily quiet now. No field guns, after weeks of incessant shelling. My ears are still ringing.

Later I have to go and attend to the men on charges. There are always men on charges. Tomorrow I will go up to the field hospital. Tonight I'll be writing letters. You know the kind, all lies and brave words. I can't believe they provide much succour for those poor families.

But I've still not told you how it was. It was as it always is, Sylvie. A mad rush forward, into the mist this time. We thought it was a good thing, the mist, but it worked just as well for the Germans. They couldn't see us, we couldn't see them, and our guns—well, you get the picture. Five days in all it went on, and I am still not sure whether we gained ground or not. The papers will say we advanced, of course. The losses were, as always, heavy.

My men went into battle bravely. I always thought it was the fear of what would happen to them if they didn't go over the top that drove them on, but I was wrong. I watched them this time. They don't fight for their country, not anymore—they fight for each other. You see, I was wrong when I said there was no such thing as comradeship.

Did I say that? If I didn't, it's what I thought, and I was wrong. I've seen valour and bravery and incredible sacrifice. Stretcher bearers, some of them conchies, take unbelievable risks to help hopeless cases, Sylvie. I have to write one of *those* letters after this one. A Corporal Bellingham. I shall say the usual stuff, but the truth is he had a horrible death, trapped for eight hours in a shell crater with his leg blown off before the stretcher bearers got to him, and conscious for most of it. He'd only been here a few months.

I hope you've not been fretting too much about me. Less than a day we spent together, it's incredible, but as we said at the time, that doesn't seem to matter. Your letters—four letters, I do not deserve such riches—have been a godsend.

I would give anything to see you, to hold you, to kiss you. Please keep writing and don't make of any silence on my part anything but the vagaries of my duties. And of the postal system, which is really atrociously unreliable.

If I could but see you again—but that is to wish for the impossible, and I am not so changed as to do that.

Take care.

Robbie

23rd November 1916

Dear Mrs Bellingham,

On behalf of the officers and men of my Company, I wish to offer you our sympathy for the loss of your husband.

Corporal Bellingham was well liked by all his comrades, and an asset to the Company. He was mortally wounded on 16th November by German fire during an advance through the Ancre valley. I am informed by those who were with him that he died instantly and suffered no pain. Unfortunately, we have so far been unable to locate your husband's mortal remains for burial.

Again, assuring you of all our sympathy in this difficult time.

Yours sincerely,

Robert J. Carmichael, Capt., ASH

18th December 1916

My dear Sylvie,
A few lines only. Hopefully you will have had my last three by now and perhaps even in an order that will make some sense! You must have quite a collection—assuming you keep them. Do you? I keep yours. The paper is worn from my reading them.

I got yours of the 10th and 16th this morning. I can see from reading them that at least one has gone missing. I write because there's a small chance of leave. Two days only, Christmas Day and the day after. I can come to Paris. Can we meet?

I shall telegram when I know—so don't panic when the boy arrives at your door.
Robbie

24th December 1916

My dear Robbie,
Can we meet?! As if there could be any answer save *YES, YES, YES.*

Just tell me when and where and I will be there, though I don't expect you'll get this in time.
I'm watching for the telegram boy.
Sylvie

28th December 1916

My dear Sylvie,
You will have received my telegram by now. I cannot say how sorry I am. There is a chance my leave may be rescheduled for next week, perhaps even Sunday, which is New Year's Eve.

I expect you'll have plans, but I'll telegram once I know, and I'll come to Paris, anyway.

I would march all the way to Berlin for just an hour in your company.

Robbie

Chapter Five

Paris—2nd January 1917

Sylvie stepped farther back from the mirror and eyed her reflection critically. The dress was new, an extravagance bought in the excitement of thinking she would be spending Christmas with Robbie. A black, tight-fitting bodice with a square neck and a high waistline, and the narrow skirt was in the new fashion, grey wool with a wide border of the same black forming the hem, which sat just below her calves. Her stockings were also black, and her buttoned boots with their French heel made her feet and ankles look elegantly narrow. The slim line of the gown would have sat better on a less curvaceous woman, but for once she looked chic, in that indefinable Parisian manner. A pity that she had to conceal it under a coat, and her outmoded grey flannel one at that, but needs must.

She was far too early. Even if his train did by some miracle arrive on time, and even if, by an even greater miracle, he was on it, she would be at the restaurant at least half an hour before him if she left now. Sylvie peered out of the window. It had been snowing again. She took the telegram from the mantelpiece and read the contents once more.

Sorry leave cancelled again. Lunch Tuesday 2nd.
1300 hours, Chartiers? Third time lucky? Robbie.

Would it be, though? She had heard so many tragic tales
of loved ones failing to return on leave because they had
been wounded or killed. But it was stupid to think that
way. Apart from anything else, Robbie was not a loved one.

'Oh, it doesn't matter what he is,' Sylvie exclaimed,
jamming her hat over her carefully brushed hair. 'He probably won't turn up, and it's incredibly stupid of me to care
whether he does or not.'

By the time she got to Chartiers, her stomach was
churning. Words and phrases from her letters to him kept
popping into her head. Silly things she had told him about
her childhood. Even more embarrassing, the way she had
poured out her innermost feelings. The things that made
her cry. Her anger, her pain. She'd even told him about
her dream. It was as if the Sylvie and Robbie who wrote
so candidly to each other were different people from the
ones who were about to be reacquainted in the flesh. Perhaps it really would be better if he didn't turn up. And
if he did—would he expect her to take him back to the
apartment, to pick up from where they had left off the last
time? She stopped abruptly, right outside the glass doors to
the restaurant, appalled by the shivery heat of desire that
clutched at her belly. *Non.* He had not once referred to it,
even obliquely, after that first letter.

Nervously checking her make-up in her compact mirror,
she pushed open the door and entered. The restaurant was
crowded, as it always was, for the food was cheap and con-
sistently good, despite the shortages. She was led past several empty tables to the back *salon*, where the huge globe
lamps that hung from the distinctive glass ceiling were
already lit despite the early hour. On the back wall, the

mirrors reflected the hive of activity as waiters worked the long gallery like ballet dancers, moving fluidly between the tightly packed tables, taking orders, pouring wine, ladling soup, imperiously ignoring requests for the bill.

She didn't see him at first. She was so convinced that he would not be there that when the waiter paused in front of an occupied table, she started to apologise. Then he got to his feet and her mouth went dry. She had forgotten how very, very attractive he was. 'Robbie,' she said, staring stupidly.

'Sylvie.' He hesitated, then kissed her, Parisian-style, once on each cheek. His fingers tightened briefly on her shoulders. 'It is very good to see you. I only have a few hours. Let me take your coat.'

He put it up beside his own coat and hat on the coat rack, which was suspended above the tables, and pulled out a chair. By some miracle, or more likely with the aid of a few francs, he had managed to secure a corner table, where they could watch the room but could also talk in relative privacy. She was quite unprepared for the surge of emotion that shook her. His hair had grown, the scar was no longer visible, though there was a new, freshly healed scar on his cheek.

'A flesh wound,' Robbie said, spotting the concern on her face. 'So trivial I didn't think to mention it.'

He looked tired, but had lost a little of the haunted look that had first drawn her to him. Nor did he look quite so gaunt. 'At least they are feeding you,' she said. 'That is more than I can say for the French army, from what I hear in the club.'

'By all accounts, your lads took a hammering at Verdun. Sorry, I know your brother is there.'

'I haven't heard anything. I have to assume no news is good news.'

'My train got in early, would you believe,' Robbie said,

picking up the menu before putting it down again distractedly. 'You'll think me an idiot, but I'm actually nervous.
I've told you things in my letters that I've never told anyone, and now you're sitting right opposite me looking so
much more beautiful than I remember, and I feel like I'm
naked.'

Sylvie laughed. 'I know exactly what you mean. I was
standing outside the restaurant just a moment ago thinking, he knows that I am a thief....'

Now Robbie laughed. 'You were only eight, and you
came out in a terrible rash.'

'I thought that was my punishment for stealing the
strawberries from our neighbour's garden. Like you being
sick after sneaking a drink of your father's whisky.'

'I was ten! Maybe that's where my preference for wine
stems from. Talking of which,' Robbie said, pouring her
a glass from a dusty bottle, 'I confess, I paid an obscene
amount for this renowned vintage, but it is a very special
occasion. A belated happy New Year, Sylvie. *Sláinte*, as
we say back at home.'

He watched her as she sipped her wine and scanned the
menu, ordering quickly but with assurance. Could she really live up to his expectations, and he to hers? But here
they were, and she was very beautiful, and they had only
a few hours, and he was dammed if he'd waste them on
futile speculation. What mattered was now. This was the
only reality.

'Robbie?'

'Sorry, I was in a *dwam*. Daydream,' he translated,
when she looked at him blankly.

'Is that a Scottish word?'

'Aye.'

'Aye,' she repeated mockingly, smiling at him over her
glass. 'Tell me more about your home. Glen Massan. Tell

me what you would be doing now, if you were there. It sounds so romantic, this castle of yours.'

'Not mine, my father's. And right now, it belongs to the army. My mother tells me they've converted it into some sort of convalescence home. I don't know what they did for Hogmanay—that's New Year's Eve—this year, but before the war, there was always a big party. Provided it did not fall on the Sabbath, of course, in which case the ceilidh—the dancing—couldn't start until after midnight.'

He talked. She laughed, asked more questions, and he lost himself for the first time since he'd arrived in France, in talking about the old days, before all this. Their lunch arrived, clean plates disappeared, but he didn't remember what he ate. The wine went down slowly. He was fascinated by her smile, by the fan of lines around her eyes when she laughed, by the way she communicated with her hands, those curious little Gallic shrugs of hers. He liked to make her laugh. Today, it was not forced. Today, she smiled as he had imagined she must have, before. As he was doing, too, talking about Glen Massan. He'd forgotten how fond he was of the place after all.

'It must be difficult,' Sylvie said, 'having your home taken over by the army.'

He was about to shrug, as he always did when asked, but the trite response refused to appear. 'I've not been back. I couldn't bear to see it so changed.'

'There is no going back for me now. Not even after the war, I think.'

He could have kicked himself. 'I'm sorry. At least my home is still standing.'

In the silence that followed, Sylvie picked up her coffee cup and drained it in one gulp. 'Whatever is left back in Picardy, it is no longer my home. I think we had better get the bill.'

Robbie looked around the empty room in some surprise.

The waiter, who had been lurking with intent for some time, making a show of polishing glasses at the nearest counter, came immediately. 'My train doesn't leave for an hour or so,' Robbie said, checking his wristwatch. 'We could go for a walk, have a digestif somewhere.'

'I would like that,' she said, handing him his cap. 'I wish you did not have to wear this uniform.'

'Not half as much as I do,' he said bleakly.

Outside, the afternoon was overcast but dry, the flurry of snow already melted from the pavements. They wandered through the faded glamour of the Galerie Vivienne with its mosaic floors and high glass canopy, down towards the Palais Royal, where the silence between them became uncomfortable. Though Robbie had promised himself an interlude from the war, the very clothes he wore made that impossible. They were at the entrance to the Tuileries. It was too cold to sit, but he drew her over to a bench all the same. 'Sylvie, I didn't join the army to satisfy some sort of bloodlust, you know.'

The animation had gone from her face. Her skin was pinched, pale with the cold, her eyes bleak with something else. 'But you knew when you enlisted that you would have to kill. And you joined of your own free will, Robbie, you were not conscripted.'

She had made her views very clear the first time they'd met, and they were implicit in her letters, but her determination to see the war only from her own, simply defined point of view made his temper rise. 'True, I wasn't conscripted. I happened to believe that I was doing the honourable thing by volunteering.'

Something in his face or his tone must have alerted her to his feelings, though he had tried to keep his voice level. 'You think I am mistaken, don't you?' she asked him.

'I think you see things very much in black and white.

War is wrong. Killing is wrong. It would be better if we all shook hands and made up.'

'I know it's not so simple, that there are treaties and pacts and alliances and— I have read the papers, Robbie, I know how all this came about, but you did not have to join in, any more than my brother did. If only there had not been such an appetite for warmongering—all the flag waving, and the jingoistic songs, and the generals rubbing their hands together because they hadn't had a war in a while and now they'd get a chance to try out their new guns, and all the men rushing to leave their families and all that nonsense about how we would teach the Bosche a lesson and be home for Christmas.' Sylvie scrubbed angrily with her gloved hands at the tears that had gathered in her eyes. 'If any thought had been given to the people who would be caught in the crossfire, the hundreds of thousands of people who have no home, no family, the refugees who camp out in the streets here in Paris, who are shipped off to England to live off charity—but no one gave any of it a thought. If we had women in charge of the governments, then maybe…'

Robbie laughed bitterly. 'You and my sister, Flora, would get along very well.'

'Yet she is here in France, isn't she? Helping the war effort?

'Easing the suffering,' Robbie said. 'There's a difference.'

Sylvie bit her lip.

He took off his cap. His scar itched, as it always did when he was upset. He could feel a headache coming on. 'When this war started, I thought it was a just one. Right or wrong, that's what I thought. And I've been raised to believe that I owe a duty to my country. Again, right or wrong, it's what I believed. I didn't realise that doing the right thing would oblige me to do so many wrong things.

Things that keep me awake at night, Sylvie.' The dull ache had quickly become a stabbing pain, but he was determined to finish, acknowledging it might well finish things between them. At least it would end as it had begun, on an honest note. 'Every day, I'm forced to break my own moral code in the name of duty. Do you think I find that easy?'

Sylvie shook her head. She was even paler now, her eyes wide, her hands clutched tightly together.

'I can't be neutral about this war, Sylvie, don't you see that? All this bloodshed, all this suffering, I can't let it be for nothing. I have to believe I'm fighting for something important. And if that makes me a murderer in your eyes, then so be it.'

'I didn't say that.'

'But you think it,' Robbie said harshly.

'Not about you,' she replied, her voice barely more than a whisper. 'You think that wartime is no place for principles, *non*?'

'If anything, I'm a bit envious that you have managed to retain yours.'

'I think you are being very much too kind,' she replied, her voice trembling. 'It is easy to have the luxury of principles when they are not challenged. I am not the one in the trenches. I feel…' She shook her head. 'You have made me feel very small.'

'Sylvie, that's the last thing…' It was the way she refused to cry, the way she was biting her lip, struggling for self-control, that was so difficult to witness. He offered her his handkerchief and she took it, dabbing frantically at her eyes, looking off into the distance where the Eiffel Tower stood stark against the fading light.

'I'm sorry,' she said finally. 'You've given me a lot to think about. I hadn't realised— Oh, Robbie, I just wish…'

'Don't.' She looked so tragic and so lovely. He felt drained, and yet looking at her, he remembered that first time, and desire caught him in a fierce grip. 'Don't wish for anything except what we have, Sylvie,' he said, unable to resist tucking the silky curl of hair, which was always escaping, back behind her ear. 'I'm here because I want to be with you. I don't hate you for what you believe in, I admire that you can still believe in something.'

'I think you do, too, Robbie, though you're reluctant to admit it.' She touched his face, her gloved fingers lightly tracing the tiny new scar, then the line of his old one. 'You believe something good will come of all this.'

Her touch was distracting. The throbbing in his head had faded, giving way to a latent throbbing in his groin. He wanted to trace the lovely line of her throat, the questioning arc of her brows. He wanted to run his fingers through the dark, vibrant curl of her hair. She wore a coat of grey wool, a garment more practical and not as stylish as her dress, but the poor cut merely drew his attention to the desirable body underneath. 'I have to, or I couldn't go on.' He'd forgotten how delightful the scent of her was, that mix of flowery perfume and warm skin and intense femininity. She wasn't wearing lip rouge. Her lips were so soft. He could feel her breath, cold on his cheek. 'Sylvie.'

'Robbie?'

He meant to say, 'Let's not talk about it anymore.' He meant to tell her that she had given him much to think about, too. Instead he groaned and pulled her into his arms.

His lips were soft, his kiss tender, so very different from the last time. Sylvie closed her eyes, wrapping her arms around his neck, drinking in the taste of him, the warmth of him. His kiss was like the kind of summers she remembered from before the war, soothing warmth building slowly to strength-sapping heat, drugging her and at the same time fluttering life into her, making her shiver for more. His tongue swept over her lower lip. His hands

were in her hair, cupping her face. Small kisses now, on
her eyelids, on her cheeks, back to her lips. Their tongues
touching, retreating, touching. So sweet, like the strawberries she could not eat, teasing her, rousing her into a
languid, sensual state in which she could not tell whose
lips or tongue were whose, merely that they kissed. And
kissed. And kissed.

A disapproving tut caused them to break their embrace.
An elderly woman with two small dogs drew them a dis-
dainful look. Sylvie blinked, blushed, put a hand to her
hair and found that her hat fallen off. The woman and her
dogs continued on. Robbie cast a quick look around, then
pulled her back into his arms, and it started again.

Kisses to make her swoon. She had thought such a thing
the product of her adolescent imagination, but now she
found they really did exist. He pulled her tighter against
him, and she ran her fingers through the closely cropped
hair at his nape, to the silky softness farther up. Kisses to
make her sigh. Kisses to make her feel like she was flying
higher than the Eiffel Tower. When they finally stopped,
dusk was falling. Her lips were swollen. 'I feel like a *jeune
fille*, not a grown woman of twenty-five,' Sylvie said, trying to make light of the matter, though it was the truth.

Robbie ran his fingers through his dishevelled hair. He
looked endearingly youthful. Her heart did a strange little
flip. 'You don't kiss like a *jeune fille*, though I know what
you mean.' He got up carefully from the bench. 'Not the
sort of behaviour expected of a British officer, my dear,'
he said in his best old-guard accent.

'This is Paris, and we are at war. Apart from Madame
Chiens, I doubt anyone will have batted an eyelid.'

Robbie straightened her hat and put his own cap on.
He checked his watch and blanched. 'I should have left
half an hour ago.'

'I could come to the train station with you.'

'No.' He shook his head emphatically. 'No goodbyes. I'll write. If you still want me to.'

'Of course I do.'

He kissed her swiftly. 'You'll get home safely from here?'

'I'll take the Métro.'

'Take care, Sylvie.'

'And you, Robbie,' she said. 'Please take the best of care,' she whispered, watching him walk briskly from the park.

Chapter Six

2nd January 1917

Dearest Robbie,

I am safely back at my apartment now. I hope you caught your train. I am due at work in half an hour, but I simply had to write to you about today.

I couldn't believe how nervous we both were, like children on a first date, right down to the kiss on the bench in the Tuileries. I am blushing just thinking about it. So silly, blushing about a mere kiss when we have— But that was different somehow; we were strangers. We still are, practically, and yet we are not. Do you know what I mean? Of course you do.

I was going to say that today was perfect. It was not, though it ended perfectly, if endings can ever be described as perfect. Our earlier conversation was difficult, but I am glad you said what you did. I need time to reflect, but I do see that I cannot sit on the fence forever. It made things easier, or I thought it did, but now I see that all it did was postpone—I don't know what, pain, definitely, some difficult decisions probably—but things I need to confront eventually.

So often when I write to you, I think you must be scratching your head and wondering what on earth does she mean? After today, I will worry less about that. Have a safe journey and keep safe.
Sylvie

2nd January 1917

Dearest Sylvie,
I am writing this on the train so won't be able to post it until I get back to camp, but I couldn't wait until then. Today was—momentous! Is that too strong a word? It doesn't feel it. I can confess now, I was worried you would not be the person I imagined, or, worse, that I would not live up to your expectations of me. You were so much more than I imagined, and I pray, if your kisses are anything to go by, that I did not disappoint, either. Such kisses, Sylvie. I had quite forgotten that kissing could be more than a means to an end.

But I am not writing to tell you how wonderful your kisses are—that I made perfectly obvious at the time. I fear I was quite harsh with you earlier today, and yet there is a part of me that is glad I was. The honesty between us, my dearest Sylvie, is extraordinarily important to me and, I hope, to you. It matters, which I confess I find a little disconcerting.

I am a soldier. That is not going to change in the near future, and even after—but I won't talk of after. It is not all that I am, but for now it is by far the biggest part of me. My job is to kill the enemy, and though it's under orders, and though we are assured that God is on our side, I can't reconcile myself to it. But I do it all the same. There will always be blood on my hands. If we are to continue to correspond, perhaps even to meet again, though I won't tempt fate by hoping for that, you, too, will have to find a way of accepting that fact.

I won't read this over, I never do, but I've a horrid suspicion I sound like a pompous ass—pardon the language! I would not have dreamed of committing such thoughts to paper before—is it the war that's making me so self-analytical, or is it you? We've just pulled in at a station and there's what looks like an entire brigade of French soldiers coming on board so I'll finish now.

Bonne nuit, Sylvie. Don't work too hard. I wish you didn't have to work in that place.
Robbie

5th January 1917

My very dearest brother,
I have not heard from you in *two months*. I tell myself, because there has been no telegram, not even one of those dreadful postcards, that you must be well, but the more time passes, the more I am afraid for you.

Henri, the last time we met we both said such dreadful things. It seemed then that we were on diametrically opposing sides, but I don't think we were, it's just that our way of coping with the loss of Maman and Papa and all the other people from our little town is different. Our tragedy is being replicated all over the Western Front, in Italy, in the Balkans, everywhere this dreadful war is being fought. It felt like we had lost everything back in the autumn of 1914. But we still have each other, and that is so much more than some of the people I meet these days.

Being reconciled to you, my dear and only brother, is my *fervent wish*, and one, if granted, that I pray will help both of us to become reconciled to the tragic loss of our parents. I will not lie to you. I still see this war as a pointless exercise whose terrible cost cannot ever be justified. But...

I said to you that I could never imagine myself killing another human being, no matter what the circumstances. I had no right to say such a thing, because I have never been forced to confront the kind of extreme circumstances that you and all the other soldiers face every day. I passed judgement and it was wrong of me. Soldiers are also men, who kill only because they have to. They are not animals; they take no pleasure from what they are forced to do—on the contrary, it almost destroys them. I know that now.

I shut out the memory of that dreadful day, but in doing so shut out everything else, including you. I am *so very sorry* that I judged you so harshly. I hope that you can find it in your heart not to judge me as I did you. Please write. I beg of you, please write.
Your own sister always,
Sylvie

12th January 1917

Dearest Robbie,
I received the letter you wrote on the train only today, even though we've both written twice since. How strange that we both felt compelled to write almost the same thing to each other. I don't know what the English word is, but in French we say *nos esprits se rencontrent*.

You say that being a soldier is the biggest part of

what you are, but for me, it is second to the fact that
you are you, Robbie Carmichael. You know now, or
at least you will if my letters are getting through,
just how much my opinion has changed. I can never
condone war, but nor can I condemn those who
fight it honourably. I have written to my brother. He
has not yet replied. I will write again to him soon,
regardless. For now, I send you a kiss, and I leave it
up to you to decide which kind.
With affectionate thoughts,
Sylvie

16th February 1917

Dearest Sylvie,
Despite the relative quiet on the front lines, perhaps
due to Jerry concentrating all his effort on blowing
up our submarines, our mail has been extremely irregular. I received yours of 12th January along with
the one you wrote just three days ago, and I confess I've spent the last fifteen minutes imagining
every possible variety of kiss that you could possibly give me.

Nos esprits se rencontrent means serendipity
in English. More than a happy coincidence, but a
meeting of minds, as you say. Not that I believe
anything so fanciful. At least I wouldn't have, before.
Now, isn't that strange? I think that's the first time
I've ever compared before—before the war and
before Sylvie—with now, and actually preferred now.
I am so glad you finally had word of your brother. It
sounds like he's been through hell, and I'm not surprised. They reported Verdun as a victory, but they
said the same about the Somme. I will be thinking
of you tomorrow, and hoping with all my heart that

Henri manages to get to Paris as promised. However it turns out—and you'll know before you get this, I suppose—at least you'll have tried. No matter how changed he might seem, remember that somewhere inside is the brother you love.

I'm being summoned, so must go. I'm refereeing a football match, would you believe. We played rugger at my school, so I'm not exactly sure of the rules, but it allows me to mix with my men. I can hear you laughing at the notion of me voluntarily seeking company—how I wish I could hear you laughing, Sylvie—but I find these days I quite like being one of the lads for a while, when I am elsewise one of *them*. Robbie

20th February 1917

Dearest Robbie,
Henri has gone back to the front, and I am *so happy* and *so sad*. You were right, he has changed almost beyond recognition. For the first two days, he barely spoke, barely did anything save lie on my sofa and stare into space. He does not drink, but he smokes, lighting one from the other, dragging on the cigarettes as if they were a drug. I suppose they are. Then, in the middle of the second day, I found him weeping uncontrollably—oh, Robbie, such raw pain. I won't repeat the details of what he told me. Horrors I could never imagine—but then you will know, of course you will know. I let him *talk and talk and talk*. I said nothing, or at least nothing meaningful, but I held him, and after a while, he started talking to me and not at me and then, only then, I could see what you promised, that inside, trapped but still there, was the Henri I know and love.

It is an exaggeration to say that he is better. I can claim only that I gave him respite, but I do think it is the beginning of something new between us. What that will be I don't know, only that at least it will be something. You will say you played no part in this, but you did. You gave me the courage to face what I had been hiding from, and that has given me hope. Oh, but Robbie, what a mixed blessing is hope, for now he has gone back...

But I won't dwell on that. Instead I will tell you my other big news. I am teaching again! Voluntary, not paid, so unfortunately I still have to work in the nightclub, but during the day I teach classes of little ones from refugee families. I thought I could not, that it would remind me too much of what I had lost. I have discovered instead that it is a way of assuaging that loss.

You see how far I have come, how far you have helped me along?
Today I dare finish—with deep affection,
Sylvie

13th March 1917

Dear Mr and Mrs Finchley,
I am writing to express the deepest sympathy of the officers and men of my Company for the sad loss of your son, Private Eric Finchley. It is customary in these letters to extol the virtues of the man as a soldier. I have been proud to serve with your son for the last eleven months, and can assure you that Private Finchley was one of those soldiers who could be relied upon utterly to follow through the course of action expected of him.

But while this earned him the respect of his

comrades, it was his enduring good humour, particularly at times when other men were beginning to show signs of battle fatigue, which earned him their abiding affection.

Your son could raise a smile in the most onerous of circumstances, Mrs Finchley, and you have my word, as a man who has endured countless such situations, that doing so is no mean feat. The intercompany football league that has proved so popular with our battalion that others have begun their own, was the brainchild of Private Finchley, and while not all of his initiatives were strictly above board, they were universally successful.

Private Finchley was mortally wounded by a sniper while on reconnaissance duty. The bullet hit him in the head, killing him instantly. Sometimes we officers gloss over the details in order to spare relatives pain, but in this instance, it is the truth. You have my word that your son died instantly and did not suffer.

I believe you have already been informed of the location of his grave, but if there is any other way I can be of service, then please do write to me.

Yours very sincerely,

Robert J. Carmichael, Capt., ASH

15th March 1917

Dearest Sylvie,

I am afraid that if I write it down it won't happen, but I am fairly certain that I can wrangle a few days' leave in a couple of weeks. I know that your teaching and your work must come first, but is there any chance you can arrange for cover? It's a lot to ask, and as usual I can't give details, but after that, it looks like I'll be otherwise engaged for some time.

We've said so much in these letters of ours, but there are some things that words can't say. I want to see you, touch you, hear you, and, yes, I want to kiss you again, too! I don't even have a photograph of you, and yet you have become— No, I don't want to speculate.

All very well for us to spill our guts in our letters— forgive the crudeness of that, too much time spent with soldiers—but is our affection for each other as real as it feels? I think so, but perhaps you don't. It's a risk I want to take, but if you don't, then tell me now. No, you probably won't be able to tell me in time.

I'll send you a telegram and you can decide whether to meet me or not. I'll understand.

With all affection,

Robbie

20th March 1917

Dearest Robbie,

I know this won't get to you before I see you—oh, please God, let me see you—but I wanted to write, just so you'd have proof if anything went wrong, of how *very much* I do want to see you, just as *desperately* as you do. I have arranged for someone to take my classes. I have arranged cover at the nightclub. I have bought a new dress and I've had my hair cut. I sound like a silly girl. I feel like a silly girl. I do know what you mean, though; I am almost afraid to think about it because the disappointment would be unbearable. I can't stop thinking about you.

Two more days. Yes, I worry that you might have changed your mind about me, but what I don't worry about is that I might have changed my mind about you. Two more days—I shall count the hours. No, that would be fatal. I shall work extra hours to avoid watching the clock.

Oh, Robbie.

With deepest affection,

Sylvie

21st March 1917

Café le Buci, 13.00.

I will wait and hope.

Hope is indeed a mixed blessing!

Robbie

Chapter Seven

22nd March 1917

Sylvie emerged from the Métro at Pont Neuf station and began to make her way over the bridge across the Seine. She paused halfway across, pulling her coat tightly around her, for although the sky was azure-blue, the breeze was chilly. Downstream, in the distance, the Eiffel Tower was hazy, looking like a watercolour painting of itself. Her stomach fluttered with a mixture of fear and anticipation. Every time she tried to imagine this rendezvous, her mouth went dry and her blood heated. It scared her how much she was looking forward to it.

She crossed to the Left Bank and began to walk up Rue Dauphine. Was this encounter really only their third? They had said nothing overtly, made no demands or promises, but it was clear from their letters that they both wanted more than a few stolen kisses. She could feel her face flushing under the narrow brim of her hat. Almost five months ago, that first time. And second time. And only time. She was a different person now. And Robbie—yes, so, too, was Robbie. It was nearly three months since they had even kissed. The desire she felt clawing at her, keeping her awake even after the busiest night at the club…

Would she be able to surrender to it in the cold light of day? And would it be the same between them, now that they knew each other?

She turned onto the Rue de Buci, her heart thudding in her chest. It was not yet twelve-thirty, but there was already a smattering of people drinking aperitifs at the cluster of little tables under the red awning. Sylvie sat down with her back against the café's long glass doors and ordered a kir. The glass clattered on the table as she set it down, but the cold, sharp wine and fruity cassis calmed her a little. She closed her eyes, trying to compose herself, for already her mind was flying in a myriad of directions, telling her that he wouldn't come, that his train would be late, his leave cancelled yet again, that he had been wounded, or worse. Would she get a telegram? But they only sent telegrams to family, and she was not family. Unless Robbie had specified— But then, why would he?

His last letter had intimated things had quieted down. He wasn't even at the front line, but men were killed in accidents behind the lines all the time. No, she was being ridiculous; he had been alive yesterday, remember? He'd sent the telegram telling her to meet him here. If he didn't turn up, it would simply mean that his leave had been cancelled, not anything more sinister. She was desperately trying to rid her mind of the image of his lifeless body lying broken and unattended in a no man's land when a tap on her shoulder made her jump to her feet with a little yelp.

'Sylvie, I didn't mean to startle you—you're as white as a sheet.'

'You're here!' She threw herself at him, wrapping her arms tight around his neck. She closed her eyes, breathing him in, pressing herself tight against him, oblivious to the stares of the other customers and the sardonic smile of the haughty waiter hovering by the doorway. 'You're really here,' she whispered, fluttering her fingers over the nape of his neck.

His arms were tight around her waist. 'Of course I am, silly,' he said, his voice husky with emotion. 'Wild horses couldn't keep me away.'

'Oui, moi aussi.'

'You've got a new coat. It suits you.'

She touched his cheek. 'Your scar has healed.'

He tucked her hair behind her ear. 'You're so lovely it takes my breath away.'

She ran her fingers along his jaw. 'I've missed you so much, Robbie.'

He kissed her forehead. *'Moi aussi*, Sylvie.'

She linked her arms around his waist and pulled him closer, running her hands over the breadth of his shoulders. 'How long do we have?'

Robbie smiled. 'Two whole days,' he said, and kissed her.

Not a polite Parisian kiss on both cheeks, but one where their lips melded and they clung to each other for many seconds before he pulled away. 'I don't have to work,' Sylvie said, already breathless, her blood already heating. 'We can spend the whole time together, if you want?' she said, though it wasn't really a question. All her doubts had vanished the moment she set eyes on him, the moment he put his arms around her.

'I know exactly what I want, Sylvie Renaud.' Robbie's smile was new to her. His mouth was the sensual, teasing curve it was designed to be.

Her breath caught in her throat and she flushed, but was relieved to note that the waiter was studiously looking elsewhere. 'Aren't you hungry?' she asked.

Robbie nibbled her ear. 'Extremely. Are you?'

She felt as if she had been caught up and tossed into the air. She felt as if she had just drunk a large glass of Calvados in a single gulp. She felt… Sylvie laughed, a husky sound she barely recognised, sensual and carefree. 'Ravenous,' she said, grabbing her bag from the seat under the little table and throwing some change down. 'Let's go.'

Robbie barely registered the journey back to Sylvie's apartment. They took the Métro. They sat beside each other, thigh to thigh, in the first-class carriage, holding hands. Did they change trains? He couldn't remember. He studied her profile, fascinated by the shell-like delicacy of her ear, the long line of her elegant neck, the shape of her nose, her jaw. Then she turned in her seat, and they gazed into each other's eyes like lovelorn adolescents. Her mouth had such a delightful curve. Her eyes were the colour of toffee today and the shadows under them were not so pronounced.

When she smiled at him like that, he could imagine himself ravishing her there and then. She would sit astride him. He'd hold her by the waist. Her hair would fall over her cheek as she leaned over to kiss him. He'd slide his tongue into her mouth as she took him inside her.

The train jolted to a halt. Sylvie took his hand. Her eyes were wide, her pupils dilated. Her hand trembled, echoing the rumble of the departing train. He was hard. Just as well he had his greatcoat on. What a preposterous thing to think!

She led him up the stairs, out into the street. He blinked. He had forgotten it was only just afternoon. He liked that she didn't try to hide her desire. He was incapable of hiding his. He couldn't believe he had been so nervous he almost hadn't come to Paris. Stupid wartime superstitions. It was bad luck to want something too much. War destroyed what was precious. Was Sylvie precious?

He looked at her profile as they finally turned into the Rue des Martyrs. Best not to dwell on that. Then she smiled at him, that amazingly sensual smile he'd always imagined, so rarely seen, and he slipped his arm around her waist, hurrying her the last few yards, and she laughed and quickened her step, and Robbie thought, *I can be happy after all*.

At the entrance to her apartment Robbie swept her up in his arms, causing a customer emerging from the pharmacy next door to applaud, and Sylvie laughed, twining her arms around his neck as he climbed the stairs. Her hands shook as she put the key in the lock. Behind her, Robbie was nuzzling her neck. The door burst open and they staggered in. She had laid a fire before she left. She had cleaned the rooms, bought coffee and bread and a small selection of food, which she stored in a box on the window ledge. The room looked so plain. She had never really felt at home here, had never made much of an attempt to make it her own. 'Flowers,' she said. 'I wish I'd thought to buy flowers.'

'You smell of flowers.' Robbie dropped his kit bag on the floor and pulled her to him. 'You smell of flowers and Sylvie. I lie in my bunk and close my eyes and I conjure up your scent. Your new coat is very stylish, but would you mind terribly taking it off?'

She did so, conscious of him watching her, and as he watched her, her confidence began to grow. His eyes, more blue than grey today, were feasting on her. His mouth was still curved into that sensual half smile. In the daylight, there were dark streaks of autumn-red in his hair. 'Shall I take off my hat, also?' she asked teasingly.

'I think that might be advisable.'

'And you must take off your coat. And your boots. And those horrible things on your legs.'

'Puttees. Supposed to keep out the damp.'

'Stop the circulation, more like.' Sylvie dropped her expensive hat onto the sofa. 'Let me help you,' she said.

'No, I can...'

'I want to.' She led him into the bedroom, and knelt before him and began to unlace his boots, then unbuckle the puttees, which were leather, held on with straps. She glanced up at him and smiled, running her fingers over his muscular calves, an unexpectedly slim ankle. She pulled off his socks. They were thick, woollen, rather badly knitted. There was a hole halfway up one, where the stitches had been dropped.

'My mother made them for me,' he said, seeing her raised brows. 'I don't think she's very good at that sort of thing.'

Sylvie folded them carefully. 'Then she must love you very much, to have made such an effort.' His feet were narrow, the arches high. She stood up and began to unbuckle his polished crossover belt. Then she unbuttoned the brass buttons on his tunic, flattening her palms over the broad sweep of his chest as she eased it from him.

Robbie kissed her, lifting her almost off her feet. 'I think you should take something off now. Let me return the favour.'

She stood motionless as he unfastened her dress, pressing little kisses onto her spine as he undid each button, his fingers warm on her skin as he slid it over her arms.

Another kiss, deeper than the last, and she removed his trousers carefully over his erection. She was breathing erratically, her skin flushing hot then cold. Another kiss. He cupped her breasts, teasing her nipples into aching hardness with his thumbs. His tongue touched hers, retreated, touched hers. She tugged his undershirt over his head. He kicked off his underwear. She caught her breath, staring unashamedly at his body in the sunlight filtering through the thin curtains. Pale Highland skin, muscles that were so close to the surface she could see them move when he breathed. He was sleekly lithe, his chest smattered with dark auburn hair arrowing down to his belly. Long legs. Strong thighs, like a runner. And…

Sylvie wrapped her hand around him, relishing the shudder that her touch caused. Silken skin. So hard. She stroked him. He shuddered again, then he kissed her again, and his kiss took her desire and ratcheted it up a notch, so that she was no longer just hot but burning.

He picked her up and set her down on the bed. He unbuttoned her chemise. It was new, cream coloured to match her knickers. He barely seemed to notice, so intent was he on tasting the skin beneath. He kissed her neck. He kissed her shoulders. He kissed the valley between her breasts, the soft undersides, and then he sucked her nipples. She was moaning, breathing erratically, her fingers plucking at his hair, at his skin, but he would not be hurried.

He eased her onto her back and pulled off her knickers. Kissing her belly. Kneeling between her legs. Easing them apart. Kissing her thighs, her knees, her ankles as he removed her stockings. Nuzzling the pulse at her ankle. Who would have thought there was so much sensation scattered about her body? Then back up again to the crease at the top of her thighs. Then between her legs, his tongue delicately parting her, delicately delving into her, making her arch up, cry out.

He pulled her towards him, easing her back down on the bed, and continued his delicious torment. She was climbing, tensing, coiling. His tongue. His fingers. His mouth. She was hot, so hot. And still he licked, stroked, sucked, teased, taking her almost there, letting her fall back again, until she let out a guttural cry and began to climb again, and he sensed there was no stopping her. Her entire body tensed, then seemed to split apart as she climaxed, yet he held her still, bringing it back when it began to ebb again, and then again, until she thought she could not bear any more, and put a restraining hand on the top of his head.

He was smiling up at her. She wrapped her arms and legs around him and kissed him greedily. His smile faded, desire making his face tense as he slipped on protection. On her back again, her arms still around his waist, finally he entered her. Slowly. Then deeper. She found that there was more she could bear after all, as he began to thrust, each stroke rousing her again in a new way, a different way, reaching deeper, until he, too, got to that unstoppable moment, when he thrust harder, faster, and it took him, too, and Sylvie with him, over, up, over, flying and soaring, to a place where there was only them, and nothing, absolutely nothing else.

They spent the afternoon in bed, making all sorts of love, taking their time, as if there was all the time in the world for their bodies to learn all there was to know about each other. In between, they dozed, talked, kissed. Kisses with no purpose but kissing, Robbie said, and then almost immediately proved himself wrong. They ate the cheese and bread in bed. 'A naked picnic,' Robbie said. 'I've never been on one of those before.'

'Have you ever swum naked—maybe in one of your Scottish locks?'

'Lochs.' Robbie shivered as he corrected her. 'Trust me Sylvie, the water's cold enough to ensure that even the sight of you naked on the shore would have no effect whatsoever.'

'What about the sight of me naked in bed?' she teased, looking at him over the rim of her glass.

Robbie took it from her, setting it down on the bedside table. 'Now, that's a different matter entirely. See for yourself.'

Sylvie laughed, made utterly brazen in the wild exhila-

ration of his presence and their lovemaking, sated and at
the same time already aroused again. She leaned over him,
trailing her breasts on his chest. 'I think I will,' she said,
and began to kiss her way down his stomach.

That evening they ate in the splendour of Le Grande
Véfour near the Palais Royal. The restaurant where Napo-
leon had taken Josephine to dine was sumptuous, a riot of
gilded wood, gold leaf, delicately painted cornicing, plush
crimson banquettes, gleaming mirrors and tiled columns
depicting various semi-naked gods and goddesses.

Sylvie, horribly aware that her only evening gown was a
very far cry from haute couture, eyed the menu nervously.
'There are no prices,' she said.

Robbie grinned. 'I have them. Trust me, you don't want
to see them.'

'We shouldn't have come here. I would have been quite
happy to eat at Le Chat Noir.'

Robbie put down his menu and leaned across the table
to take her hand. 'First of all, stop fidgeting with your
dress. I told you before we left your apartment that you
look divine, and I meant it. Second, stop worrying about
the cost. Apart from the fact that I've been stuck in the
trenches with nothing to spend my pay on for nearly two
years, I'm actually quite well off.'

'You would need to be rich to afford this place, I think,'
Sylvie said, sneaking a covert glance at the woman in the
next booth, who was positively dripping diamonds.

'Well, I am, rather, as it happens,' Robbie replied, looking slightly abashed. 'I inherited a fair bit of money from
my grandfather, and my business—well, it's actually quite
a large concern.'

She wondered why it hadn't registered before. The signs
had all been there. The cut of his uniform. The references

to his school. And the castle. How could she have forgotten the castle? 'Why didn't you say?'

'It's hardly the sort of thing one drops into the conversation. Besides, I can't believe that it matters, except that I can easily afford to treat you to a posh meal.'

'Which will probably cost as much as I earn in a year waitressing.'

Robbie pressed her hand. 'I rather took my life for granted before. I had no idea how privileged I was. It doesn't matter a hoot now, my money. All that matters is that we're here, and the food is reputed to be excellent, and as far as I am concerned, the company—by which I mean you, Sylvie—could not be better. Let's order, I'm starving.'

She was content to let him choose, impressed by his expertise when he did. 'You certainly know your way around a menu.'

'My sister would say I'm a show-off. I saw her briefly last week, I haven't had a chance to tell you about it. Flora is one of the few people I know whom the war has changed for the better.'

'How so?'

Robbie frowned. 'She was always a wee bit timid. You know, happy to do what she was told, not too much to say for herself. Now, though she plays it down, she's a bit of a force to be reckoned with. She's achieved wonders with the work she's doing behind the lines. I can understand why my mother's a bit in awe of her these days.'

'Her husband is serving here in France, isn't he?'

'Geraint. Fine chap. I've never seen anyone so happy as Flora was on her wedding day.' Robbie took a sip of his martini. 'This war has a lot to answer for. They've never lived together, never had any sort of married life. One night of a honeymoon, then nothing but days snatched here and there since. It's not right.'

For the first time that day, the spectre of war had cast

its shadow over them, Sylvie thought as she took a sip of her own aperitif. 'You think their marriage was a mistake?'

'Yes, I do.'

'Have you never been in love?' Sylvie asked.

Robbie shook his head. 'I thought I might be once, with a girl called Annabel. She was pretty, fun to be around. My parents liked her, which was a bonus. You've no idea the fuss my mother made when Flora married the son of a Welsh miner.'

'What happened—with Annabel, I mean?'

Robbie shrugged. 'The war. I stopped writing. She found someone else. Though I think it would have come to a natural conclusion, anyway. The fact is, we didn't care for each other half as much as we thought we did. We sort of fell into it, really. Everyone thought we were suited, and we liked each other, and there was nothing stopping us, and—you know the kind of thing.'

Sylvie smiled sadly. 'Yes, I do. I thought I was in love once,' she said. 'A friend of Henri's. We grew up together. We liked each other. We liked the idea of falling in love. For a while, I thought we might get married, then he met someone else, and instead of being jealous I realised I was glad.'

Robbie grinned. 'Not as glad as I am,' he said, taking her hand again, 'because otherwise you wouldn't be my best girl.'

The teasing look was back in his eye. 'Best girl,' she said, repeating the unfamiliar English phrase with a smile.

'Very best,' Robbie said, kissing her fingertips again. 'Very different, and very best. It's not like how it was with Annabel, Sylvie. You and I, I mean. You do know that, don't you?'

It was the way he was looking at her that did it, that mixture of teasing and tenderness, the hint of anxiety in his tone that told her how very much it mattered, and made her see, with a shock, just how very blind she had been. She loved him. She had actually fallen in love with him.

For a few precious moments the knowledge made her feel quite euphoric, but the implications were terrifying. She would not deal with them. Not tonight. Not yet. She wanted to bask for just a little while in the glow. She wanted to savour the joy of just being with him. She loved him so much. What harm was there in pretending, just for a few hours, that it meant she would be happy with him forever after.

'Sylvie? You do believe me, don't you?'

She smiled across the table at him, gazing into his beautiful eyes, the colour of the sea in winter. 'I do. And you believe me, too, don't you, when I tell you that nothing has ever been like this for me, too? *Nothing*, Robbie. Do you believe me?'

'I do,' he said, taking her hand. 'I really do.'

Chapter Eight

Robbie lay awake, watching the dawn light filter in through the thin curtains. Sylvie was sleeping on her side, her delightfully curved rear brushing his thighs. He had dozed, but had not dared sleep for fear of dreaming. They came to him in dreams, the men he had lost, and the friends, too, a long line of them, snaking on and on into the distance. He could never see their faces, had only a blurred sense of their presence as they solemnly filed past him, rather horribly like one of the parades they used to have at school in honour of some visiting dignitary. He didn't know if he cried out during those dreams. So common-place, disturbed nights were, that no one ever mentioned them until they got to the stage when the poor lad had to be carted off. Shell shock. Not that they were allowed to call it that these days.

Only another twelve hours or so and he'd be on the train back there. He didn't want to think about it. He hadn't thought about it once since he got here, but now he couldn't stop. It was a habit with him, with all the officers, to be matter-of-fact about the prospect of death. He never thought about surviving the war. Never thought about the things he would never have. A wife. Children. And now, in a moment of horrible clarity, which struck him not like a blinding light but like a sharp blade, he knew that it was this woman sleeping beside him he wanted to be their mother. This was the woman he wanted to marry. This woman that he loved so deeply he couldn't understand how he hadn't realised it before now.

He allowed himself a few more brief moments of dreaming. Sylvie beside him at the altar. Sylvie at Glen Massan as it was before the war. Sylvie in his bed in his flat in London. Sylvie in five years' time, in ten years' time, twenty. Smiling at him lovingly. Holding his hand. Telling him that there was no one like him, nothing like this. Nothing.

He roused himself when it became unimaginably painful. Determined to make the most of the day and escape these melancholy thoughts, he suggested they take a trip to Versailles.

It was cold, but bright and sunny. The famous fountains were still, the gardens rather sad and bare with little sign of foliage, but they spent a pleasant few hours wandering hand in hand around the grounds before lunching at a café in the town, talking of anything but the fact that he had to go back to the trenches. Time played games, cooperatively dragging its heels for a while before leaping forwards, two hours in a single bound.

It was late afternoon when they returned to Paris. As the light began to fade, it became impossible to cling to the illusion that the clock was not ticking inexorably towards that last hour.

They arrived back at the Rue des Martyrs in a subdued mood. The two days that had once seemed to stretch before them endlessly were almost at an end, and the things they had not said hung over them like a leaden cloud. 'When do you have to leave?' Sylvie asked.

Robbie looked at his watch. 'Soon.' He drew her into his arms, breathing in the scent of her. It would be a mistake, to make love to her again. It meant too much now. How had it crept up on him, this sudden all-enveloping significance? It would be best if he left now. Yet his lips sought hers hungrily, and she pressed herself against him urgently, and his body responded, blood rushing to his groin, pulses quickening in anticipation as she ran her fingers through his hair. She tasted so sweet and he wanted her so much. Once more. Just once more.

He picked her up and carried her through to the bedroom. They undressed each other reverently, made love slowly, looking into each other's eyes, tenderly touching, rocking into a climax together, holding each other so tightly he could have sworn there was no skin between them.

Afterwards, a terrible melancholy gripped him. He wanted to stay here, holding her like this forever. Was Flora right after all? He had been so sure she was wrong, so sure that it was much better not to have so much at risk, but now? Doubts assailed him. Hope gripped him. He loved this woman. Oh, how he loved this woman. Did that really mean he had to say goodbye? He needed to think. Edging out of bed, he scooped up his clothes and headed for the bathroom.

Sylvie opened her eyes as the door closed softly on Robbie. It had been almost too much this time, but the need to make love to him, to touch him, to tell him without words how she felt for him had been overpowering. Now it was over. Truly over. From that moment last night, when she'd realised she loved him, she had known it. All through the night and today, she had managed to ignore it, wanting to eke out every single precious moment. But there could be no more.

She lurched out of bed and pulled on her dressing gown, heading through to the other room to light the fire. It took three attempts to strike a match, her hands were shaking so much. She mustn't let him see her like this. She mustn't let him know just how much she cared. She was fairly certain he was going to end it, anyway. Pointless to wish there was another way. Heartbreakingly pointless. She could not survive another loss, and the plain fact was that Robbie was almost inevitably going to become another statistic. His luck couldn't hold forever. She couldn't cope with the loss and he couldn't cope with the hope. It was this, telling herself that it was for him, that brought her some element of self-control.

By the time he emerged, dressed in trousers and under-shirt, she was setting a pot of water to boil.

'Coffee?'

He shook his head.

'Wine?'

'Sylvie, we need to talk.'

'Yes.' She sat down beside him on the sofa, careful not to touch him, aching to touch him. 'I will spare you,' she said gently. 'I know what you are going to say. It is *au revoir*. Not *adieu*, but goodbye.'

For a moment, she thought he was about to deny it. He flinched, paled, struggled for words. 'Why do you say that?' he asked eventually.

Sylvie wrapped the tasselled sash of her dressing grown around her hand. 'Because it matters too much now, Robbie.'

He looked at her searchingly. 'Does it?'

She nodded.

'Is that really a reason for us to say goodbye?'

She tightened the sash, because he sounded as if he needed to be persuaded, and she knew that he didn't really, that it was simply her own desperate desire making her imagine it so. 'You told me, when we first met, you told me that you survived because you didn't have anything to lose.'

'I was wrong about that. I was wrong about a lot of things. I see things differently now. I don't know what it is that I've got back, but you've given me it.'

'L'humanité?'

He smiled briefly. 'I would settle for that.'

She touched his hand fleetingly, but even such a slight contact threatened to overset her. 'It was the same for me, Robbie. Since I met you, I feel as if I have clawed myself out of a very black tunnel. I will never be the same, but I am better. I have my brother back—a little. I am teaching. But I don't think I could cope with another loss. One that would mean so much.'

'Because I'm living on borrowed time,' Robbie said, his voice flat. His fingers strayed to the long-healed scar on his skull, a habit he thought he'd outgrown. 'We're going up to the front as soon as I return to duty. My luck can't hold out forever. You're right.' He looked at her as he had that first night in the club—haunted, hopeless. 'Fear and caution are a fatal combination.'

A chill ran through her. She would have given anything not to be having this conversation. 'What do you mean?' Sylvie asked.

'Worrying about what you've got to lose makes you cautious, and that makes it more likely that you'll be killed,' Robbie said brutally. 'It's how it works, it's one of the unwritten rules of war. When you go over the top, you can't think of anything but what you have to do. It's how you survive. But now I've got the most precious thing of all to lose. You've come so far, endured so much. I don't want to be the one responsible for sending you back into that pit of despair.'

'There really is no way, is there, for us?'

Again, she was unable to keep the glimmer of hope from her voice, but again he shook his head.

'Can we at least write?'

'Do you really want to be one of those women who live for the post? My father can't bear to open the telegrams anymore, my mother tells me.'

'But I won't know what's happening to you.'

His self-control was back in place, and hers was crumbling. Her voice sounded pitiful. Robbie pulled her close. He smelled so familiar and so unique. 'Isn't that best?' he asked softly.

She shook her head, but he ignored her, kissing her gently, achingly. She wanted it to go on forever, that kiss. She clung to him, tasting her tears, his tongue, clinging to him desperately until he gently disengaged himself. 'I have to go,' he said, disappearing into the bedroom.

Numbly, she listened to the sounds of him dressing, packing up his kitbag. A few more minutes and he would be gone forever. She could not believe it. It was not possible. Yet it was the only thing possible. He was there, in his greatcoat, wearing his cap, and she really thought he must have heard the sound of her heart breaking as she got to her feet, pressed herself up against him for one last kiss, forced herself to step back, because she would not have him remember her crying.

He tucked her hair behind her ear. *'Au revoir, ma belle,'* he said.

'Don't look back,' she said. *'Je t'aime,'* she added as the door closed behind him.

16th April 1917

'We'll have to survive with what rations we have for now. Looks like we'll be here for a few days at least. Keep a close eye on McNair, Sergeant.'

'Funked it, didn't he? Lucky I was watching his back, or he'd be a goner.'

Robbie shook his head. 'He's had a long war. Between you and me, if there's any chance at all of having him sent back up the line, I'll do it. But keep an eye, I don't want him doing himself damage. You know where to find me if you need me.'

Robbie made his way back down the straggling line of his men, currently camped out in craters and what was left of the German defences. So much for the promise that it would all be over in forty-eight hours. First the delay because the French didn't want to fight on Easter Sunday, and then the snow. And now, though they'd taken Observation Ridge and Feuchy and had even moved on to Monchy-le-Preux as planned, their supply lines were struggling to keep up. 'Which makes you wonder if they ever really believed we'd get this far so quickly,' Robbie muttered to himself. The CO was claiming a victory, but the casualties had been appalling. And though the Canadians had been successful at Vimy Ridge, word was that farther south in the French sector things weren't going so well. He wondered if Sylvie's brother was part of that battle. He missed her appallingly. They hadn't written, as they'd agreed.

'Ah, Carmichael, CO wants to see us. Orders.' Captain Hartigan smiled wearily. 'Blasted mail! I'm on tenterhooks. My wife's expecting. Our first. Can't help but worry, you know.'

'I expect you'd have heard if something was wrong.'

'Yes. Of course, quite right,' the younger man said, looking marginally relieved.

'Do you mind if I ask you something, Hartigan?

'No, old chap. Fire away.'

'How do you cope? Knowing that your wife and child are back in England, I mean, and you're stuck out here.'

'That's precisely how I cope. Knowing that they're waiting for me is enough to sustain me. It's quite simple, really. Why are you looking at me like that, Carmichael?'

After the briefing, on which he was quite unable to concentrate, Robbie walked into what was left of the village of Monchy-le-Preux. The cavalry's horses were tethered in the open. Some of the wounded were still on stretchers at the advanced dressing stations, for the ambulances were having a hard time getting through.

He sat down on a wall beside the ruins of a house, and wished that he smoked. Hartigan's simple certainty had rocked him to the core. How he missed Sylvie. He missed talking to her—for their letters had become a conversation. Without them, he'd lapsed into that netherworld, where everything was in shades of grey. It would be easier, he'd said, for her not to know. But it wasn't easier for him. Had he been selfish? Was it as bad for her, or worse? Was she coping? Did she miss him? Was Henri alive? Had she managed to persuade that traumatised little girl at the school to speak yet? Had they managed to persuade the authorities to provide the children with a meal? He wondered if Flora could help there. He should have thought of that. Flora would like Sylvie. Flora, who said that every second she spent with her husband was worth any sacrifice.

And she was right. Robbie picked up a stone and hurled it at the nearest crater. 'Face it,' he said to himself angrily, 'you were wrong on all counts.' Waiting to go into battle in the cold light of dawn on Easter Monday, his Webley service revolver in his hand, he had thought of Sylvie. He'd tried not to, but she was there with him. Now that he was safe—at least alive, relatively unscathed—he could face another fact. He was going to make damned sure he stayed alive, because the first thing he would do when this battle was fought was find her and tell her he how he felt, and the second thing he was going to do was persuade her to marry him, because his little sister was right. Every second was too precious to waste.

Paris—10th May 1917

The nightclub was quiet tonight. The temporary jubilation that had restored Paris almost to its hedonistic self when the Americans joined the war had abated as the casualty lists had started to come through from the latest offensive on the Western Front. Today, the newspapers were full of the fact that Nivelle had been replaced as commander-in-chief by Pétain, a move that rather contradicted the claims of victory.

At least Henri was out of it for the moment, Sylvie thought. A chest wound, sustained near the village of Soupir. Not serious, he had insisted in the postcard from the field hospital. She hoped he would have the sense to make his recovery slow. How strange that after almost three years of fighting, he'd ended up not much more than one hundred kilometres from home.

She picked up her tray and began to collect glasses, ignoring the half-hearted attempts to engage her in conversation. The British, too, had been fighting hard. The newspapers claimed victories for them alongside heavy casualties. Was Robbie still alive? Was he wounded? So many times she had written to him only to burn the letters, but her resolve was weakening. He'd said it would be better not to know, but not knowing was so much worse. She told herself that she would sense if something had happened to him, but she didn't really believe it. Without him in her life it was so much harder to carry on. He had been wrong about that.

And she had been wrong, too. She placed the empty wine bottles in the back room and began to wash the glasses. She'd thought she wouldn't be able to bear losing him, but by trying to keep them both safe, she had already lost him. Another day, another letter even, would have helped. Just telling him how she felt would have helped. She'd thought that an honourable sacrifice. Now she thought she'd been a fool.

'Sylvie, what is wrong with you these days?' *Monsieur le patron* glowered at her. 'I've more chance of being rewarded with a smile from my mother-in-law than you. Didn't you hear me? Get a bottle of the vintage burgundy from the cellar. Take it over to the officer sitting at the table in the far corner, but make sure you tell him how much it costs before you open it.'

'Sorry.' It was the same at the school. Only this morning, little Thomas had asked her why she was so sad. *Petit* Thomas, who had so much more to be sad about than she did.

Sylvie wiped the dust off the bottle and set it on a tray with two glasses. '*Bonsoir.* Monsieur says to tell you…' He caught the bottle as it fell from her nerveless fingers. 'Robbie!'

Tears, sudden and uncontrollable, streamed down her face. 'You're alive,' she said, gazing up at him in wonder. He looked exhausted. He'd lost weight. His hair had grown. 'You're here. Oh, God, you're really here. I have been so— I can't tell you— It has been so— I can't believe you're here.' She scanned every inch of him anxiously. 'You're not hurt?'

'A few minor scratches.'

'You're sure?'

'I'm fine, I promise. What about Henri?'

'He's wounded, but he says only lightly. What are you doing here?'

'My love, don't cry. Darling Sylvie, please don't cry.'

'I'm not. I'm— What did you call me?'

'Darling Sylvie. I'm here because I think about you

every waking moment. I'm here because I needed to tell you I'm so sorry for being so blind and so stupid. Most important, I'm here to tell you I love you so very, very much.'

She stared at him, unable to comprehend what he'd said. 'But you can't,' she said. 'You said…'

'I know what I said, but I was wrong. Utterly wrong. I felt your presence with me when I went over the top the last time. You give me something to fight for, Sylvie, a reason to keep going. I see that now.'

She shook her head dazedly. 'You love me? You really love me?'

'Desperately. Completely. I haven't been able to bear it, not knowing how you are, what you're doing. I kept thinking, is it the same for you?'

'Yes. Oh, Robbie, yes, but we said…'

'That it would be too painful to lose each other, I know. Sylvie, I…' He stopped suddenly, staring down at her intently. 'I'm sorry. I've just blindly rushed in and I haven't given you a chance to speak. Do you still think the same—that it's too big a risk?'

Did she? She tried to imagine the pain of losing him, but all she could think about was that she had a shot, a wonderful chance, at happiness, and surely that was worth any risk. She touched his face, reassuring herself that he really was here, and how only a few moments ago she'd have given anything to be able to tell him how she felt, and suddenly it was easy. And very simple. 'I love you, Robbie.'

He caught her to him, holding her so tightly that she could scarcely breathe. He kissed her urgently, threading his fingers through her hair. His breathing was ragged. Her heart was hammering. 'Do you mean it?' he asked raggedly.

'I mean it. I love you. I kept thinking of that last time,' Sylvie whispered. 'I haven't been happy in so long, but you made me feel happy to be alive. Before I met you I felt nothing. I thought I was safe, beyond pain, but I didn't realise I was beyond joy, too. I was so foolish.'

'Not just you. We've both been stupid. But there's still time to rectify that.'

This time his kiss was deeper. Only the slow catcalls of the nightclub's customers brought them back down to earth. 'I forgot,' Sylvie said, blushing. 'I'll get my coat. I'll speak to *Monsieur*, he'll understand.'

But when she made to pull away, Robbie caught her. 'Not yet. We might as well finish the floor show first.'

'What do you mean?'

He smiled down at her, the wicked, teasing smile she had thought never to see again, and she felt quite light-headed with joy. 'Come on.'

He led her, protesting, through the tightly packed tables and onto the dance floor. The customers were cheering now, some of them standing. 'Robbie! What are you doing?'

'I promised myself that if I got out of that last scrap I'd do two things. I've done the first, which is to tell you I love you. I'm just about to do the second,' he said, dropping onto one knee in front of her. 'Darling Sylvie, will you marry me?'

An expectant hush fell over the customers. Sylvie looked down at the love of her life and thought she might burst with happiness. 'Yes,' she said, 'darling Robbie, I will marry you tomorrow if you'd like.'

The nightclub erupted into wild cheers as he kissed her, but she was barely aware of it. A louder cheer greeted the pop of a champagne cork, but she was barely aware of that, either. 'Now you can get your coat,' Robbie whispered in her ear, 'because even in Paris there's a limit to public displays of affection, my darling.'

Forever With Me

Chapter One

Base Hospital Number 5, Boulogne-sur-Mer—
11th November 1918, Armistice Day

The church bells had begun to chime at eleven that morning, and ten hours later they were still ringing. In the two weeks since Lille had been liberated by the British, all but guaranteeing an Allied victory, bunting and flags had bedecked the Boulogne Casino building in which the hospital was based. Earlier today, the bunting had been torn down by wildly cheering staff and was now strung from the windows of the cafés and bars in the streets of the old town. Raucous laughter and communal singing, which was more exuberant than tuneful, erupted from the open doorways. Children, too excited to go to bed, hung precariously out of windows, waving flags and calling out greetings to the joyful revellers. Passers-by stopped to shake hands, to embrace and sometimes even to kiss.

Everyone, it seemed to Sheila Fraser, was, like herself, intoxicated not by alcohol but by the notion of peace. A world finally, blessedly, free from war, surely forevermore.

The crowd was giddy with excitement, the mood one of unfettered joy tinged with an air of abandon. It was like a hundred New Year celebrations back in Glen Massan rolled into one. What form would their celebrations take back there tonight? It was a strange thought. She found she felt more remote, more disconnected from home as time passed. She missed her mother, of course, but everyone else that mattered was elsewhere. She had managed to meet up with her best friend, Flora, a few times here in France, but Flora's brother Robbie was on active service somewhere in the north, and Alex…

She pushed that memory to the back of her mind. There'd been time enough to reflect on the past and worry about the future. Having volunteered to form part of the skeleton staff who remained on ward duty on this most auspicious day, she was anxious to join the gaiety. Tonight, like everyone else, she was going to celebrate being alive.

At the far end of the street, a crowd had formed around an accordion player. French soldiers and British Tommies, American Doughboys and Anzacs, doctors and orderlies alike danced with nurses and VADs, with local housewives and good-time girls, and with each other, too. A *poilu* grabbed Sheila's hand and pulled her into his embrace. Laughing, she allowed him to kiss her cheek extravagantly and waltz her round the square before his place was taken by an American soldier.

It was on her third circuit, in the company of a British Tommy, that she noticed the man watching her intently from the sidelines. He was tall, in the distinctive pale blue uniform of a French officer. His long brown boots encased lean, muscular legs. His tunic was well cut, emphasising the fact that the body underneath was well built. He wore no cap. His hair was dark brown, cut close to his head. He had a striking face with strong features and an extremely sensual mouth quite at odds with the overt masculinity he exuded. Sheila's stomach gave a little flutter. He wasn't exactly handsome, but there was something about him that made her look backwards over her shoulder as the

Tommy's friend whisked her off on yet another circum-navigation of the square.

She was conscious of the Frenchman watching her the whole way round. Sheila was used to men looking at her. Her blonde hair led them to make all sorts of assumptions. She'd learned the hard way not to encourage them after that one fatal misjudgement when she'd first arrived, wet behind the ears, in France, intent upon proving she could do the job of any qualified nurse. Her first taste of freedom had gone to her head. Her first experience of infatuation, she was determined, would be her last. Poor judgement on her part, and a callous disregard on the part of her lover's, had severely compromised her reputation in the hospital. Recovering from that had been a painful experience that had cost her dearly. Even now, almost three years later, she still blushed when she remembered the whispers, nudges and cold shoulders she'd had to endure, and felt ashamed when she recalled how foolish she had been to think herself favoured for her ability rather than her figure. She had learned an important lesson. No man, especially no man with the authority that particular doctor wielded over her, was worth more than her integrity. She had resolved in future to concentrate entirely and only on her vocation.

It had paid off. She had an excellent reputation in the hospital for being reliable, a cool head in a crisis, and wore her two efficiency stripes proudly on her blue dress. There was nothing a fully trained nurse could do that she could not, and several times, during the worst of the fighting, she'd taken on the role of anaesthetist during surgery. Soon all that would be over, but she was determined not to swap her VAD uniform for that of a maidservant again. This war had changed everything. She wasn't that naive wee Highland lass anymore. There was, literally, no going back.

But today was the day they had waited four years for, and tonight, for once, she was not going to worry about what people thought, and enjoy herself. Even Matron had been seen dancing in the streets earlier in the day, according to Daisy, the American nurse who'd come on duty as Sheila finished her shift. *If it's good enough for Matron,* she thought defiantly, *it's good enough for me.*

She had come full circle round the square once again. A crowd of hopeful partners competed for her attention. The intriguing Frenchman stood to one side. It seemed to her that the men in the crowd kept a respectful distance from him, though the women could not take their eyes from him. It wasn't his uniform, but the way he wore it, and the natural air of authority that clung to him. The day's growth of stubble was dark on his jaw. His eyes, in the dim light, seemed almost black. Lines, exhaustion or experience or both, fanned out from the corners of them. He was rather intimidating. And very attractive. Even as the alarm bells began to ring in her head, he had stepped out in front of her.

'Voulez-vous danser, mademoiselle?' he asked, taking her hand firmly in his, sliding his other arm around her waist and launching them into the whirling crowd.

He led her with a confidence that didn't surprise her, though the occasional stumble told her he wasn't by inclination a dancer. 'You didn't give me the opportunity to say no,' Sheila said breathlessly.

He smiled down at her and tightened his hold on her waist. It unsettled her, the way her body responded to him with a little frisson of excitement that rippled through her belly, making her pulse leap. Especially since she'd kept the lid well and truly closed on that aspect of her life.

'Would you have refused me?' he enquired teasingly.

'Would it have made any difference if I had?'

He pulled her closer, resting his chin on her neatly tied VAD cap. 'No.'

She couldn't help but laugh, even though her instincts

told her this was a potentially hazardous situation. He was a man with a decidedly dangerous air. She had forgotten what it was like, the thrill of being held, the rush of blood. It made her reckless. She ought to walk away now, her sensible head told her, but she was so tired of being sensible, and it was just a dance after all, so she rested her head on his shoulder and allowed herself to drift against him. It was an effort to pull away when they came full circle, though she did it, albeit reluctantly.

But he shook his head, and pulled her still closer. 'Not yet,' he said, and his words were exactly what her body wanted to hear, and it was Armistice, and so she made no further protest, and allowed him to lead her back around the square.

He really should get back to the hospital, Luc Durand knew. On any other night, he would have gone before now. Correction—on any other night, he would still be there, operating. But tonight was different. For four years he had been working flat out at a driven pace even his former fiercely ambitious self would have found exhausting, determined to plug the gaping void in his life. The pain of Eugenie's loss had faded in the face of the myriad other losses he had witnessed. The guilt had proved more stubborn. Work had been his cure. He wasn't sure if he *could* slow down. What if he discovered that his cure had been merely a temporary distraction?

He had come out onto the streets of Boulogne in an attempt to try to lose himself in the celebrations, thinking that doing so would make this longed-for peace feel more tangible, but the more he watched, the more unreal it felt. Surreal, in fact.

It was the blonde girl's zest for life that had caught his eye. Everything about her was exuberant, joyous, carefree. If she were a drug, he would prescribe her for depression. She was slim, the army-issue greatcoat dwarfing her frame, at the same time accentuating the lithe way she moved. The handkerchief-style cap, tied at the neck, proclaimed her to be one of the British VADs. Beneath it, her hair gleamed bright gold. Her eyes were dark, sparkling with humour. She was more than pretty; she was the sort of woman who would always turn heads.

Her smile seemed to connect directly with his groin. How did she do that? Was it the way her mouth curved upwards at the corners? The way her upper lip was short, pert, compared to the fullness of her lower? Or the pinkness of her lips compared to the paleness of her skin? She must be perfectly well aware of what that smile did, as if she smiled in that particular way only for him.

His body was showing definite signs of interest. In more than four years, he hadn't felt the slightest glimmering of desire. There was something both reassuring and exciting to discover he *could* still be aroused. Perhaps the atmosphere had infected him. Perhaps he was finally accepting that, with the war over, his guilt might also be finally laid to rest. Whatever the reason, he decided he was going to enjoy it, at least for a little while.

The music had slowed. The dancers had thinned to a few couples now as the crowd dissipated. Luc slid both arms around her narrow waist, pulling her closer. He had forgotten how good it could feel to hold an attractive woman in his arms. He slid his fingers under the knot of her cap to touch the nape of her neck. Such a delicate spot. Such soft skin. He bent his head, pressing his lips to her throat, under the line of her jaw.

She sighed. A tiny sound, innately feminine. That, too, he had forgotten, how delightfully different, such a perfect contrast, was a woman's body to his own. They were no longer dancing so much as swaying together. Her fingers were curled into his hair. His lips brushed her cheek. The urge to kiss her was overwhelming, and then she turned her face so that their mouths met and his pulse jumped, began to race. They stopped moving. Their eyes met, and he saw his desire reflected in her eyes. And then he kissed her.

It was a tentative kiss. The barest touch of his lips upon hers. The sort of kiss from which she could easily pull away, Sheila thought. She ought to pull away, because the very fact that she didn't want to, really, really didn't want to, ought to have had her running in the opposite direction. Dancing with him, just dancing with him, had left her dazed, drugged and at the same time tightly strung, her nerves jangling, her heart beating too fast. She felt as though she ought to leave, but then he cupped her face in his hands, and something in her expression must have betrayed her, and his lips found hers again.

He kissed her, and this time it felt like he'd always been kissing her, like he'd been made to kiss her. His lips formed perfectly over hers. Hers formed perfectly under his. He tasted sinful, and he made her want to behave sinfully. Shockingly so. She kissed him back, relishing the taste of him and the feel of him, her body clamouring for more as she raked her fingers through his hair, as he angled her head to kiss her more deeply until a catcall from a passing soldier made them both jump. They stared at each other, her astonishment, her passion, reflected in his enlarged pupils, in the slash of colour across his cheeks.

They were alone in the square. 'It's late,' Sheila said, aware that was somewhat obvious.

'*Oui.*'

She could feel his breath, quick and uneven. He made no move to release her. 'I should probably go,' she said.

'*Vous êtes fatiguée?*'

She had never felt less tired in her life. But to say so— she was under no illusions about what he would infer from that. Under no illusions, either, about what she wanted. Just a dance, only a kiss, and yet she had never felt so—so…

'Vous êtes fatiguée.'

This time it was not a question but a statement. There could be no mistaking the disappointment in his voice. No mistaking the way her body clamoured, either. Was it the three years of locking herself away, or was it the atmosphere, or was it him? All of it, everything, though mostly him. She tried to remind herself of the salutary lesson she'd learned, but it seemed so far away and so ir-relevant, tonight of all nights. *'Non,'* Sheila said, before she could change her mind and flee, *'je ne suis pas fa-tiguée, monsieur.'*

He laughed, a low growl of a laugh that sent shivers running down her spine. 'Luc,' he said, 'my name is Luc.'

'Et moi, je m'appelle Sheila.'

'Sheila,' he repeated, smiling down at her wickedly. *'Embrassez-moi encore.'* Kiss me again.

Chapter Two

He gave her no time to reply before pulling her into the shadow of a building on the corner of the square. This kiss made her blood roar, made her mind blank, set her skin on fire, left no room for rational thought. His tongue touched hers and she felt an answering shiver deep down in her belly. He leaned into her, pressing his body against hers, leaving her in no doubt as to the state of his arousal.

She angled her head back to deepen the kiss, and pulled him closer, sliding her hands under his tunic, digging her fingers into the taut muscles of his buttocks. They kissed until their breathing was ragged, but this time when he lifted his head and made to release her, she pulled him back, kissing him with a passion she didn't know she possessed. She was kissing him because she didn't want it to end, because she didn't want to think about what that meant.

They had to stop just to catch their breath. Distant laughter from a shuttered bar echoed down the narrow street. 'I have a room,' he said urgently, 'not far from here.'

Under any other circumstances she would have been appalled at such an assumption being made, but tonight, with this man—Luc, his name was Luc—she felt no need to pretend. His need was naked. So, too, was hers. *'Oui,'* she said, taking his hand. 'Let's go there.'

* * *

He closed the door softly behind them. The room was an annex to a larger house, with its own entrance. An armchair, a table, bookcases, a bed, Sheila noticed vaguely as Luc turned on a lamp. Then he pulled her back into his arms, and she was leaning against the locked door and he was kissing her again.

The fire was out. The room was cold, but she didn't feel it. Luc ran his hands down her arms, up from her waist to cup her breasts. She fumbled with the buttons of his tunic. He pulled it off, dropping it unceremoniously onto the floor. Her own coat followed, and her cap. He threaded his hands through her hair, tugging it free of the pins that held it in place, spreading it out over her shoulders.

His thumbs caressed her nipples through the layers of her blue uniform dress and her underwear. She whimpered, tugging at his undershirt, and finally encountered his skin. She ran her hands up his back, relishing the way his muscles clenched.

Their kisses were wilder now. He fumbled with her belt and she yanked it off. She undid the buttons of her dress for him, eager for his touch. It slid to the floor. She kicked it away. He moaned, dipping his head to the swell of her bosom, cupping her breasts, teasing her nipples into a tantalising, aching hardness.

'*Mon Dieu,* I did not think— I have not— I did not intend…' His breathing was laboured. He ran his hands through his hair. 'If we do not stop now— If you want to stop, tell me now, because…'

She felt as if she was dangling on a precipice. She knew the risks she was taking, but she didn't care. Not tonight. The world felt poised, balanced on the cusp of a new dawn, and while it was, only this existed in the gap in between. She didn't want to think about tomorrow. Tonight, she wanted only this. 'No,' she said, and the word made her feel as if she was flying. 'No,' she repeated, more for herself than him. 'I don't want us to stop.'

He picked her up in his arms. The bed was narrow but high. He laid her down on the hard mattress and helped her slide out of her petticoat. When he took off her stockings, he kissed her ankles, her knees. Stepping back, he quickly removed the rest of his clothes. She did the same, tossing her brassière and knickers carelessly onto the floor. Now that she had abandoned herself, she felt utterly without shame, deliciously liberated.

He stood naked over her for a long moment, desire etched in his expression. His erection was thick, jutting up towards his belly. His body was lean and hard, just as she had imagined. *'Que vous êtes belle,'* he whispered, then dipped his head to take her nipple in his mouth and sucked.

Heat enveloped her. She shivered, moaned and wrapped her legs around him. She was already on the edge. She leaned into the hard wall of his chest, feeling the roughness of his hair on her cheek, flattening her palms over his torso, his belly, round to his back and down to his buttocks.

He took her other nipple in his mouth. She reached for him, wrapping her hand around his erection. The skin was silky. She stroked him. He groaned and claimed her mouth again in the wildest of kisses. She stroked him again. *'Attendez,'* he said urgently, leaving her side briefly to rake through a drawer in a chest over by the fire.

'Standard issue,' he said, returning with the condom, turning away from her to pull it on before joining her on the bed. 'I had not thought I would have need of it.'

His fingers slid into her. He was lying half over her, his erection nudging into her side. His lips were on hers again. His fingers were stroking, sliding, stroking. She tensed, arching under him, her body alight, coiled, desperate for release. 'Please,' she begged, with an urgency that should have embarrassed her but didn't.

She heard that low growling laugh again. He pulled her upright to sit on the edge of the bed while he stood in front of it, tilting her to wrap her legs around his waist before nudging his way inside her.

He was being both careful and gentle, but that was not what she wanted right now. She was only just clinging on. She dug her heels into his flanks. He thrust. She gasped, her muscles tensing around him as he pulled her tighter up against him, his hands under her buttocks, and thrust higher. She leaned back on her elbows and arched her spine, and he thrust higher again.

Her body was singing for release, but she didn't want to let go. Not yet. She braced herself, and when he thrust again, she met him, arching upwards, drawing a long groan from him. He thrust again, and she found if she tilted her own body upwards he plunged even deeper.

His eyes were dark pools, focused on hers. She watched him, fascinated, enthralled by the reflection of every thrust on his face. She didn't want it to end. She clung on, the frisson of each withdrawal so intense it was almost her undoing.

'Mon Dieu,' he gasped, his voice with a gravelly edge to it now. He was close. She could feel him swelling inside her, but still she held on. Then he slid his hand from under her buttocks and touched her, circling her, thrusting at the same time, and suddenly everything was pulsing and her climax ripped through her, making her cry out, shuddering, arching, clinging, tightening around him, and he cried out, too, a carnal, animalistic sound, as he came as wildly as she.

Panting, Luc withdrew. The woman on the bed was a picture of abandon, her golden hair splayed out behind her, her breasts rising and falling. He could not believe what they'd just shared. It felt quite unreal and at the same time, on a visceral level, as real as anything ever could feel. His body thrummed. He couldn't remember feeling this alive since— No, he wasn't going to try to remember, and besides, it had never been like this. He was astonished to discover, as he looked, that his body would very much like to repeat the experience. That was what four years' abstinence did for you, he thought, dragging his eyes away and grabbing a towel to wrap around himself. Four years' abstinence and a vibrant blonde and the end of the war.

'I'm just going to…' He headed for the door, and the bathroom, because if he stayed he would end up in bed with her, and though his body heartily approved, his mind was already wrestling with the consequences. He knew nothing about her. He had no doubt that she had wanted him every bit as much as he had wanted her, but he wasn't at all sure how she'd feel now that their passion was spent. Or at least partially spent, he thought ruefully, looking down at his persistent hardness. He knew, because he couldn't help overhearing the talk in the mess, that this sort of thing went on all the time among the staff, but never having indulged, he had no idea of the post-coital etiquette.

From wild elation, his spirits plummeted. Luc swore under his breath. Etiquette! *Sacre bleu,* he had just made love to a complete stranger, and he was worrying about etiquette. What had he been thinking? How could he have allowed himself to become so carried away? He should have stayed at the hospital. He should not have danced with her. He should not have kissed her. He should certainly not have brought her back here. Though honestly, truly, he couldn't regret it. Blame it on the Armistice. Call it an aberration. Blame it on the girl. Not a girl, a woman. And he would not do that. All she had done was dance when he asked her. Kissed him back when he kissed her. Wanted him when he had wanted her.

No, he could not blame the girl. Woman. Sheila. Who was probably wondering where the hell he'd gone, maybe even thinking he'd abandoned her. Perhaps she knew more about how these things played out? No. Even in the heat of passion, her lack of experience was apparent. He was certain this was as much an aberration for her as it was for him.

Zut! Confused and irritated with himself because he was, after all, a thirty-five-year-old man and not a callow youth, Luc made his way along the draughty corridor and back to his room.

Sheila was tightening the belt of her overcoat when the door opened. He—Luc—was still clad only in a towel, and it was a very small towel. A shocking image of her hands raking down that torso, of her legs wrapped around that waist, made her blush painfully. She dragged her eyes away from his body and snatched her cap from the floor. It was ruined. If Matron saw it— But she would make blooming sure that Matron didn't see it.

'You're leaving?'

He spoke English with the most delightful accent. 'Yes,' Sheila said briskly. The truth was she was running away. The truth was she couldn't believe that she had allowed herself to get so carried away, and with a man she'd just met! It was a tiny consolation that she was unlikely ever to meet him again, that the backlash that had followed her last indiscretion would not be repeated. Not that the last time had been anything like this in any way. It made her burn up, just thinking about how wildly she had behaved. Mortified, she jammed her cap on, stuffing her hair up under it anyhow.

Luc was still standing at the door, blocking her exit. What was he thinking? Was he expecting her to stay? Had she broken some sort of unwritten rule by not being quick enough to make her escape while he deliberately lingered in the bathroom? She groaned inwardly. She had absolutely no idea, but she wasn't about to betray her ignorance. Far better that he thought her a floozy, because then, on the off chance that he had a conscience, it wouldn't bother him enough to seek her out to apologise. Though if any-one ought to apologise, it should be her. She had practically devoured the poor man. 'Well, *bonne nuit*,' she said, looking expectantly at the door.

'It is almost morning.'

If she didn't know better, she'd have thought he sounded as confused as she felt. As if! To a man as lethally attrac-tive as him, this sort of thing was probably commonplace. Though there had been that remark about the condom. Which meant nothing save that he most likely thought to flatter her. 'Almost morning!' Sheila pinned on one of her brightest smiles. 'Then I'd better hurry. I'm due on duty at eight.'

Still, he blocked the door. The longer she remained here, with him half-naked and dishevelled, reminding her of just how shockingly she had behaved, the more embarrassed she became. It wasn't just what she had done, it was that looking at him, her body became frightfully interested in doing it all again right now. That was another thing that had never happened before. Nice, pleasant, enjoyable, it had been, before her memories were coloured with the bitter aftertaste of how it had unfolded afterwards. Not a single one of those epithets could possible apply to what had just occurred between her and this man—Luc—on that narrow bed.

'So this is *au revoir*?'

It wasn't really a question. She'd be daft to think it was

a question, and she wasn't daft. Sheila nodded firmly. Finally, he stood away from the door, but as she made to pass him, he caught her, wrapping his arms around her and pressing her close against his naked torso. Her legs brushed his naked legs. Underneath that scanty towel, he was naked. Naked. Naked. Naked. And…

'Oh!' Her breath left her as he kissed her. She closed her eyes, and she could smell the scent of their intimacy on him. His tongue touched hers, and her belly clenched. Then he let her go.

'Bonne nuit,' he said roughly. 'It was an evening I will never forget. On a day the world will never forget.'

She was too confused to reply properly. She managed a brisk goodnight that made her sound uncannily like Matron and had her cringing even as she closed the door behind her. Desperate to escape what she was fast beginning to think of as the scene of her crime, Sheila ran along the corridor, down the stairs, and out into the dawn.

Back at Number 5 General, safe in her hut, which was thankfully empty, she quickly changed into the dressing gown that her mother had sent her the Christmas before. It was more like a coat really, fashioned from hand-woven dark brown tweed that Màthair had woven herself. Though rough on the skin, it was deliciously warm, and was much envied by her fellow VADs. It was a symbol of Glen Massan and home. So many things she'd experienced since coming here at the end of 1915, so changed was she by it all, that her wee Highland village seemed like another world, another life.

Now that the war was over, she thought as she made her way to the shower block, she would go home, but only for a visit. She wasn't the Sheila Fraser who had been born into service at the Big House. Whatever the future held for her, it certainly wasn't going to involve going back to working as a maid for Lord and Lady Carmichael. She'd earned the right to more than that, and she was determined to claim that right.

Chapter Three

Glen Massan, Argyll, Scotland—March 1919

'I've managed to get the trustees to fund the position, but remember, Sheila, the new chief surgeon will have the final say with regards to taking you on,' Flora Cassell said. 'He arrives tomorrow, and the Alex Carmichael Trust Hospital will be under his management. We've pulled off a bit of a coup in persuading someone so distinguished to come and work here.'

Sheila smiled wearily at her childhood friend. 'I really do appreciate it. I hate having to involve you, I was so determined to get something on my own merit, but—well, it's been a tough few months.'

'It's just so unfair!' Flora jumped to her feet and began to pace back and forward between the window and the fireplace of the small parlour. 'You worked your socks off as a VAD. The wealth of experience you picked up nursing at the front, you'd think it would be invaluable, wouldn't you, to say nothing of the sacrifices you've made for your country, yet it counts for absolutely nothing.'

Sheila grimaced. 'Less than nothing, according to some of the rejections I've had. I am not a qualified nurse, so I can't be employed to do the job I've been doing for the past four years unless I start all over again with the General Nursing Council.'

'That's a damn disgrace.'

'Flora Carmichael! If I have to ask you one more time to mind your language…'

Both women looked up as Lady Carmichael entered the room. 'It is Flora Cassell now, Mother! If I have to remind you one more time that I'm twenty-eight and a married woman…'

Her ladyship closed the door behind her and took a seat by the fire. 'Your language is atrocious. I blame that husband of yours. He will have you waving the red flag and tying yourself to railings, if you are not careful.'

'His name is Geraint, Mother, as well you know. And though it is true he has opened my eyes to politics, my views are entirely my own,' Flora said with a tight smile.

'Why you require any views at all on such matters is quite beyond me.'

'You're over thirty, Lady Carmichael—you'll be eligible to vote in the next General Election,' Sheila said mischievously. 'Don't you think you ought to acquire some opinions yourself before it's called?'

Her ladyship shuddered. 'I shall vote as the laird instructs me. Good day to you, Sheila. I presume my daughter has informed you that she has been pulling strings on your behalf?'

'She has, and I've just been telling her how grateful I am.'

'Mother, do you know, the only positions Sheila has been offered since she was demobbed are as a lady's companion and a lady's maid?'

'Where is the shame in that?' Lady Carmichael demanded. 'Reliable staff are in short supply these days, and as I said to Mrs Fraser myself just the other day, Sheila, the laird and I would be delighted to rehire you. Especially after all you did for poor Alex.' At the mention of her youngest son, her ladyship's expression crumpled. 'I can't tell you how much of a comfort it was to the laird and I that Alex was not among strangers at the end. We will be eternally grateful to you for that.'

Lady Carmichael dabbed a tear from the corner of her eye. The death of her youngest, favourite son just a month before the end of the war had taken a severe toll on her austere good looks, though she bore the loss more stoically than her husband. Sheila had been horribly upset when she had first encountered the laird on her return, stooped and frail, his expression so distant, a shadow of the man she had last seen striding out over his beloved moors.

It had been such a shock when Alex had been admitted. Of all the thousands of young men who had been wounded, it was incredible that her best friend's baby brother should end up under her care. She was glad of the small miracle, though, glad that the last face he had seen had been a familiar one.

So many parents, wives, sisters and sweethearts she had comforted over the past few years, but it was easier to speak in false platitudes to strangers. She doubted she could have done the same to the laird and his wife, whom she had known all her life. But Alex had been so dosed up with morphine, he hadn't even realised he'd been wounded. He'd recognised Sheila, though. He'd held her hand, and reminded her with that endearingly quirky smile of his, of the time he'd snatched a kiss from her under the mistletoe when he was twelve years old. 'I'll be twenty-one in a month,' he'd whispered. 'Coming of age. The war will be over then. The laird will throw a big party, and I'll beg a kiss from the prettiest girl in Glen Massan. That's you, incidentally. Looking forward to that. But think—may need to practise.'

She had kissed his cheek. He had died a few moments

later. Poor Alex. Poor Lord Carmichael. And yes, poor Lady Carmichael, too. But the war was over, and Sheila was determined that Alex's death, like all the others, would have some purpose. She would not be forced back into the box from which she had escaped.

'Since you seem set on taking up this post, I must wish you luck, Sheila,' Lady Carmichael said, getting to her feet. 'However, if things do not work out, please be assured that there will always be a position for you here at Glen Massan Lodge.'

'You're staying here, even though Glen Massan House will no longer be yours?' Sheila asked in surprise.

Her ladyship grimaced. 'I would prefer to leave. It is one of my daughter's better suggestions, to move to a place where the past is not on the doorstep to haunt us, but the laird—he's never known anywhere else.' She turned away, dabbing at her eyes with the black-edged handkerchief that had become her constant companion. 'What pains me, my husband finds a comfort, and so we will stay at Glen Massan. At least we have left a fitting memorial to Alex in the form of the hospital. You will excuse me now, I must go and find the laird. If I do not stand over him at meal times, he quite forgets to eat.'

The door closed behind her. 'She might be old-fashioned, but she's a trouper,' Sheila said admiringly to Flora.

'She is. I worry how she'll cope when I leave here, but...'

'She'll be fine, Flora. I'll be here to keep an eye on her, don't forget—providing this new surgeon likes the cut of my jib. Besides, you must be desperate to join Geraint now that he's been given a date for his release from the convalescent home. Isn't he getting impatient?'

'Very.' Flora smiled, a secret little smile that made Sheila rather envious. 'I still can't believe he's made such a full recovery. He'll have a limp for the rest of his life, but there was a time when we thought he wouldn't walk again. Though he's so determined, I shouldn't have doubted him'

Sheila pressed her friend's hand. 'All I've had to worry about is finding a job. Between Geraint being wounded and losing Alex, you've had it rough.'

Flora shook her head. 'It's my father I'm worried about. It wasn't just Alex's death, it started with the requisition. His whole world is utterly changed. When the army informed us that they would be closing down the hospital and handing the house back, I hoped it would be the boost he needed, but then he just—I don't know, sort of abdicated. He told Robbie it was up to him to do what he wanted with the estate, but Robbie is rebuilding his wine business now the war is over, and he spends as much time in France as London. You haven't met his wife, Sylvie. She's lovely and I've never seen Robbie so happy.'

'How did your mother take to his marrying a foreigner?' Sheila asked laughingly.

'French is preferable to Welsh, apparently, and a school teacher is an improvement on a miner's son,' Flora said wryly. 'It was Robbie's idea to establish the trust in Alex's name, and the laird's idea to have it dedicated to treating ex-servicemen. When it looked as if Geraint would still be in convalescence for some months, I agreed to come up here and manage the handover from the army to the trust, but now I *have* to be with Geraint. So you see, it's been a blessing, really, that you came along looking for something to do, because I can leave with a clear conscience. Do you know, in four years of marriage, we've never actually lived together.'

'You must miss him madly.'

'Oh, much more than madly,' Flora said with another of her secret smiles. 'You wouldn't believe the things I say in my letters. Sometimes I think the paper might burst into flames.'

Sheila laughed, though she was rather taken aback. 'My goodness, I never thought I'd hear you say such a thing.'

Flora blushed. 'I love my husband in every way,' she said with a touch of defiance. 'I don't see why I should pretend we don't—you know—or that I don't enjoy it.' She narrowed her eyes. 'You've been away from Glen Massan for more than four years, Sheila Fraser, but the one thing that hasn't changed about you is that you're still the bonniest lass in the Glen. Don't tell me there weren't men tripping over themselves to ask you out, over in France. Was there anyone special?'

An image of herself naked under the lean, thrusting body of her Armistice-night lover popped into Sheila's head, making the blood rush to her cheeks.

'I knew it, there was someone,' Flora exclaimed triumphantly. 'Spill the beans. Was he one of the doctors?'

Another face, Dr Mark Seaton's, replaced the previous image. *You've got hold of the wrong end of the stick, poor girl, and now everyone else has, too. Frankly, my dear, you're becoming an encumbrance.* Sheila shuddered, not so much at the memory of Mark's contempt as her own naivety. 'There was no one special,' she said.

'I don't believe you. What happened, Sheila?' Flora looked at her with concern. 'Oh, no, did he die? I'm so sorry.'

'No, no. Nothing like that.' Sheila turned her face away from her friend's anxious gaze. 'You know what it was like out there, no time for anything but work, and nothing more important, either.' Which was true, had always been true for her, even when she had thought herself in love, even if the man she thought herself in love with had believed otherwise. She managed a weak smile. 'There's nothing to tell.'

Flora looked unconvinced, but to Sheila's relief, decided not to press her. 'You'll meet someone special, I'm sure of it.'

'I'm not interested in finding a husband. I don't *need* a husband. I want to stand on my own two feet, and I want to be judged on my own merit, and I intend to start by securing this post at the hospital,' Sheila said with conviction. 'Though I have to tell you,' she added wryly, 'it's not easy, living in the village again, sleeping at home in my old bed, buying groceries at the shop, as if the past five years haven't happened.'

Flora rolled her eyes. 'Don't I know it. You heard my mother, talking to me as if I was still a wee lassie. Is yours the same?'

'I love her, I really do, but she simply doesn't understand why I don't want to slip back into my old life. She can see I've changed, but she doesn't know the half of what it was like out there, and I don't want to disillusion her. I feel like I'm pretending, all the time I'm here. Don't you feel sometimes, there are those of us who were there, and those who weren't? And between us there's this thing called the war that we're all desperately trying to put behind us, but it's there all the same.'

Flora frowned. 'It will always be there, and it's just as much a part of those who were left behind. We've all changed, Sheila. Look at my father. Look at that memorial in the village to the fallen. Geraint says the trick now is to look forwards, not backwards. We have to rebuild something better from the ashes of the past.'

Sheila grinned. 'It sounds like Geraint is going to have competition when he finally gets up on his political soapbox.'

Flora looked sheepish. 'His enthusiasm is infectious.

But he's right,' she said. 'We need to embrace change. A brave new world and all that.'

Just how much she had changed would surprise even Flora. For a moment, Sheila considered unburdening herself to her friend. It was not embarrassment that stopped her. She hadn't been in love, but she'd thought she was, and Flora would not condemn her for behaving improperly. As to Sheila's lack of judgement, however—would Flora be able to overlook that? This job was far too important for her to take the chance. 'Since we're swapping slogans—actions speak louder than words. I'll make a success of this job, and then maybe everyone will see I'm not just the chambermaid from the Big House who's become too big for her boots.' Or think that she clung to the coat-tails of her lover to advance her career. 'Thank you for setting this up for me, Flora. I won't let you down, and if I make a success of it, who knows where it might lead.'

'Let's not get ahead of ourselves. First, you have to make a success of your interview. In my experience, these high-flying surgeons can be an arrogant lot, especially when dealing with a woman.'

'Trust me, I know the type.'

'That sounds like the voice of bitter experience.'

'It is, believe me,' Sheila said, noting too late the questioning look on Flora's face. 'That impertinent manner of yours, Miss Fraser,' she continued quickly, in an excellent imitation of Lady Carmichael, 'will likely get you into trouble. I suggest you remember your place in the order of things and stick firmly to it.'

Flora's peal of laughter told her she had successfully averted any potential reference to Dr Mark Seaton. Good! It could stay that way.

Chapter Four

It had been a long drive, through countryside that had become less and less familiar with every passing mile. Which was a good thing, wasn't it? This was, after all, a new chapter in his life. An exciting new challenge. An opportunity to deploy all the skills and techniques he had worked so hard to acquire. A chance to finally leave his past behind.

The last leg of the journey was along a ribbon-like road that seemed to be carved into the hillside. The sheer drop was breathtaking. Far below in the valley, a track snaked alongside the path of a river. At the bottom of a steep descent, he passed through a village before turning through two large gate posts into a wide, curved driveway. Glen Massan House, the sign read in florid script, and beside it, a familiar-looking military sign read Argyll War Hospital. Soon, as soon as he could manage it, the house would reopen in another incarnation under his management. Though he mocked himself for it, he couldn't help but feel a burgeoning sense of pride.

Passing a small lodge of grey granite, Luc drove along a wide, winding driveway, catching glimpses of a sparkling blue stretch of water before pulling up in front of the large house. Stepping out of the car onto neatly swept gravel, he noticed with amusement that it was bordered by the army's trademark white-painted boulders.

The house itself was built of pale grey granite and stood on a promontory facing out over the loch. A mass of turrets and sloping roofs, with a larger turret bolstering one side, it was a real Highland castle. He hadn't been expecting that. The car engine ticked as it cooled, but there was no other sound to disturb the scene. Though he knew the army had vacated the place only a few weeks before, it felt eerily empty, the windows shuttered, the huge door closed. Funnily enough, it had felt like a huge door opening when he received the letter offering him the position. He had been so excited by the prospect, he hadn't really considered the implications. The terms of the trust responsible for setting the hospital up were somewhat vague, for though it wasn't run by the military, it would be in effect a privately funded military hospital, with ex-servicemen for patients. At this moment in time, however, there was no hospital at all, only an empty shell that he would have to equip and staff.

He was a surgeon, he knew nothing about such administrative matters, but help was on hand in the form of a family member from the trust, a Mrs Flora Cassell. A few discreet enquiries had reassured him. She had a formidable reputation for administration, which would leave him free to concentrate on what he'd come here to do. Save lives. Make lives better. He turned towards the house, where the huge front door was opening. That would be her now presumably. He stepped forward, a professional smile on his face, and removed his hat.

There were two of them, both considerably younger than he had expected. The taller one had a cloud of copper hair. Beside her, the other woman, also tall and slim, had bright gold hair cropped in the new fashion to her shoulders. Dark brown eyes, fixed on him. A pink mouth that turned up at the corners, the plump bottom lip contrasting with the shortness of the upper.

She wore no army overcoat, no neatly tied VAD cap and her hair was shorter, but it was her, all right. She had inhabited his dreams too many times for comfort since that night for there to be the slightest vestige of doubt, and now here she was standing in front of him, looking as stunned as he felt. What the hell was she doing here?

When he stepped forward, the redhead did so, too. 'Forgive me, I hadn't expected you to be so...' She stopped, disconcerted. 'What I mean is, I had expected someone much older. Welcome to Glen Massan, Doctor. I am Flora Cassell.'

He shook her hand distractedly. *'Enchanté.'*

Flora Cassell stared at him. The other woman—Sheila!—was determinedly looking anywhere else but at him, obviously as flabbergasted as he was. He looked pointedly at her.

'Oh, yes,' Mrs Cassell said with a faint start, 'may I present Miss Sheila Fraser who, I hope, will be your right-hand man, so to speak, in the coming weeks.'

A heart-rending plea from those speaking brown eyes begged him not to admit to their previous acquaintance, something he was more than happy to do. 'Miss Fraser,' Luc said, with a slight nod of the head.

'Doctor...?'

'Durand.' She had come slowly forwards to stand on the gravel beside him. She held out her hand. He took it. A frisson of shared memory shot through them and she snatched her hand away as if it had been electrocuted. In the bright spring sunlight, she looked more mature than he remembered and far lovelier, though the sparkle had gone from her eyes. Now he knew why the accent of the landlady in the little inn he'd stayed in last night had been vaguely familiar.

'Doctor Durand?'

As if she could not quite believe it. *'Vraiment,'* he said, and was rewarded with a ghost of a smile.

'I am afraid I have some packing to do and must beg to be excused,' Flora Cassell said. She gave Sheila a look that, if Luc didn't know better, might have been construed as a wink. 'I'll leave you in the capable hands of Miss Fraser, Dr Durand. She was raised in the village here. There is no one who knows the house and the estate better, outside my immediate family. I am certain she will prove satisfactory to your needs.'

Of course Flora did not intend the double entendre, Sheila thought as she turned from her friend's fast-disappearing figure to face the man who held her professional fate in his hands. The man who had, for one torrid night, been her lover, who was no doubt, thanks to Flora's unwitting remark, remembering exactly that. If only the ground would open up or the sky fall or a thunderbolt would strike. Why did these things only ever happen in books? And why, why, why, did he have to be so much more devastatingly attractive than she remembered? It wasn't fair. Flora had certainly been impressed by him. That little look she had given her, as if to say, 'Well, look at this handsome stranger who's fallen into your lap.' Luckily, she had no idea that, while he was undoubtedly handsome, he was no stranger!

Doctor Luc Durand. Doctor! She hadn't even noticed the medical insignia on his uniform. Not that she had been paying much attention to his uniform that night, being much more concerned with the man underneath. The man who would now be her boss. She could feel her face flaming. She had to get control of herself. She was not going to allow history to repeat itself, absolutely not! 'You didn't tell me you were a doctor,' she said, turning to him accusingly.

'I hardly though it mattered at the time. I don't recall that you even told me your surname.'

He sounded equally defensive. The realisation was both reassuring and disconcerting. 'Those rooms of yours—why weren't you living in the hospital grounds like the rest of us?'

'I was on secondment only, to several of the hospitals run by the Americans. It was easier to rent a room than fight for space with the permanent staff. And I like my privacy.'

She was horribly flustered. She couldn't look at him without imagining him naked, without remembering the way he had felt, his mouth on hers, his skin, the low growl of his laugh, the harsh cry he'd let out when he'd climaxed. She closed her eyes, trying to blot it all out, but it only made it more vivid.

'I suppose it made it easier for you to entertain women,' Sheila said. For heaven's sake, now she sounded petty, jealous, even, but it was too late to retract her words.

'I am not in the habit of *entertaining* in that manner,' he replied.

She eyed him with disbelief. He wasn't classically handsome in the way that Douglas Fairbanks was, but he was unforgettable, and even out of uniform he had an air about him that commanded attention. 'Next you'll be telling me I was an exception,' Sheila said sarcastically.

'It's the truth.'

Was he teasing her? He didn't look as if he was. He looked—no, it would be better if she didn't look at him like that. She narrowed her eyes. 'How much of an exception?'

'The only one.'

His answer would have made her reel if she wasn't reeling already. 'Why me?' she blurted out.

'I have absolutely no idea.' When she said nothing,

because she could think of absolutely nothing to say, he shrugged, a very Gallic gesture, and smiled wryly. 'I saw you dancing. You had such *joie de vivre*. I thought you were like—I don't know, the spirit of the night. I wanted to capture it, what you possessed. You think that sounds fanciful?'

'I think it sounds rather delightful.' She ought not to have told him so, but these past few months had rather knocked the stuffing out of her *joie de vivre*. 'It was like no other night, that night,' she said softly.

'Certainly, I am not usually given to dancing.'

'That much was obvious,' Sheila said, smiling faintly at the memory.

He was standing close enough now for her body to protest that it wasn't close enough. His hair had grown since she'd last seen him, curling over the starched white collar of his shirt. His eyes were dark brown in the light of day. He said he'd made an exception for her. That she was the only one. *In how long,* she wanted to ask him. She wanted to tell him that for her, too, he had been an exception, but how could she explain what she meant without explaining too much, without sounding as if he meant too much? 'It all seems like a dream now,' she said. Which was not at all what she meant to say, but his nearness was confusing her.

'Do you regret it?'

Did he? She studied him, his striking but not quite handsome face, the strong, lean figure that looked just as good in his civilian suit as in uniform. Embarrassed and appalled by this outrageous twist of fate as she was, she could not deny her body's response to him. 'Regret it, no. But I definitely think we should forget it,' Sheila said resolutely, 'especially if we are to work together.' She tried to sound as if it were something to be taken for granted, their working together, but it came out as a question all the same.

'That is still to be decided,' he said firmly, 'especially in the circumstances.'

She should have guessed. He was going to send her packing. This job, no matter how temporary, mattered to her. She could not let him dismiss her without even giving her a chance to prove herself something other than easy. She *would* not let that happen. 'Doctor Durand,' Sheila said urgently, grabbing hold of his sleeve, 'let's both agree to forget that night. You say nothing, and I say nothing. Not to anyone. Let's pretend we've just met, that we're complete strangers. Let me give you the guided tour. Let me tell you a little more about myself and my nursing experience. I can help you, Dr Durand. Let me help you. Please. I need this job.'

There was an edge of desperation to her voice. He couldn't reconcile this anxious, almost insecure woman with the one he'd met on Armistice night. One minute she was smiling, the next she sounded as if she was going to burst into tears. What on earth was going on?

Luc disengaged himself, because even the touch of her fingers on his jacket was making him think of the other ways she'd touched him, and threw his hat into the back seat of his car. There was no doubt that he needed assistance. Surely the formidable Mrs Cassell—who didn't look at all formidable—would not have suggested Sheila Fraser to him if she was going to be a waste of space. This hospital was to be named after Mrs Cassell's dead brother. It was her former family home. The lands that would provide funds for the place were her family's estate. And Sheila—would he now have to call her Miss Fraser?

Luc grimaced. What mattered was that she knew the family, the locals, the house. He would be a fool to dismiss her out of hand. But would he be a fool to think they could work together after what had passed between them?

He surveyed her covertly, with the barrier of his car between them. In the light of day, he was embarrassed by the passionate way he had responded to her, by his complete loss of control. Forget what had happened between them, she had said, pretend they'd never met. Was it possible?

Since Eugenie, he had dedicated himself to his work. His work had been his wife, his mistress, his life. Not once since his marriage ended so tragically had he wanted another woman until he'd met this one, so very different from Eugenie in every way. Was that why he had been attracted to her? Had it been some sort of final exorcism? Or perhaps a symbolic new start. The end of the war. The final burying of his past.

He laughed inwardly at himself. What nonsense. Eugenie was dead, and the gap she had left had been filled—with his work. He had no room in his life for anyone else. He was perfectly content as he was. Alone. With his work and his patients. He was most certainly not interested in pursuing a dalliance with Sheila Fraser, no matter how attractive he found her. It would pass. The only thing that interested him about Sheila Fraser was her ability to help him with his work. And absolutely nothing else.

Luc reached into the car for his leather-bound notebook and slammed the door behind him. 'Very well, let us agree that we have never met.'

She caught his sleeve. 'You promise you won't say anything, because this is a small village, Dr Durand?'

'I don't gossip, Miss Fraser, and I've no more desire to have anyone know our rather unconventional history than you have.'

'Thank you.'

'Do not thank me yet, Miss Fraser. *Alors*, let us take this tour, and you will persuade me why I will find you an indispensable—what was it Mrs Cassell said?'

'Right-hand man.'

Luc eyed the extremely feminine form in front of him and smiled. 'That remark, *mademoiselle*, could only have been made by another woman.'

Chapter Five

Sheila led Luc—no, it had to be Dr Durand from now on—into the house. 'This is the Great Hall,' she said, her voice echoing in the huge empty space. 'Most of the original furnishings are still in storage, in the stables and the attics,' she explained. 'Lord and Lady Carmichael have no room for it since they've moved into the Lodge.'

'What about the rest of the family?' Luc asked.

'Flora and her husband, Geraint, are setting up home in London. Geraint is hoping for a career in politics. That's also where the eldest son, Robbie, lives, with his wife, Sylvie. She's French, apparently, like you. He was discharged from the army in January this year and has gone back to his wine-importing business. The youngest—Alex—well, as you know, he was killed in battle in October.'

'I am sorry,' he said.

'I was with him at the end,' Sheila surprised herself by saying.

'Really? That must have been extremely traumatic for you.'

Sheila shook her head. 'I'm glad it was me and not a stranger. His name has been added to the family crypt. It's a lovely place at the far edge of the loch—you should visit it, if you get the chance. His body is interred in France though. I think Lady Carmichael would like to visit the grave, but I doubt the laird is fit for it. Màthair said…'

Luc raised a questioning brow.

Sheila laughed. 'Màthair,' she repeated slowly. 'My mother. It's Gaelic. I don't speak it myself, but she's fluent.'

'And she lives in the village—I think it is called Glen Massan, yes, the same name as the house?'

'She does, and it is.'

'It must be good to be home, after being in France for— how long?'

'Almost three years, after a year in a hospital in Glasgow training before that. I joined the VADs at the outbreak of the war.' Sheila gazed up at the wall over the huge fireplace. 'I gained a huge amount of experience. I want to put that to good use. I don't want you to think you have to take me on just because of—because we…'

She broke off, mortified, cursing herself for having resurrected the subject when they had only just agreed it hadn't happened. She could see it in his eyes, too, the memory of it. The air between them was suddenly charged. Their eyes locked. She had no idea how it happened. She had no memory of moving, or of him moving, either, but one of them must have. Or both. His fingers feathered along her jaw. She tilted her head. He dipped his. For just a fleeting moment, their lips met. The memory of that first kiss, just as tentative, just as irresistible, kept her transfixed. She sighed, the merest breath, then she jerked back. Or he did. Or they both did.

'As I said, I don't want any favours, Dr Durand,' Sheila said briskly, turning away, throwing open the first door she came to. 'The drawing room,' she announced.

Neat rows of iron bedsteads flanked the walls of the huge room. The bare wooden boards were scrubbed clean. Through the white paint covering the walls, traces of the original wallpaper pattern could still be glimpsed. The plasterwork of the ceiling formed a geometric pattern that looked to be quite intact. Luc wandered farther in. The fireplace, which was probably marble but had also been painted institutional white, was flanked by a pair of statues, one carrying a torch. The other, which looked as if it should have matched, was both headless and minus her torch.

'My heavens, it looks like the Western Front out there.' Sheila was standing in the bay window, gazing out in horror at the gardens, though to call them gardens would be a gross exaggeration. The churned-up lawn scarred with practice trenches and criss-crossed with duck boards looked all too familiar, along with what looked like the remnants of a walled garden full of piles of rusting machinery. 'You should have seen it before. And this room— it was so beautiful.'

'Tell me, I'd like to know.'

Luc listened as she described the room in a level of detail that surprised him. She took him by the arm and showed him where each of the gilded sofas, the inlaid tables, the fire screens and armchairs with footstools had been placed. The animation he remembered from their first meeting had returned to her face. Her eyes sparkled as she recounted stories of the parties that had been held here, of the games she had played with the Carmichael children in her youth.

Leading him through a concealed door in the panelling, she took him into another room, where the inbuilt bookshelves, now empty, proclaimed its former use. 'I can't remember how many times Lady Carmichael chided me for hiding in here, my nose stuck in a book,' Sheila said.

As she stooped down to retrieve a piece of paper that was wedged in the skirting, the movement tightened the folds of her gown against her pert bottom. He suddenly

remembered her legs wrapped tightly around his waist,
her heels digging into his buttocks.

'I don't understand why it was such a crime to be caught
reading,' Luc said, hoping his voice didn't sound as stran-
gled as it felt. 'Were the books so very valuable?'

'Oh, it wasn't my reading them that was the problem.
The laird was always encouraging me to borrow books,
but Lady Carmichael wasn't keen on my reading them
when I was supposed to be working. I was her maid, didn't
Flora tell you?'

'You were a servant?' It seemed so at odds with her
confidence and her obvious intelligence, but at least it explained her intimate knowledge of the house and all its furnishings. He tried to imagine her in a maid's black gown
and apron, cleaning the huge grate, dusting the shelves,
running up and down the steep staircases they had passed,
and discovered that he didn't like the idea of her in such a
menial position one little bit. 'I thought you were a friend
of the family.'

'Flora and I have always been friends. We went to the
village school together, until she was old enough to be
packed off to finishing school and I was old enough to
make a living from scrubbing out pans. My grandmother
worked here, and my mother before me. It's a family tradition.' Her smile had faded. There was still a sparkle in
her eyes, but it seemed to Luc it was more belligerent now.
'What else was I to do?' she demanded. 'My mother's a
widow, and I'm her only child. She taught me how to sew
and how to clean because that's all she knows. I worked
my way up here from scullery maid, and I never once relied on my influence with Flora. In fact, if you must know,
Lady Carmichael did her best to prevent us being friends.
It's to Flora's credit that she didn't succeed.'

'Sheila, I didn't mean to imply…'

But she ignored him. 'I've no formal qualifications,

Dr Durand. Even if I'd wanted to leave, where would I go, other than to another position in another house where I didn't know anyone? When I applied to be a VAD, they took one look at my hands and accepted me because they needed people willing to swab the floors of the hospitals and wash the sheets. Have you any idea how hard it was for me to persuade them I could do more! And even then...'

'Sheila...'

'Even then,' she continued remorselessly, 'I had to work harder than everyone else. This face, this hair—oh, I'm not such a hypocrite as to say that I wish I looked different, but you've no idea what a handicap it is. Especially after...' She looked down at the bit of paper she'd retrieved, biting her lip, then glared at him. 'It's different for men. I don't suppose your dashing good looks have ever held you back.'

'You think I am handsome?' He was so taken aback by her tirade that he said the first thing that came into his head.

'Not handsome exactly, but you know perfectly well how attractive you are. I wasn't the only woman who couldn't take her eyes off you on Armistice night. I bet the theatre nurses drew lots to be on your rota.'

'I choose my own theatre nurses on the basis of experience and skill.'

'And yet, I am living proof that you have a weakness for a pretty face—you see, I've heard it all before. You'll be telling me next that you're so dedicated to your profession that women are a distraction you can't afford.'

'I am. They are.' He was struggling to keep his temper, unsure how the conversation had taken this turn, confused by her aggression. 'I told you the truth when I said you were an exception, and I told you the truth when I said I don't notice how my nurses look, but only what they do. I am not some sort of surgical lothario. I don't abuse my position.'

She went quite pale. 'What have you heard?'

'About what?'

'About me. What did they say?'

She looked quite terrified for some inexplicable reason. 'Until I received Mrs Cassell's letter, I didn't even know your full name,' Luc said patiently. 'How could I possibly link Miss Fraser with the VAD I knew only as Sheila until today? I'm not sure what your previous experience is, Sheila—Miss Fraser—but I assure you, when I am working, I am not a man but a surgeon. I think like a surgeon and I act only as a surgeon. If you and I are to work together, then I will expect you to do your job and nothing else.'

He meant it, every word. It had been one of the few things about his work that Eugenie used to tease him about. 'You talk about the nurses as if they are some other sort of species, not women,' she'd said to him once, and he remembered how surprised he'd been, to realise it was true. Perhaps it was the fact that Sheila Fraser wasn't in uniform that was making it difficult for him to stop thinking like a man. Perhaps if she wore some sort of apron and cap. But she'd been wearing a uniform the night he met her and he'd only had eyes for the woman beneath. 'I don't think this is going to work,' Luc muttered.

'Because I'm not a trained nurse? Because I was a skivvy before the war and you think I was nothing more than a skivvy during it, you'll not be wanting my help.'

He hadn't even realised he'd spoken aloud. The flush faded from her cheeks, and the light from her eyes. Her shoulders slumped. She looked quite dejected, and he was struggling to keep pace with the changes in her mood. He caught her as she turned away, gently turning her towards him, holding her by the shoulders, forcing her to meet his gaze. 'I don't know what this *skivvy* means…'

'Cleaner. Servant.'

There was a shimmer of tears in her eyes, but she widened them, determined not to let then fall. Whatever was going on in that mind of hers, he couldn't help but admire her spirit. 'Let me tell you something that might surprise you. My father was a humble baker. I was raised in the apartment above the shop in Paris. It was my job to scrub down the table where he worked before I went to school and to sweep the floor. I know how to lay a fire, and how to clean out the oven. I, too, have been a—a skivvy.'

'Can you bake bread?'

He was relieved to see the spark of interest in her eyes. 'But of course,' Luc replied. 'One of my earliest memories is standing on a box kneading dough at my father's side in the bakery. I could never rival my father, though, he was a true artisan.'

'Was?'

'He died six years ago, two years after my mother. At least they were spared the war.'

'I'm sorry, Luc. Doctor Durand.'

'Moi aussi.'

'Did your father expect you to become a baker?'

Luc shook his head. 'I have always wanted to be a doctor. From an early age, I was fascinated by how the human body worked.'

'You must have had to study very hard. I don't know how it is in France, but here, doctors tend to come from wealthy families.'

'It is the same in France.' Luc grimaced. 'I had nothing in common with them. I went to different schools, I lived in a different area of Paris and I had to work to supplement my bursaries—sometimes two or three different jobs at a time.'

'You must have been very determined.'

'Very,' he said grimly, thinking of those early days. 'I know all about having to prove yourself, Sheila—Miss Fraser. I know all about earning respect. I don't care that you were a servant before the war. All I'm interested in is what you are now.'

'You mean you'll give me a chance?'

She looked almost incredulous. He had never suffered from lack of conviction. Lack of funds, lack of background, lack of the right family, but never lack of conviction. It touched him, her determination not to give in to the pressure to conform. *'Oui,'* he said. 'I mean I will give you a chance. I'm a surgeon. I don't know the first thing about running a ward or ordering supplies or keeping patients clean and fed. I know what I want this hospital to do, I know what kind of patients we can help, but I don't have the first idea about how to get them here, and how to release the funds from this trust, either.'

'I'm not a lawyer.'

'No, but you can talk to the lawyer on the board. You're in a unique position here, as far as I'm concerned, because you understand both sides—the medical and the administrative. That will allow me to focus on what I do best.'

'But, Luc, Dr Durand, really, I think you're expecting too much from me. I'm not qualified...'

'You're not listening to me. You have the perfect qualifications.'

He raised his brow enquiringly and waited.

'It's a huge responsibility.'

'Says the woman who without doubt had the care of wards containing fifty, sixty, a hundred men at a time?'

'There was always a nurse on call.'

'Did you rely on her?'

'No, I preferred to stand on my own feet, so long as it didn't put the patient at risk.'

'Voilà. So you will take the position?'

'Not if you're offering it out of pity, or because...'

He shook his head wryly. 'No, it has nothing to do with that. I want you to work for me because I think you deserve a chance, and because I think you are the best person for the role, *d'accord*?'

Her smile was slow to arrive, but eventually it came. *'D'accord,'* she said. 'Thank you.'

His hands were still on her shoulders. He was supremely conscious of her not as an administrator but as a woman, as *the* woman his body craved. He couldn't take his eyes of her lips. He remembered how soft they were, how they had clung to his as she kissed him, and he wanted desperately to kiss her again. She had made no attempt to move. Was she feeling it, too, this attraction, this pull that was almost overwhelming?

He moved towards her. She tilted her face to him compliantly. Because she wanted to, or because she felt obliged? Slightly sickened, Luc altered course, brushing his lips once to each of her cheeks, and once again, Parisian-style.

'D'accord,' he said stiffly as she stepped back. She wasn't looking disappointed—that was him, projecting his own emotions onto her. He turned away. 'Now I think it would be best if we continued our tour. I would like, if you please, to see the rooms that were used as operating theatres first.'

Chapter Six

One month later

'I think that covers everything, Dr Durand.' Sheila closed her notebook and sat back. 'I'll sort out the details of which of the clan artefacts are to go into the new Carmichael Room with the laird, and I'll pull together a report for the next meeting of the trustees covering the details we've discussed.'

'Thank you, Miss Fraser.' Across the table from her, Luc smiled politely before turning his attention to the woman seated primly by Sheila's side. 'Over to you, Matron Mac-Donald.'

The older woman glanced sideways and pursed her lips. 'I see no reason for Miss Fraser's presence while we discuss specific medical matters, Dr Durand.'

Luc sighed heavily. 'I have several times explained Miss Fraser's role to you, Matron, and several times also mentioned that she served with distinction in France for three years.'

'Perhaps, but only as a VAD. She is not a trained nurse.'

'But she is responsible for ensuring that your trained nurses have everything they need to function properly, including comfortable accommodation and a place to relax when they are off duty. I believe she has being trying to discuss that with you for some days now.'

'It's fine,' Sheila said, aware of the other woman's jealous eye upon her. 'Whenever Matron MacDonald can spare the time…'

'She will find the time today, won't you, Matron?' Luc snapped. 'It's not as if we have any patients yet.'

Matron MacDonald coloured deeply. 'My apologies, Dr Durand. I will meet with Miss Fraser as soon as this meeting is over.'

'Excellent!' Luc said, flashing Matron a disarming smile that made her colour for quite a different reason.

With a coquettish flutter of her eyelashes, Matron MacDonald embarked upon a detailed list of medical queries and issues. Listening with one ear, pencil poised lest she be required to take action, Sheila allowed her attention to drift to Luc. There was no sign of the temper that had made him snap at Matron a few moments ago. He was giving her his undivided attention, taking notes without looking at his book, keeping his eyes focused on her. He often disagreed with things she said, but he never talked over her, and he always explained his reasons when he did. He encouraged her to voice her own views, and on occasion acted upon them.

'Which,' Matron MacDonald had told Sheila in an unguarded moment a few days before, 'is almost unheard of, especially for such a very distinguished surgeon. So refreshing. We're so privileged to work with him. Confidentially, if it were not for his presence here, we would have had a great deal of difficulty finding staff willing to work in a hospital in such a remote location.'

Today, however, Matron was as starched as her apron as she got to her feet at the end of the meeting, her brusque nod in Sheila's direction in stark contrast with the effusive smile she aimed at Luc.

'I'd better get on, too,' Sheila said as the door closed behind Matron, 'unless there's anything else.'

'Just one more thing,' Luc said. 'I'd like you to attend the meeting of the trustees with me.'

'Me?'

He got to his feet, rubbing his hand over his eyes and came round to the other side of the table, perching on top of it. 'Yes, you. The author of the report you are going to write. They will have questions, and you are in a far better position to answer them than I am.'

'But the men on the board, they know me from before, Dr Durand.'

'Please, when we are alone, can we dispense with the formalities?'

'I can't call you Luc.'

'You just did, Sheila.'

He smiled at her. Not his usual polite, strictly business smile, but the one she remembered from Armistice night. The one she'd tried very hard *not* to remember from Armistice night. The one that made her stomach knot and her heart flutter in a most unbusinesslike way. 'They won't take me seriously. The board, I mean. They'll look down their noses at me. "That's wee Sheila, who used to be the chambermaid at the Big House," they'll say. "What the devil does she think she knows about anything beyond laying fires and setting tables?"'

'Are you telling me that after all your wartime experiences you are afraid of a few men in suits?'

She opened her mouth to deny it, then stopped. She tried to picture herself sitting round a table much larger than this one, a lone female face surrounded by local dignitaries. 'Most of them have known me since I was a wee lassie. The laird. His solicitor and his accountant. Colonel Patterson from the other Big House.'

'But you are not a—what do you call it—*wee* lassie

now. You told me the day I arrived here that you wanted a chance to prove everyone wrong. I am giving you that opportunity. Why won't you grasp it?'

'I— Because I—because I— It's not that I'm afraid of them, Luc. It's just that I don't...'

'You won't let me down, if that's what you're worried about.'

'How did you know I was going to say that?'

He shrugged, smiling at her. 'Because these past few weeks, I think I have come to understand you a little.'

She smiled back. 'Quite a lot, I'd say.'

'When you are here with me, you are so confident, so sure of yourself. You are doing an exceptional job. Even Matron would admit that.'

'If you tied her down and forced her.'

'She may be old-fashioned, but she is a fair woman. Others may be less so and attempt to judge you based on assumptions. Don't let that affect you, Sheila. And don't be ashamed of where you come from, either.'

He was so confident, so very sure of himself and his abilities, it was difficult to believe he came from such humble origins. He clearly spoke from experience, she had no doubt about that. What pain lay behind his words? And what courage! It made her own insecurities seem petty.

Sheila tossed her head back. 'You're right. I will go to the meeting, and I'll answer whatever questions they throw at me, and if one of them so much as mentions my past I'll remind them that the war has changed everything. Which it has,' she added soberly.

'Complètement,' Luc agreed.

She thought a shadow passed over his face, but it was gone before she could be certain. 'Thank you,' she said, 'for having such faith in me. And before you say it, yes, I agree, I should have more faith in myself.'

'So now you can add mind reader to your list of attributes.' Luc wandered over to join her at the window. 'What am I thinking now?'

Over the past month, they had both taken enormous care not to get too close physically. They had never referred again to Armistice night, but there were times when she knew he'd been thinking of it. A look in his eye. The way he jerked his hand away if she brushed it accidentally. On such occasions awareness was strung like a wire between them. It lasted the merest of seconds but left her heart pounding, her throat dry. It was there now, though neither of them was looking at the other. He was just inches away from her, and the urge to lean into him was almost overpowering.

'I'd prefer not to know what you are thinking right now. Much safer for both of us, I suspect. It's a beautiful view, is it not?' Sheila added hurriedly.

'Very beautiful,' Luc whispered.

But he wasn't looking at the view. 'It is,' Sheila said, horrified to find herself blushing. 'Over yonder, right at the edge of the loch, that's the family tomb I was telling you about. There's a path through the rhododendrons. It's a pity they're not in bloom. I could show you, if you'd like.'

'I'd like that very much.'

His shoulder brushed hers as he angled towards her. Trance-like, she reached up to touch his hair, running her fingers through the soft silky waves at his collar. He touched her cheek. His thumb caressed her jaw. She lifted her face. He drew her forward. His lips hovered over hers. For an aching moment, she thought he would pull away, and then, suddenly, his lips were on hers.

It was the sweetest of kisses, all the more so for being so much longed for. She wrapped her arms around his neck. His fingers tangled in her hair. His mouth clung to hers. She closed her eyes on the world and kissed him back. It was like sunlight dancing on the skin after a long cold winter, that kiss, warming her from the inside. It was languorous and heady, like honey and wine. She was floating, bathed in the smell of him, the heat of him.

When finally it ended, they clung together, poised in the embrasure of the window, staring wide-eyed at each other, speechless. They had broken all their own rules, but it was impossible to deny this bubble of attraction that enfolded them, this thirst they had slaked. No, not slaked; this longing was far from slaked.

Sheila was the first to move, casting an anxious glance first at the closed door, and then out of the window, to the empty gardens. 'Luc…'

'Don't say it,' he said.

She had no idea what she was going to say. That it shouldn't have happened. That it couldn't happen again. That was what she should be saying, but she couldn't bring herself to. She stared at him helplessly. She had worked so hard to make him into Dr Durand, her superior, and now the illusion was stripped away. Though she knew getting it back was a matter of self-preservation, she did not want to. Not yet.

He smoothed his hand over her hair and kissed her brow. 'We have been working so hard, I forget sometimes that the war is really over. It is a beautiful day, and we are in a very beautiful place and you are a very beautiful woman. I am tired of being Dr Durand,' he said, echoing her thoughts, 'and though I have the greatest admiration for Miss Fraser, I find I would very much like to spend some time with Sheila before the hospital claims my soul. Do you think we could, just for today?'

She couldn't imagine wanting anything more, right at this moment, though she knew, simply from wanting it so much, that it would be a mistake. But would it? He was offering a moment out of time, away from reality. An escape. An illusion. Something that they could pretend had never happened, just like before. She knew, even as she thought it, that she was lying to herself, but she didn't care. Not when she could still taste him on her lips. Not when he looked at her like that, his eyes slumberous with the passion that smouldered between them, his smile the most tantalising curve.

Sheila nodded before she could change her mind. 'Yes, I think we could,' she said, and surrendered to sweet temptation.

She decided to make up a picnic and found an army-issue haversack hanging on a peg in the old garden room that had become a repository for abandoned pieces of kit. Looking out of the dusty window, she remembered having a conversation with Flora in this very room, not long after the start of the war, when her own thoughts were already far away from Glen Massan, concentrated on her first hospital placement. Outside in the grounds, the army had erected neat lines of tents. Inside, Flora had been confiding her attraction to the man who would later become her husband. Sheila, who had thought herself so much more worldly wise, had cautioned Flora against surrendering to that attraction.

Flora had ignored her advice and followed her heart. So, too, had Sheila, in the heady first months of freedom in France, though the consequences had been very different from Flora's happy ending. Four years on, and Glen Massan's grounds were once more being tended by the men who had left to fight. Not all had returned, but every one who had, and who had wished to reclaim his job, had been encouraged to do so. And here Sheila had returned, too. The former maid, now in charge of the rebirth of Glen Massan House, restoring the grounds to a new and functional purpose, minus Lady Carmichael's beloved croquet lawn. If Flora was here now, with the roles reversed, what advice would she give Sheila?

She turned away from the window, smiling at her own whimsy. Being in love coloured everything Flora said. Flora wanted the world to fall in love as she had, but Sheila had tried love on for size and hadn't liked the fit of it at all. She wasn't about to make the same mistake again.

'And since that is one thing I am absolutely certain of,' she said firmly to herself as she made her way to the kitchens, 'then today can do no harm whatsoever.'

Chapter Seven

Sheila led the way through a narrow gap in the tall rhododendron bushes, whose lilac, magenta and fuchsia flowers were just beginning to unfold from the large, fist-like buds. The path behind the bushes was rutted and narrow, wandering through a wood, through which the occasional glimpse could be had of the sparkling waters of the loch, and the hills beyond.

She walked with the easy stride of one used to being outdoors, the heavy boots she wore emphasising her slender ankles, the skirt of her dress swinging out to give him tantalising glimpses of her calves. It was warm, she had told him, for spring in the Highlands, laughing as he shivered in the breeze, which seemed to blow permanently off the loch. She wore no coat but instead a long woollen garment in navy blue, which apparently her mother had knitted. Her hair floated behind her in silken strands. Her skin was healthy from being in the fresh air, the colour of cream. Freckles speckled her nose. The vibrancy that had first attracted him to her was like a field of electricity, an almost tangible spark of energy surrounding her.

The path widened and Luc caught up with her, taking her hand, enjoying the warmth of her fingers as they twined with his. They talked of politics, because there was so much to discuss. The Paris Peace Conference. The new workweek that would be introduced in Britain and in France. Momentous changes that the war had brought about, but today they'd had enough of the world, and the subject paled.

'That book you were reading the other day, when you were having lunch, are you enjoying it?' Luc asked.

Sheila made a face. 'Virginia Woolf. Not particularly. It's beautifully written and frightfully clever, and before the war I'd have lapped it up, but these days I find I want something less weighty.'

'Such as?'

'You'll laugh at me,' she said, 'but I think I'm a wee bit in love with an ape man called Tarzan.'

He did laugh. And because her eyes were dancing with fun, and because her mouth was curved into the most teasing of smiles, and that smile connected straight with his groin, he caught her to him. 'Tell me about him.'

'Well, he lives in the jungle, naturally, so he spends most of the story half naked, but that's fine because he's very athletic, and very good-looking. He's a bit of a hero, too, forever doing good deeds.'

'Every woman's dream, in fact,' Luc said ironically.

Sheila chuckled. 'He's not so very different from you. I think the work you do is much more than heroic. I've been reading some of the case studies you wrote up for the medical journals. You work miracles, Luc. You don't just save lives, you make life so much better for those dreadfully disfigured men and their families. You make them feel human again.'

He was accustomed to being thanked, accustomed to his skill being lauded, but his standards were so high, his aim always for perfection, that more often than not he felt undeserving of both. 'I think it is never enough, what I do,' Luc said. 'I think there must always be more.'

'From what I've read, you're already achieving the impossible. Your patients must think you a real hero. I know I do.'

She meant it, and it touched him to the core. He had been lonely before coming here to Glen Massan, he realised with a shock, and with a further shock realised that Sheila was the reason he wasn't lonely now. It panicked him, this knowledge, so he thrust it to one side, and said the first thing that came into his head. 'So if I went to live in a jungle, you'd desert this Tarzan for me?' She blushed delightfully. 'And if you did, *mignonne*,' he said, 'would you be half naked, too?'

An image of her, not half but fully naked, flashed into his head, and he was immediately aroused. He wanted to kiss her again. Was this what he'd intended when he'd suggested this outing? He'd been so befuddled with that kiss, he hadn't been thinking straight. And Sheila, what had she wanted?

'Tarzan doesn't have a mate,' she said, interrupting his thoughts. 'He's too busy saving lives. You see, you do have a lot in common.'

The truth is, you don't have time for a wife, you're too busy saving lives. Eugenie's accusatory words rang in his ears. Abruptly, he let Sheila go, making a show of gazing up at the sky, hefting up the haversack, which had fallen unnoticed to the ground. 'I hope it's not going to rain. We haven't had our picnic yet.'

'Luc, what's wrong?'

He forced a smile. 'Nothing.'

They walked to the end of the woods in silence. Beside her, Luc was frowning, lost in thought. Sheila racked her brain but couldn't understand what she'd said to make him retreat into himself. They emerged at the edge of the loch, and the promontory upon which the church stood came into view. As ever, the haunting beauty of the ruin made her stop in her tracks.

'*Mon Dieu*, it must be very old,' Luc said.

'Fourteenth century,' Sheila replied, 'though apparently there was a monastery on the site for hundreds of years before that.'

They followed the perimeter wall round to the gate and entered the ancient churchyard. Luc bent over the headstones, most of which had sunk into the soft ground, tracing the inscriptions with his fingertips. The wrought iron enclosure that housed the Carmichael family crypt stood at the far end, facing out over the loch. The large Celtic cross that bore the names of those interred was made of the same grey granite as Glen Massan House. The gold lettering of the newest inscription stood out brighter than the rest.

Alexander Gordon Maxwell Carmichael
Lieutenant of the Argyll and Southern Highlanders
Laid down his life for his country 10th October 1918
aged 20 years
Virtutis Gloria Merces
Beloved son, the battle is over, but you will live forever in our hearts

'Glory is the reward of valour,' Luc translated. 'Do you believe that?'

Sheila frowned, shaking her head. 'I've witnessed the results of valour and they're far from glorious, but...' She broke off, staring at the words on the tomb. 'I believe we have a duty, those of us who are left, to make sure that they didn't die in vain. You'll think that sounds awfully pompous but...'

'*Non*, I think it is true. I came here to Scotland hoping to escape France and all the memories. I wanted to forget the war, but it's not possible, is it? It has shaped us.'

A cloud scudded over the sun, casting a shadow on the tombstone. There were fresh flowers in an urn. Lady Carmichael's doing, Sheila knew, for the laird had been unable to bear coming here after the ceremony. She wondered where they had come from, those flowers at this time of year. She opened the gate and laid her own spray of dried rosemary on the plinth, kneeling down to say a private prayer.

When she had finished, the sun was shining again. Luc was standing to one side of the railings, gazing out over the loch. She slipped her hand into his.

'*D'accord?*' he asked.

She nodded, her smile tinged with sadness. 'If you could go back to being the person you were before the war, would you?'

'*Non,*' Luc said without hesitation. 'When I said it had shaped us, I didn't mean I wished it undone. When I said there was no escaping the war, I meant it would be wrong to pretend—or to try to pretend—it didn't happen. It did, and here we are, and you are right, we have a duty to make all that sacrifice worthwhile.' He grinned. 'Now you will think I sound pompous.'

She brushed her lips against his hand. 'I think you put it perfectly.'

They left the chapel enclosure, and Sheila led the way towards the path that wound up the hill. Luc followed her up the steep climb, arriving at the top, slightly out of breath as she was, exclaiming with surprise as they skirted the protective hedge of yellow-flowering gorse to the hollow of grass on the other side.

'*C'est magnifique,*' he said, gazing out at the vista, the loch, the hills, Glen Massan House and the village beyond.

Sheila spread out the old blanket she had packed, but left the food in the rucksack. The sun was warm, and the gorse protected them from the breeze. Luc took off his jacket, collar and tie and lay back, resting his head on his clasped hands. His shirt was unbuttoned at the neck, leaving his throat exposed. His shirtsleeves were rolled up, the corded sinew on his forearms standing out under the soft smattering of hair. His eyes were closed. She stretched out beside him, his skin pale compared to hers.

'Do you regret coming here?' she asked. 'To Glen Massan?'

He rolled over onto his side to face her. 'How could I, when it allowed me to meet you again?'

Sheila could feel the blush stealing over her cheeks and dipped her head. 'Luc, I don't know what you thought, but I've never done anything like that before. I had no idea what you expected of me—afterwards, I mean.'

He smoothed his hand over her hair, gently tilting her chin up to meet his gaze. 'So that is why you ran away? I had a feeling that you had shocked yourself as much as I had, but I didn't know how to ask. Am I permitted to say that it pleases my ego, your saying that?'

'I didn't think your ego would be in need of pleasing. You are the dashing Dr Durand.'

His laughter was softly ironic. 'Not so dashing, I assure you. While you were getting dressed in such a hurry, I was hiding in the *salle de bain* agonising over what the etiquette was in such situations.'

She couldn't help laughing, touched to see that he looked faintly embarrassed.

'I know, it is ridiculous, *non*?'

His fingers were tangled in her hair, lightly stroking the sensitive skin at the nape of her neck. 'It was not just worrying about etiquette that kept me there,' he said.

'No?' She could see the pulse beating at his throat, the first hint of stubble on his jaw. The honey scent of the gorse reminded her of their kiss earlier.

'I was worried that if you were still naked when I came back, that I would not be able to hide the fact that I wanted to make love to you again.'

She remembered him standing there dressed only in a towel. She remembered how shocked she had been at her body's response to him, how determined she had been not to betray herself. How different would things have been had she stayed? How much more complicated? But she had not, and what was the point in speculating about what might have been when he was here now, and metaphorically speaking she was once again standing in the doorway, and she could choose to walk away or to stay?

His fingers had stilled. She had been silent too long to pretend there was not a question to be answered and she knew it would not be asked again. Tomorrow they would return to being Dr Durand and Miss Fraser. Today…

'Would it shock you,' she said, reaching over to smooth his hair to feather her fingers over his nape, mirroring what he had done to her, 'if I told you that I was thinking the same thing?'

Luc tensed. For a fraction of a second he hesitated, but though there were a hundred reasons for him to get up and walk away, he could think of only one thing. He wanted her, and she wanted him.

He rolled her onto her back, taking her unawares. She lay beneath him, her hair spread out behind her, her eyes wide with surprise. 'Would it shock you if I told you that I have spent a great deal of time wondering what we would have done if you had stayed?' he asked.

'And if I told you that once again, we'd been thinking the same thing?'

'I would tell you that I would be astonished if it was the exact same thing,' Luc whispered.

'Why don't you tell me, and we can compare notes.'

He laughed. 'Why don't I show you instead,' he said, and kissed her.

The kiss started where the other had left off. Heat flared between them. She twined her arms around his neck and arched under him. He fumbled with the belt that held her knitted jacket in place and pushed the garment aside. Her hands fluttered up and down his back. He rolled onto his side, pulling his shirt over his head.

He kissed her again, shuddering as she stroked his skin. Buttons. He cursed. 'Why does this thing need so many buttons?'

'I wouldn't have thought they'd be a problem to a surgeon as skilled as you,' she said, undoing them.

'I'm not a surgeon, *aujourd'hui*, I am a man.'

She laughed, a throaty sound that made his muscles clench. 'Patently.'

He sighed with satisfaction as her blouse parted, revealing the soft contours of her breasts under the white cotton of her underwear. 'And you, *ma belle*, are just as patently a woman,' he said, taking one of her dark pink nipples into his mouth and sucking.

She bucked under him. He continued to suck though the flimsy material. Her brassière also buttoned up the front, but this time his fingers cooperated. He buried his face between the valley of her breasts, teasing her nipples with his thumbs.

'Is this what you imagined?' he whispered, cupping her fullness.

'Yes,' she answered, flattening her palm over his chest. 'And this.'

'And this?' he asked, kissing her again, shuddering with pleasure as her tongue touched his.

'And this,' she said, her hands on his buttocks, arching against him, so that his erection throbbed between her legs.

He groaned, sliding down her body, pushing her skirts

and petticoats up and tugging her knickers down. 'And this?' he said, lifting her to him. 'Did you imagine this?'

He licked into her, and she made the most delightful of sounds, intensely feminine. 'No,' she said. 'I have never— oh! Dear heavens, yes.'

She was wet, soft, pink. He licked again, and she shuddered, and again, tasting her, teasing her, rousing her and tensing as his own arousal pulsed. She clutched at his shoulders and moaned his name as his tongue stroked her. She dug her heels into the ground, arching up under him as she climaxed.

He had never been so aroused as she tugged at his shoulders, rolling him onto his back, lying over him in a tangle of clothes and hot skin, kissing him frantically. Tiny kisses, on his eyes, his cheeks, his jaw, back to his mouth. Her hands fluttered over his chest, his belly, to the fastenings of his trousers. He kicked himself free of them and his underclothes. She knelt between his legs as he had done between hers. Her nipples were hard, pert, pink as she leaned over him, taking his shaft in her hands.

'Did you imagine this?' she asked, circling her fingers round him, stroking him slowly.

He couldn't speak. He couldn't do anything but concentrate on not peaking too soon. Not yet. She stroked him again, watching him. Her eyes were dark, her cheeks flushed. 'Did you imagine this?' she asked, taking the weight of him in her palm.

He groaned, feeling himself contract. She bent farther over him, her nipples brushing his belly. 'And this?' she said, kissing his chest. 'And this?'

Her mouth claimed his as she mounted him, taking him deep inside her with one thrust that made them both gasp. It was only then he realised he had no *préservatif.*

He ached for her, but he forced himself to tell her so, through gritted teeth. 'We have to stop,' he said.

She shook her head and lifted herself up, sliding down slowly this time, her hands gripping his shoulders. Luc cursed. 'Sheila.'

'Tell me when,' she said, and thrust again, and he thought fleetingly what a compliment of trust she had paid him, and then he all but lost control.

He kissed her deeply. She was so tight around him, he thought he might just pass out from the pleasure of it. She leaned farther over him, her breasts crushed against his chest, taking her weight on her hands, and thrust again. He squeezed his eyes shut. He didn't want to come. He didn't want it to end. Then she thrust again and he felt her pulse, heard her guttural cry, and he knew he couldn't hold on any longer. Calling out her name, he lifted her away just as his climax took him, twisting him from the inside and turning him inside out.

Chapter Eight

Sheila lay back, gazing up at the sky, waiting for her heart rate to return to some semblance of normality. Beside her, Luc, too, lay on his back, his chest heaving. He was naked. What clothes she had on were in complete disarray. She felt weightless and weighted, as if she were two people, one humming with pleasure, the other already wondering how on earth she could have behaved so wildly.

She sat up and began to straighten her underwear, to pull her blouse over her chest. 'I can't imagine what you must think of me,' she said.

He sat up and caught her hands, forcing her to still. 'I think a great deal of you.' When she made no reply, he frowned. 'Sheila? What is wrong?'

'This. We shouldn't have. You'll think...'

'What?'

'That I'm— That you don't want...' Now was the time to tell him about Mark Seaton, but she could not. 'I don't want you to think less of me,' she said instead, turning her face away.

'Do you regret that we made love?' Luc asked her.

'Do you?' she asked, unable to keep the defensiveness from her voice.

'No, but perhaps I should. Perhaps this was a mistake.'

'You think so?'

He sighed. 'If you think so. I don't know.' He got to his feet and began to put on his clothes.

Sheila finished dressing while he had his back to her. What an idiot she had been! If only she hadn't kissed him. If only she had told him she was far too busy to take time off. For more than a month she'd managed to resist him. She'd worked hard and she'd earned his respect, and now it was destroyed, and for what! A few fleeting moments of pleasure.

Her body protested that it was more than that, but she ignored it. So she'd made another mistake, but this time she wasn't going to go down without a fight. 'Luc, this doesn't have to change things,' she said urgently. 'It was a mistake, but surely it needn't prevent us working together?'

'Of course I want us to work together. Is it not obvious how much I appreciate you, and how much I have come to rely upon you?'

He broke off and stared out at the view over the loch, taking deep breaths. When he turned back to her, his expression was sombre. 'Our relationship is important but does not take precedence. The success of the hospital is what really matters. My work means more than anything to me.'

'I understand. I feel the same way, Luc.'

'You mean that?'

'Yes, I do.' He looked dubious. Now was the time to tell him about her experience with Mark, because then he would be convinced. She steeled herself. 'Luc, I…'

'Sheila, I need to explain something first.'

Luc paced over to the edge of the gorse. 'What you said earlier, about your ape man being too busy saving lives to have a mate, it was true. About me, I mean. I was married. Before the war. Her name was Eugenie.'

Shelia felt as if she had been kicked in the stomach. Her

knees gave way, and she dropped onto the blanket. 'Married,' she repeated dumbly. Luc was married! She thought she might be sick. Surely he would not have—with her—not if he was married. *Was* married. Did that mean he was no longer married? Or that his wife… 'Oh, God, Luc, she died, didn't she? In the war. I'm so sorry.'

He held out his hands to ward her off. 'I don't want your sympathy, Sheila. I want you to understand.' He sat down, keeping a careful distance away, clasping his hands around his knees. She could see he was having to work himself up to speak, so she forced herself to wait, though the questions roiled in her head.

'I have always been ambitious,' he said, finally breaking the silence. 'I have always wanted to be the best at anything I tried. My father was the same.' He looked up to smile wryly. 'I am prejudiced, of course, but he really did make the best bread in Paris, I think. When I announced that I wanted to be a doctor, I was just seven or eight. He didn't laugh at me, he simply told me that if I wanted it enough and worked hard enough I would succeed.'

His expression was distant. Sheila's skin was clammy. She had no idea where this story was heading.

'When you want something so badly,' he continued, 'when you have to work so hard for it, it means more to you, but that's no excuse. Eugenie, my wife, and I, we agreed it would take four or five years for me to establish my career, and then we would settle down, have a family. And I meant it, Sheila. At the time,' he said earnestly, 'I really did mean it.'

'But it took longer?'

'No. It actually took less time, but then it wasn't enough. There were always new techniques to learn, new methods to try. It was a bone of contention between us, the number of hours I was spending at the hospital. We began to argue.

I began to resent her because she made me feel guilty for being at work when I should want to be at home with her.'

'Did you love her, Luc?' It was a painful question to ask.

'Yes, I did. I did love her.'

And now she had her answer, and it was even more painful. She had no right to feel jealous, and no reason, either, and so she chose to twist the knife. 'What was she like?' Sheila asked.

'Young. Pretty. Fun. Clever enough to be bored waiting at home for me, and then bored enough not to wait at home for me. When the war broke out, she took a job in a munitions factory. Clerical work at first, but when demand for shells increased, she moved to the factory floor working shifts. It meant we were hardly ever home together. I think—no, I know—she meant to prove a point to me, and she was right. I had grown arrogant. I would never have said it, or even admitted it if she'd challenged me, but I did think my work was more important than hers.'

There was a time when Sheila would have defended his view, but not now. The servants' hierarchy at Glen Massan she had taken for granted was something that appalled her now. Young, naive and anxious to please, she'd accepted the doctor, nurse, VAD hierarchy that mimicked it in France until experience taught her differently, just as experience since the war had taught her, to her dismay, that few people thought as she did. 'It was the way of things before,' she said, because it was true, even if she didn't believe it was right.

'An explanation, but not an excuse. I put myself first. That was selfish and unfair of me. I paid a heavy price for my arrogance.'

'What happened?'

Luc closed his eyes, and began to speak very fast. 'We had arranged to go out for dinner. Things had been strained between us—we had hardly seen each other for weeks.

Eugenie swapped shifts at the factory, and I agreed to be home early, but then an emergency came up at the hospital and I stayed on. When I got home, I found a note saying that she'd decided to go to work. "At least there, I know I am wanted," it said.'

His fingers were kneading the blanket as he spoke, curling and uncurling around a fold in the fabric. Sheila discovered she was holding her breath.

'I went there—to the factory. I was angry because I knew I was in the wrong. When I got there…' He choked, took a deep breath. 'I walked into the aftermath of an explosion. Commonplace in those early days, such accidents. It wasn't a large explosion, but it was enough. Eugenie and three other women were— They died.'

Luc threw back his shoulders and gazed straight at her. His face was grim rather than sad. 'She wouldn't have been there if I had come home as I promised. I blamed myself for a long time after that, but I don't anymore. It was an accident. A tragic accident, but it wasn't my fault. The dead are dead. So many of them, since Eugenie, that it is impossible to imagine. But it is as you said, Sheila, there has to have been a point. I cannot bring Eugenie back, but I can dedicate myself to using my talents to save others. It's the least I can do. It is all I can do. So you see, there can be no room in my life for anything else. Or anyone else. Not in that way.'

He was warning her off. 'So we need to put our feelings to one side and work together professionally for the good of the hospital,' Sheila said. She sounded hurt. She couldn't understand why she sounded hurt when he was offering her exactly what she wanted.

'Exactly. We did before,' Luc said.

He didn't sound convinced, but that was most likely her imagination. She was deeply moved by what he had told her, and touched that he had confided in her what was obviously so painful, but she had no idea how she felt about what he'd said, save that she was extremely glad he had pre-empted her own sordid confession. What mattered most was exactly what he said. Their work. The hospital. She, too, could be wedded to her vocation. 'Yes, we did,' she said, telling herself it wasn't a lie because they had, up to a point.

She leaned over to press his hand. 'Thank you, Luc, for trusting me with this. I do understand.'

His fingers curled tightly around hers. 'I have never spoken to anyone about that day. When Eugenie died, I told myself that part of me had died with her. Until I met you, I have not wanted any woman, and since I met you, I have not been able to stop wanting you. But I will. I have to. It is the only way.'

She nodded. She had what she wanted: his respect, his trust and his support. Far more valuable, she reminded herself, than something so ephemeral as attraction. Or love.

'What was it you wanted to tell me?' Luc asked.

She felt uncomfortable with her own lack of disclosure, especially after Luc had bared his soul like that, but her emotions were in a turmoil, and when she tried to assemble her thoughts to confess all, her brain simply refused to cooperate. Aware that Luc was still waiting on a response, Sheila forced herself to smile and busied herself with the haversack. 'Nothing important. We haven't eaten our picnic,' she said, beginning to unpack it. 'I don't know about you, but I'm starving.'

She barely saw him for the next ten days as the rest of the hospital staff settling in, and Luc's attention turned to the imminent arrival of the first patients. Sheila did as they had agreed and concentrated on her work. For the most part, she managed. When she did not, when she caught herself staring at him, it was never for long, and as far as she could tell no one, not even Luc, noticed. The fact that he spent most of his time with the medical staff made it easier.

The first patients arrived towards the end of April. 'Long-term cases,' one of the younger nurses told her as they went through stores one day. 'Some of them absolutely hopeless. But Dr Durand, he says no case is hopeless. He doesn't make any promises, mind, but there's just something about him that sort of inspires trust in the patients,' she said with a dreamy smile. 'You can see it in their faces when he talks to them. He never minces his words, none of this stiff upper lip, old son nonsense. No, he tells them it's going to be a long and painful process, and he tells them it's going to be tough, and they respect him for that, Miss Fraser, and every single nurse in the hospital does, too. It makes our job a lot easier, let me tell you.' The nurse laughed self-consciously. 'Listen to me, going on like a love-struck schoolgirl. Mind you, I'm not alone. Most of the nurses have a crush on him. What do you think of him?'

'I find him very professional,' Sheila said determinedly, and carried on counting bandages.

The first board meeting, which she attended with her trepidation kept well under wraps, was for her a landmark. The board members, predictably, tried to direct their questions to Luc, but he was so adept and resolute in redirecting them back to Sheila that they were forced to engage with her. And once she began to speak, her voice stopped quavering, she stopped sitting like someone there on sufferance, and they actually seemed impressed by her knowledge.

'Thank you for having faith in me,' she said to Luc afterwards as she tidied up the papers in what had formerly been the room where the laird managed his estate.

'I did nothing except give you the opportunity. You are the one who took it,' he replied.

'I did, didn't I!' she said, smiling broadly, relieved that it was over but delighted with how it had gone. 'That toffee-nosed lawyer was even calling me Miss Fraser by the end of the meeting, although it looked as if it might kill him.'

'I rather thought he was afraid you would kill him when he tried to tell you your figures were wrong.'

'Was I rude?'

Luc shook his head. '*Formidable*, not rude.'

He was smiling at her. Not the Dr Durand smile, but Luc's smile. Their eyes met and it was there between them. Awareness. Tension. He lifted his hand as if he would touch her, then let it fall. 'I have my first jaw reconstruction scheduled for tomorrow.'

She asked him for details, at first because she didn't want him to leave, and then because she was genuinely interested. He talked, and she became immersed in the discussion, which moved from this first patient to the next five.

'One of the men lives in Cornwall,' he said, 'and he'll be with us for several months. It's so remote here if you don't have access to a motor car, which, let's face it, most people don't. It makes it almost impossible for families to visit, something that I believe is crucial to the patients' well-being. We need to find a way to provide guest accommodation for visitors.'

Sheila smiled. 'I think that's a wonderful idea. There are some old tied cottages that belonged to the estate that could perhaps be used. Although the board might balk at the expense.'

'You pull a proposal together and we'll present it together at the next board meeting. What chance do the board have against us both?' Luc said. 'We make a formidable team, you and I.'

This time he did reach for her, putting a hand on each of her shoulders. Their eyes met again. She tilted her head in invitation. His mouth hovered over hers, then moved to her cheek, and he kissed her, Parisian-style, as he had once before, then turned abruptly away. 'I think I'd better go,' he said.

The door closed softly behind him. Sheila stared after it for a moment, then began to gather up her papers.

Chapter Nine

It was the first of May, and Sheila was heading back to the village with her mother after an early-morning walk on the moors. It was a beautiful morning, with the sun just rising over the hills, the sky pale blue tinged with pink and gold.

'I'm glad you're home,' Mrs Fraser said. 'I know Glen Massan is the last place you want to be—no, don't deny it, I'm not daft—and I don't blame you, either. You've had four years away from the place—you must feel as if your wings have been clipped.'

Sheila smiled in relief. 'Flora said you'd understand.'

'Flora's got an old head on those wee shoulders of hers. A chip off the old block, as they say—and I mean her mother, not her poor father. Her ladyship would never admit it, but she misses Flora terribly. I missed you, too, lass, but I know you have your own life to lead. I'm proud of you, you know. This terrible war has created opportunities we never had in my day. I'm glad to see you've got the gumption to take yours, even if it does offend her ladyship.'

'Thank you. It means a lot to hear you say that.'

'Will you be staying on in your role at Glen Massan, now the hospital's up and running?'

Her mother's tone was diffident. Sheila laughed. 'Why do I get the feeling that's a leading question?'

'Just because I want to know if my own daughter will be staying at home!' Mrs Fraser exclaimed indignantly. 'Well, if you must know,' she admitted when Sheila drew her a sceptical look, 'we were wondering about Ronnie Oliphant's wee laddie.'

'I didn't even know Ronnie was married.'

'To Shona. They got engaged before the war. I told you, I'm sure I told you. You remember, he was reported missing but he was actually in hospital. When he finally came home, he told Shona he didn't expect her to keep her promise because of his injuries, but she wouldn't hear of it. So anyway, to cut a long story short, they had a bairn about a year ago. A wee boy. He's got something wrong with his mouth. The doctor said he needed an operation, but he'd have to go to Glasgow, and it was going to cost a small fortune. It's a crying shame for the wee mite, it's so disfiguring and I just wondered…'

'Màthair, you know the hospital is only permitted to accept military patients. The laird is absolutely adamant on that.'

'It just seems wrong, a place like that on our doorstep, and the village relying on that old doctor who has one foot in the grave himself,' Mrs Fraser exclaimed. 'There's hardly a soul in the village that hasn't worked for the Carmichaels at one time or another, and besides, Ronnie Oliphant *is* military. He gave a leg and an eye for his country. Couldn't you have a word with that charming French doctor of yours?'

'How do you know he's charming?'

'You mean apart from reading between the lines of what you *don't* say?' Mrs Fraser said with an arch look. 'Well, there's Morag and Mhairi who work in the kitchens, for a start. And there's Mrs Watson from the shop. She was awfully impressed when she saw the doctor out swimming in the loch the other morning. He must have the constitution of an ox to brave that water. But it's not his charm I'm interested in. You're always telling me that he's able to perform miracles, Sheila. What's wrong with him performing a wee miracle for one of us?'

'Because the rules were laid down by the laird.'

'The laird! He gave up his estate. He's no right to any say in the matter, if you ask me.'

'Màthair, if I didn't know better, I'd say you'd been talking to Flora's husband. You sound quite revolutionary.'

'I just want what's fair, and I'm not the only one. The Carmichaels have a duty to this village. We need someone to speak up for us, Sheila, and no one's in a better position to do that than you. They're all talking about you, you know. So I said I'd ask.'

They had reached the crossroads where Sheila turned to go to the Big House. 'I can't promise anything,' she said, torn between pride and a horrible feeling that her mother was reaching for the sky.

'You can promise to try, that's all I ask. And, Sheila,' Mrs Fraser said, catching her daughter's hand, 'it's the laird you must speak to, not that doctor of yours. I don't want him to do something that might compromise his position just to please you.'

'What do you mean?'

'Do you think I'm blind and deaf? I know there's something between the two of you.'

'We work together, Màthair, that's all.'

Mrs Fraser laughed and gave her a kiss on the cheek. 'Aye, of course it is,' she said.

Sheila walked past the Lodge towards the Big House, her head whirling. Unable to face her office just yet, she headed for the grounds. The walled kitchen garden, which had been used for target practice in the early days of the requisition, was being rebuilt, but it was too early for work to have started for the day. She perched on a pile of bricks stacked in a sunny spot in the far corner where once the herbs had grown and tried to sort out her thoughts.

She wasn't in love with Luc; her mother had that one all wrong. She admired him, yes. She enjoyed his company. They understood one another. Trusted one another. Valued each other's opinion. She liked him. In fact, yes, she'd go so far as to say she counted him a friend. A good friend. Whom she also found very attractive. But that was beside the point, because acting on that attraction was strictly out of bounds, because…

She closed her eyes and saw his face. She let herself remember the way he kissed her, the way he touched her, the way her body responded to him, and for a delightful few moments, she couldn't remember why on earth they would deny themselves something so pleasurable, and so perfect.

She opened her eyes and forced herself to face reality. Luc had been very clear when he'd told her about Eugenie. He was married to his work; it would always come first. Whatever he felt for her, he would not allow it to develop into anything more meaningful. She had assured him she felt the same, and she'd meant it. She'd been so sure the ghost of Mark Seaton would help her keep her promise.

But what she felt for Luc was nothing like what she felt for Mark Seaton. *Luc* was nothing like Mark Seaton. He'd made it very clear how much he valued her work, and how much he relied on her. He didn't want to lose her. But if he discovered what she really felt for him…

'No!' Sheila jumped to her feet and began to pace the paved walkway that ran diagonally across the garden. 'No,' she muttered, but now it was there, the truth refused to be dislodged. She was in love with Luc. It was so obvious, even her mother had realised it, but she'd been so determined…

She came to an abrupt halt. If her mother knew, then

who else had noticed? The nurses, the other doctors, the staff? There would be talk. She knew from bitter experience what kind of talk there would be. Not everyone valued her the way Luc did. Some resented her. Some thought she had too much influence. What if the talk reached the board? And Luc?

He would feel sorry for her. Or he'd be embarrassed. Or he'd think she'd lied to him. Any of it or all of it, she couldn't bear it. He'd think she was a poor wee soul, and though he might keep her on out of pity, everything would be spoilt. She began her pacing again. 'He mustn't know, he absolutely must not ever find out,' she said. 'Màthair knows, but she wouldn't talk about it. Though how she knows— I have to stop talking about Luc. That must be it. If I can guard my tongue, and if I can find a way to erase the kisses, and forget we ever made love, and…'

Sheila groaned. What was she thinking of! She was in love with him. That wasn't going to go away. And yet nothing could come of it. It would be torture having to see Luc every day. The only option was for her to leave.

She made her way back to Glen Massan House with a heavy heart. Thinking about leaving it made her feel sick, but though she cudgelled her brain, locked away alone in her office for the whole morning, she could come up with no other solution. She had to go.

'You've been avoiding me,' Luc said, closing the office door behind him.

Below the desk, Sheila clasped her hands tightly together. It was a week since she'd realised she was in love with him, but every time she saw him, her resolution to leave faltered. Every hour, every day with him was precious. 'You've been very busy,' she said, 'and so have I. I've finished the proposal to convert the tied houses into guest accommodation.'

'I know, I've read it. It's excellent. I'm sure we'll carry the day,' Luc said, crossing the room to perch on her desk. 'You look tired.'

'How did the surgery go today?'

'Fine. The initial procedure was fairly routine. It will get much trickier later. What's wrong, Sheila?'

'Nothing.'

'That's the smile you give Matron MacDonald. Have I upset you?'

'No.' He drew her an odd look, obviously quite unconvinced. Unwilling to have him probe further, Sheila launched into the second most important topic, which was keeping her awake at night. 'I was wondering, Dr Durand, what would happen if the terms of the trust were broken—if you took on a patient who was not referred by the army, for example?'

'We couldn't. The terms are quite explicit.'

'Yes, but what if you did,' she asked impatiently. 'Surely the demand from the army will dry up at some point in the future. Then you'll run out of patients.'

Luc sighed in exasperation. 'Sheila, my tenure here is for five years. Unfortunately, thanks to the war, we won't run out of patients in that time, but just to be clear, the terms of the trust are very precise. It is the one point, as you know, upon which Lord Carmichael is adamant. The hospital named for his son is for the military only. If I deliberately broke the rules, I'd probably be dismissed. Does that answer your question?'

'Even if it was a life-changing case?'

Luc got to his feet, his eyes narrowing. 'What life-changing case?'

And that answered that question, Sheila thought. She couldn't possibly risk asking Luc to give even a consultation until the laird agreed, because Luc wouldn't be able to resist operating. 'There isn't one,' she said, shuffling the papers on her desk. 'It was a hypothetical question.'

She was so busy concentrating on not looking at him that she didn't notice him move until his hands were on her arms, and he pulled her out of her seat. 'It's because I almost kissed you, isn't it?' he demanded, 'after the board meeting. That's why you are avoiding me.'

She was so surprised, she could think of nothing to say.

'I knew it,' he said, misreading her silence. 'I know you don't want this complication any more than I do. If only you were not so— I don't understand it.' He smoothed his hand over her hair. 'What is it about you, Sheila Fraser, that makes it so impossible for me to resist you?'

If she moved, he would put his arms around her. She allowed herself to imagine resting against his chest, her cheek on the starched white cotton of his coat, and to pretend that he was falling in love with her. It was not such a big step. He had just admitted he found it almost impossible to resist her. But even as she thought about giving in, he was getting ready to leave.

'Forget it. I'm sorry. I have ward rounds in ten minutes.'

Sheila sat back down at her desk, picking up a paper at random and giving him a prim smile. 'Then I'll let you go. Unless there was anything else, Dr Durand?'

'No, thank you, Miss Fraser. Good day.'

As the door closed behind him, Sheila dropped her head into her hands. One more minute, a few more seconds, and she would have given into temptation and kissed him. Would it have been so wrong?

She lifted her head and straightened her shoulders. 'Face facts,' she said to herself. 'Luc doesn't love you. And if he did love you, he'd want you out of here because you'd just be a distraction. You can live without Luc, but you can't live without a purpose. So you have to go and find another job. Now.'

Without giving herself any further time to think, she picked up the telephone and asked to be connected to the Lodge. There was something important she had to do before she left.

Chapter Ten

'I need to speak to you.'

'I'm very busy, Miss Fraser.'

He had been using that brusque, businesslike tone in his dealings with her since their last meeting three days ago. Sheila closed the door of what had been the old sewing room behind her and leaned against it. She felt quite nauseous. 'It's important.'

Luc folded his hands on the blotting paper. 'Well?'

She pulled herself up to her full height. 'I want you to accept my resignation.'

He looked momentarily thunderstruck, but quickly recovered. 'Nonsense. There is no need for such drastic action. I think I've proved to you in these past few days that I am perfectly capable of maintaining a professional distance. You need have no fears on that score.'

Sheila crossed the room and sat down on the chair opposite his desk. 'It's not that. Not about us, I mean. I—I met with the laird.' Just the memory of it made her stomach muscles clench.

'About the tied houses?'

'No. Another matter. I think— If you don't accept my resignation, Luc—Dr Durand, I think the laird will have me dismissed.'

'What on earth are you talking about?'

She had his full attention now, but she couldn't bear to meet his eyes. Keeping her hands tightly clasped to stop them shaking, she recounted the gist of her meeting. 'He was absolutely furious,' she concluded. 'He said that he wanted Alex to be remembered as a soldier, not some sort of Good Samaritan. And when I—I pointed out that the Carmichaels had an obligation to give something back to the village that had done so much for them, he completely lost his rag and I am afraid—I am rather afraid that I rather lost mine.'

'Rag?' Luc gazed at her blankly.

'Temper. I lost my temper, and I said some things that were rather dreadful. Even if they were true,' Sheila said, remembering indignantly the high-handed way her former employer had spoken to her. 'He reminded me that I was a servant, and he said that things had come to a pretty pass when the laird of the manor had a servant lecture him on what to do. I couldn't ignore that.'

'No,' Luc said with a ghost of a smile.

'It's not funny. I told him that he was living in the past, and that clinging on to Glen Massan even though it wasn't his anymore was making things frightfully hard for Lady Carmichael. And I told him that if he thought Alex would have ignored the needs of the villagers then he didn't know his son at all. And that's true, Luc, but it was an appalling thing to say. He went quite ashen then, and showed me the door. I tried to apologise, but it was too late. I think I've well and truly burned my bridges there. I don't expect I'll even get a reference. Not one I can use, anyway.'

'What on earth did you suggest to provoke such an extreme reaction?'

Sheila stared down at her feet. 'You know that hypothetical case I mentioned? Well, it wasn't strictly hypothetical. It's Ronnie and Shona Oliphant's wee boy.' Unable to restrain herself, she launched into a description of the child's condition. 'Oh, Luc, it would break your heart to see him, and his parents are at their wits' end.'

'*Attends!* Wait a minute. You mean you have already spoken to them, made promises to them?'

Luc jumped to his feet, swearing heavily. 'You had no right, quite apart from the fact that you are not qualified to make any sort of clinical judgement. *Sacre bleu*, are you so frightened that I might try to kiss you that you go behind my back like this? You undermined my authority. You also ignored my advice that the laird would be implacable on the subject. I thought we trusted each other, if nothing else. Did it not occur to you that we could have done a better job of persuading the laird together, once I had been able to form a view on whether surgery was even possible?'

'As you've just so forcefully reminded me, the laird can't be persuaded.'

'If only you had let me see the boy first. If I could have operated, then shown the laird the proof...'

'Can't you see,' Sheila said despairingly, 'that's exactly what I was afraid of. I know you. You would have operated, despite it being against the rules. And then we would both have been dismissed. I couldn't allow you to risk your career like that. I know how much it means to you.'

'You should have consulted me, Sheila. You should have trusted me.' Luc sank onto the window seat, rubbing his eyes. 'I am sorry. I thought that we had sorted matters between us, but I see that we have not. We can't continue like this.'

It was what she believed. It was what she'd come to tell him, but hearing him confirm it was so much more difficult to bear. 'No,' she said sadly, 'we can't.'

'I will leave,' Luc said heavily.

She thought she had misheard him. 'What?'

'I can go back to France. There is a big demand for surgeons with my skills. This is your home. I cannot drive you from it.'

'No!' Now it was Sheila's turn to jump to her feet. 'You wanted to get away from France. You wanted to make a new life here, Luc. Anyway, the laird won't allow me to stay, I've told you that. And besides, Glen Massan isn't...' She tailed off, because that wasn't true. Glen Massan was her home. It would be painful to leave it, now that she had redrawn her place in it, to start somewhere without family or friends. Without Luc.

She steeled herself. 'No. It's not your fault. I do find it impossible to work with you, but not for the reasons you think. There is something I haven't told you.'

And it was surprisingly easy, after all this time, to tell him. Mark Seaton mattered so little now. 'I was not long arrived in France,' Sheila began. 'The end of 1915. I'd done well in my training, and I thought I knew a lot more than I did. I wanted to do more than mop floors and wash sheets, though I didn't shirk doing plenty of that, too. I thought it was because I was talented, that he favoured me. I was too naive to realise that doctors didn't request VADs to help them, too full of myself to notice that his asking for me was putting the nurses' nose out of joint, to say nothing of what my sister VADs were thinking.'

Sheila risked a glance at Luc. 'His name was Dr Mark Seaton, do you know him?'

He shook his head, his gaze not wavering from her face. She rushed into speech, anxious to have it over with. 'It was forbidden for VADs to be alone in the company of officers, but that was part of the fun then, flaunting rules. He was handsome and fun and I didn't need much persuading to think myself in love, and not much more persuading to show him how I felt,' Sheila said.

She could feel her cheeks heating, but she was determined to finish now. 'I thought he loved me, too. Turns out, once he'd got what he wanted from me, he didn't even want me in his operating theatre anymore. And when I made it clear I thought we had a future, he virtually laughed in my face. He had plans for a career in Harley Street after the war, and the likes of me didn't fit in with those plans. He accused me of gold-digging, and warned his colleagues to steer clear because, though I was free with my favours, it would cost them dear in the long run. You can imagine, in a hospital, the kind of gossip that generated.'

'He sounds like a complete bastard,' Luc said.

'But one with influence. He had me transferred, which was actually the best thing he could have done. I worked doubly hard, and I made sure no one did me any favours. It was easy to get over him—in fact, it was easy to keep well clear of any man—but it wasn't so easy to get over the consequences. You can see now why I was so appalled when it turned out you were to be my boss.'

'You thought I was like this man?' Luc exclaimed in horror.

'No! But I didn't know anything about you save that you were a surgeon. I couldn't take the risk.'

'Why didn't you tell me sooner?'

'I was embarrassed. I was determined to prove myself to you first. I was going to tell you that day on the hill, but then you told me about Eugenie.'

'So why tell me now?'

Sheila swallowed. 'Because I need you to understand. Mark made me realise how important it is to me to stand on my own two feet, to have people respect me, for me to respect myself, and to do that, I need to be honest.' She took a deep breath. 'I'm in love with you, and it's not going to go away, and it's going to get in the way, so that's why I have to go.'

She risked a glance at him. His eyes were glazed. He

looked—oh, God, he looked horrified. 'You said it yourself, it won't work. You don't want any distractions, and I certainly don't want to be the kind of woman who sits at home out of the way, waiting.'

'I don't want a woman to sit at home waiting for me.'

'I know. So—' Sheila fumbled in her pocket '—I've put it in writing for the board. I've put all my papers in order. I thought it best if I went straight away.' She thought she was going to faint. Or lose her breakfast. It was the strangest thing, this feeling that she had to get out of there as quickly as possible, and the languor that seemed to be keeping her pinned to the spot. She wouldn't cry, and she wouldn't change her mind. 'Goodbye, Luc.'

'Sheila, wait.' He grabbed hold of her. 'You can't just...'

She had to get out of here. 'Goodbye, Luc.' She grabbed the door, threw it open and fled.

Three hours later, Luc stood outside Mrs Fraser's cottage. Sheila's mother—unmistakably Sheila's mother, with her fair hair and brown eyes—didn't seem particularly surprised to see him.

'I'll fetch her,' she said, disappearing up a narrow flight of wooden steps. Returning a few minutes later, she picked up her shawl and draped it over her shoulders. 'I'll be back in an hour, no more. I warn you, whatever you've got to say, it had better not make her even more upset. You might be charming and you might be a miracle worker, but Sheila is my daughter.'

'What do you want, Luc?'

Sheila was hovering at the foot of the stairs. She glared at him, though he could see in her eyes what it cost her. He wanted to sweep her into his arms and kiss her pain away, but he knew her too well to think she would allow that. He needed to do this properly.

'Won't you sit down?'

She pulled out a chair at the scrubbed wooden table, and he sat opposite her. 'Well?' she said.

'I've just come from Mr Oliphant's house. We're going to have the boy in for some preliminary examinations next week.'

'Luc! For heaven's sake, did I not warn you…'

'You said a great deal, and I listened, and now I want you to listen to me.' The urge to pace the room was strong, but he repressed it. 'I've spoken to the laird. It seems your tirade didn't miss the target entirely. I persuaded him that you were right.'

'How on earth did you do that?'

'By threatening to resign if he didn't agree, of course.' He shook his head reassuringly. 'It would never have come to that. You had already done the spadework and pricked his conscience. "Shook me to the bones and made me take a good look at the self-pitying excuse of a man I'd let myself become" is what he actually said.' Luc grinned. 'Not only did he agree to the Oliphant boy's surgery, but he says he will put a proposal to the trustees to establish a clinic for the village based at the hospital.'

'Luc, that's wonderful news.'

He was pleased to see the light return to her eyes. 'That is not all. It seems your remarks about Lady Carmichael also hit home. The laird has had a bit of an epiphany all round. He will be making plans for them to leave Glen Massan and settle in London. That, I am sorry to tell you, is not wholly down to you. He has just received a telegram telling him that he is expecting his first grandchild.'

'Flora?'

'The eldest son, Robbie, and his wife.'

'Oh, Luc, you'll think me silly, but a new life, a new generation, it's…'

'Symbolic. The laird seems to think so, too. "Time for us all to move on and leave the past behind." A sentiment I heartily endorse and the real reason I'm here.' He couldn't stay still any longer, and pushed the chair back, coming round to the other side of the table to sit beside her. 'I love you, Sheila. I think I have been in love with you for weeks, only I have been too stubborn to admit it. Only when you told me that you were leaving did I realise that nothing was more important than being with you.'

'Oh, Luc. Don't say it just because you feel responsible or feel sorry for me.'

'I have never meant anything more in my life. I love you.'

'But your career, the hospital…'

'Our hospital. That's the point, *chérie*. It can be a joint endeavour,' he said, taking her hand. 'I thought I had to choose, but I realise now I was wrong. Only—only this is not just about me. You need to want it, too.'

'I don't know what you're actually suggesting,' Sheila said.

He laughed. 'Nor do I. I have no idea at all what I'm suggesting, except that I love you, and I want to be with you, and whatever that means, I'll move heaven and earth to make it happen, but just, please, tell me that you will have me, because if you don't…'

She threw herself into his arms, laughing, crying, shaking. 'I love you so much, you can take me pretty much any way you want.'

He kissed her then, and she kissed him back, twining her arms around him. He pulled her onto his lap, and their kisses deepened. 'If we don't stop, then I might find myself quite literally taking you right here,' Luc said, tearing his mouth free.

Sheila laughed and scrabbled to her feet, turning the lock in the door. She held open her arms. 'Take me, Luc, I'm yours.'

And with a low growling laugh, he did just that.

* * * * *

Historical Note

I have endeavoured to make the historical element of these stories as faithful to the facts as possible. Any errors are entirely my own, and I apologise in advance for them—because experience tells me that someone, somewhere, will point out at least one!

My reading list for this story was huge, but I'd like to single out two books that were a great source of inspiration. First of all, Vera Brittain's *Testament of Youth*. I first read this many years ago, and reread it as part of my research. It has dated. To modern eyes, Ms Brittain can at times seem, frankly, a bit of a whinge, but for me it's still one of the most moving personal accounts of the War I've read. Vera before the War was the inspiration for Flora; Laird Carmichael's fear of telegrams stems from a line of Vera's that every ring of the doorbell could be one of *those* telegrams; and Vera's tragic account of the Christmas leave when she waited in vain for the return of her fiancé, Roland, inspired my happier reunion between Sylvie and Robbie at New Year. The second book is Lyn MacDonald's amazing *The Roses of No Man's Land*, which gave me a wonderful insight into the life of the VAD and inspired Sheila's story. To Ms MacDonald, I owe the description of Armistice Day in Boulogne, as well as the background to the Harvard hospitals and their associated teaching schools where Luc learned so much.

Glen Massan House doesn't exist, nor did the Argyll War Hospital. Glen Massan, for those of you who enjoy insider detail, is a real place in Argyll, a beautiful river flowing through a valley that is full of trout, with some icy cold pools where I used to go swimming as a child. Flicking through Ian Gow's excellent *Scotland's Lost Houses* made me realise how many of Scotland's stately homes were requisitioned at the beginning of the War, and sadly how many of them were lost to the families forever. The Great War made white elephants of stately homes and the aristocratic lifestyle, and the army, unfortunately, left the buildings that had been requisitioned in a bit of a state.

Both Robbie and his brother, Alex, join the Argyll and Southern Highlanders, which happens to be the regiment associated with my own home county, and hence also theirs. Robbie joined the Argyllshire Battalion, which was sent to France in May 1915 and merged with the Highland Division. All of the action mentioned in his story was that seen by the Highlanders. He had just returned from the Battle of Ancre, part of the Somme initiative, in November 1916 when he first wrote to Sylvie. In fact, the Highlanders surrendered to the Germans at the end of this battle—one of the few facts I've changed. The final action in Robbie's story was part of the Battle of Arras, in which Sylvie's brother also saw action with the French army. Alex I assigned to one of the Renfrewshire Battalions of the Argylls. They were posted to Gallipoli in 1915 and arrived at the Western Front in April 1918 following a lengthy period in Egypt.

On Armistice Day, Sheila was working at General Hospital Number 14, Boulogne-sur-Mer. This was based in the casino and in 1917 had been taken over by a Harvard Unit. The hospital took mostly British patients, with a small number of Americans and some civilians during the worst of the air raids in 1917 and 1918. Previously run as an evacuation hospital under British management, it was transferred to the American team because of their surgical expertise.

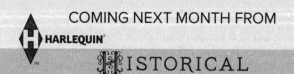

REQUEST YOUR FREE BOOKS!

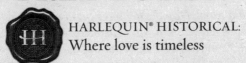

HARLEQUIN® HISTORICAL:
Where love is timeless

2 FREE NOVELS PLUS 2 **FREE GIFTS!**

YES! Please send me 2 FREE Harlequin® Historical novels and my 2 FREE gifts (gifts are worth about $10). After receiving them, if I don't wish to receive any more books, I can return the shipping statement marked "cancel." If I don't cancel, I will receive 6 brand-new novels every month and be billed just $5.44 per book in the U.S. or $5.74 per book in Canada. That's a savings of at least 16% off the cover price! It's quite a bargain! Shipping and handling is just 50¢ per book in the U.S. and 75¢ per book in Canada.* I understand that accepting the 2 free books and gifts places me under no obligation to buy anything. I can always return a shipment and cancel at any time. Even if I never buy another book, the two free books and gifts are mine to keep forever.

246/349 HDN F4ZY

Name   (PLEASE PRINT)

Address   Apt. #

City   State/Prov.   Zip/Postal Code

Signature (if under 18, a parent or guardian must sign)

Mail to the **Harlequin® Reader Service:**
IN U.S.A.: P.O. Box 1867, Buffalo, NY 14240-1867
IN CANADA: P.O. Box 609, Fort Erie, Ontario L2A 5X3
Want to try two free books from another line?
Call 1-800-873-8635 or visit www.ReaderService.com.

* Terms and prices subject to change without notice. Prices do not include applicable taxes. Sales tax applicable in N.Y. Canadian residents will be charged applicable taxes. Offer not valid in Quebec. This offer is limited to one order per household. Not valid for current subscribers to Harlequin Historical books. All orders subject to credit approval. Credit or debit balances in a customer's account(s) may be offset by any other outstanding balance owed by or to the customer. Please allow 4 to 6 weeks for delivery. Offer available while quantities last.

Your Privacy—The Harlequin® Reader Service is committed to protecting your privacy. Our Privacy Policy is available online at www.ReaderService.com or upon request from the Harlequin Reader Service.

We make a portion of our mailing list available to reputable third parties that offer products we believe may interest you. If you prefer that we not exchange your name with third parties, or if you wish to clarify or modify your communication preferences, please visit us at www.ReaderService.com/consumerschoice or write to us at Harlequin Reader Service Preference Service, P.O. Box 9062, Buffalo, NY 14269. Include your complete name and address.

HH13R

A Mouse, the heavier hand had scrawled next to the bit
about the ceremony, and underlined it.

Not of the upper ten thousand, her shocked eyes
discovered next.

Preferably an orphan.

Her stomach roiled as she recalled the look on
Lord Havelock's face when she'd told him, that fateful
night at the Crimmers, that she'd just lost her mother.
She'd thought he couldn't possibly have looked pleased
to hear she was all alone in the world, that surely she
must have been mistaken.

But she hadn't been.

She tottered back to the tea table and sank onto the chair
the waiter had so helpfully drawn up to it. And carried on
reading.

Not completely hen-witted, the sloppier of the two
writers had added. And she suddenly understood that
cryptic comment he'd made about finding a wife with
brains. Suggested by someone called…Ash, that was
it. How she could remember a name tossed out just the
once, in such an offhand way, she could not think.

Unless it was because she felt as though the beautiful little dainties set out on their fine china plates might as well have been so many piles of ash, for all the desire she had now to put one in her mouth.

Good with children, not selfish, the darker hand had scrawled. Then it was back to the neater hand again. It had written, *Modest, Honest* and *Not looking for affection within Matrimony.* And then the untidier, what she'd come to think of as the more sarcastic, compiler of wifely qualities had written the word *Mouse* again, and this time underlined it twice.

But what made a small whimper of distress finally escape her lips was the last item on the list.

Need not be pretty.

Need not be pretty. Well, that was her all right! Plain, dowdy mouse that she was. No wonder he'd looked at her like—what was it Aunt Pargetter had said—like his ship had come in?

Getting to her feet, she strode to his bedroom door and flung it open. Somehow she had to find a sample of his handwriting to see if he'd been the one to…to mock her this way, before he'd even met her. And then she would… She came to an abrupt halt by his desk, across the surface of which was scattered a veritable raft of papers. What would she do? She'd already married him.

*Don't miss
LORD HAVELOCK'S LIST,
available from Harlequin® Historical
September 2014.*

HARLEQUIN®

ℋISTORICAL

Where love is timeless

COMING IN SEPTEMBER 2014

The Lone Sheriff
by
Lynna Banning

A WOMAN DETECTIVE?
NOT ON HIS WATCH!

As if tracking down train robbers weren't hard enough,
now Sheriff Jericho Silver's backup has arrived and *she's* a
gun-toting, head-turning beauty. She sure spells trouble.

Madison O'Donnell had the perfect life—a beautiful home and
all the ladies' luncheons she could stomach—but it left her
bored to tears. Now a widow, she's determined to fill her days
with daring deeds and wild adventures.

Jericho is equally determined that she'll be on the next train
home. But this is one lady who won't take no for an answer….

Available wherever books and ebooks are sold.

www.Harlequin.com

HH29799

COMING IN SEPTEMBER 2014

The Gentleman Rogue

by

Margaret McPhee

INESCAPABLE, UNDENIABLE AND IMPOSSIBLE TO RESIST!

In a Mayfair ballroom, beautiful Emma Northcote stands in amazement. For gazing at her, with eyes she'd know anywhere, is Ned Stratham—a man whose roguish charm once held her captivated.

But that was another life in another part of London.

With their past mired in secrets and betrayal, and their true identities now at last revealed, Ned realizes they can never rekindle their affair. For only he knows that they share a deeper connection—one that could make Emma hate him if she ever discovered the truth….

Available wherever books and ebooks are sold.

HISTORICAL

Where love is timeless

COMING IN SEPTEMBER 2014

Saved by the Viking Warrior

by

Michelle Styles

"THERE IS NO ONE. I TRAVEL ALONE. I LIVE ALONE. ALWAYS."

Battle-scarred Thrand the Destroyer has only one thing on his mind: settling old scores. But with the beautiful Lady of Lingfold as his prisoner, the unyielding warrior starts to dream of a loving wife and a home to call his own.

Cwen is also seeking justice, but she knows the fragile alliance she's built with Thrand will only last as long as they share a common enemy. Unless they can find a way to leave revenge to the gods to forge a new life together.

Available wherever books and ebooks are sold.

www.Harlequin.com